Some Questions Have No Answers

JANE BLYTHE

Cover designed by Q Designs

Created with Vellum

Acknowledgments

I'd like to thank everyone who played a part in bringing this story to life. Particularly my mom who is always there to share her thoughts and opinions with me. My wonderful cover designer Amy who did an amazing job with this stunning cover. My fabulous editor Lisa for all the hard work she puts into polishing my work. My awesome team, Sophie, Robyn, and Clayr, without your help I'd never be able to run my street team. And my fantastic street team members who help share my books with every share, comment, and like!

And of course a big thank you to all of you, my readers! Without you I wouldn't be living my dreams of sharing the stories in my head with the world!

June 7th
8:52 A.M.

This was not how she had expected the first day of her new job to turn out.

She'd moved here to escape her old life, create a new one, a quiet, peaceful one, one where she could finally manage to put the baggage of her past down and move forward, find happiness. It wasn't like she thought it would be easy or that everything would be perfect. She had accepted a job as a deputy in the small town of River's End after all, so she'd known she would be dealing with crimes.

Sydney Clark just hadn't expected this.

She was crouching, balanced precariously on the edge of the river, and desperately hoping she didn't topple over because she didn't know how to swim. The river ran through the forest, and the tall trees sheltered her from the heat of the sun, it wasn't quite summer yet, but you'd never know it from the weather. Picking a town where a river was one of the main highlights might not be the smartest decision for someone who hated the water, but she'd been ready to move on, and River's End had been looking for a new deputy to join the Sheriff's office, and so she'd jumped at the chance to start a new life.

The sight of the body—the reason for her presence at the water's edge—made her queasy, not that she would dare let anyone know that. She was a cop, and she'd seen dead bodies before, just nothing like this.

Still as much as she wanted to throw up the single piece of toast she'd quickly eaten on her way out the door this morning, she couldn't do that, not on her first day. What would her colleagues think of her? She was the only woman in the Sheriff's office and one of only two who hadn't grown up in River's End so she felt like she had to prove herself. It didn't help that her five colleagues were all ultra-tough, former military men who she was totally still intimidated by, there was no way she would make a fool of herself.

So to that end, she shoved away the nausea and focused on the body, forcing herself to think clinically and logically and not let her emotions get in the way. She could do this, this was her chance at letting go of the past, and she wasn't going to give it up for anything, certainly not some deranged killer who got off on torturing people.

Facts.

As long as she focused on facts then she could get through this.

Fact number one; the body had been dumped in the river just south of town.

Fact number two; the body hadn't really been *dumped* it had actually been purposefully staged.

Fact number three; the place the killer had chosen to leave the body was secluded, but it was almost summertime, and people were at the river fishing, swimming, boating, and a dozen other things meaning that he knew the body would be discovered promptly.

Fact number four; this location was a safe place to leave a body, there were no houses, no businesses, no buildings whatsoever within a mile, which meant there were no security cameras in the area and no people around to stumble upon him.

Fact number five; this killer was one sadistic monster.

Fact number six; she knew fact number five because the victim had been horribly burned before having their neck sliced from ear to ear so deep she could actually see bone.

Fact number seven; she was doing a bad job of trying to hold it together. Her hands were sweaty, and it had nothing to do with the hot late spring morning, but despite the heat she felt ice-cold inside.

"Not what you expected on your first day, huh?" Sheriff Abe Black asked as he strolled across the grassy bank toward the river's edge.

Sydney startled at his deep voice and prayed that any traces of the horror she was feeling were wiped from her face. She'd never worked a homicide before, and while she'd seen some pretty awful things, this was definitely top of the list.

When she'd moved to River's End she'd thought she would be mainly dealing with traffic violations, maybe some drunk tourists, the odd brawl, possibly a theft, but not murder, and definitely not torture and murder.

Not that this would make her quit.

She'd already lived through hell, and if she could make it through that then she could make it through this. When she had decided to become a cop it was for this very reason, she wanted to save people, she wanted to bring justice, she wanted to do for others what those cops had done for her over a decade ago.

Straightening her spine, she looked her new boss in the eye. "No, not how I expected to start this job, but I'm ready to work this case to the best of my ability, sir."

"Not sir," he said blandly, "Abe. So what do you think, Sydney? You getting a feel for this guy?"

"This is the second murder, right?" she asked. When Abe had called her this morning to tell her to go straight from the house she was renting to the crime scene, he had only given her a very brief rundown of the case.

"Second in the last week," Abe confirmed.

"Both found like this?"

"Both found with their throats cut, submerged in the river with a rope around their neck tied to a tree."

"Both were young women?" Sydney asked. The woman in front of her was yet to be identified, but she appeared to be in her early or mid-twenties.

"Yeah," Abe said softly, and from the look on his face, she assumed that he knew who the woman in the water was.

"You know her."

"Her name is Elena Martinez. Her grandparents moved to River's End nearly twenty years ago. She used to come every summer to visit with them, moved here permanently just a few months ago."

"I'm sorry," she said, feeling a pang of empathy. She knew what it was like to see someone you knew, someone you cared about, lying dead at your feet. "You knew the other victim as well?"

"First victim was Naomi Franklin, twenty-four, lived in River's End all her life, she was a friend of my little sister." The way he said it implied that his sister hadn't taken the news well.

"So he targets young women, that means he has to have a ruse of some sort." She was twenty-six, and yeah okay she was a cop, and she'd dealt with monsters before so she was beyond cautious, but all women —or almost all—were inherently careful when it came to their safety. "He lures them in, then he has to have a place that's secluded so he can torture them. Their feet are badly burned, they would have screamed, he needed someplace they wouldn't draw attention. Then once he slits their throats he brings them to the river, choosing places where he's unlikely to be spotted while leaving the bodies, but also where he knows they're going to be found fairly quickly, so it seems like he's local, or at least has good local knowledge. He seems smart and controlled, making decisions that will keep his identity a secret, and leaving the bodies in the water could have been his way of trying to get rid of any forensics he might have left behind. Yet it's important to him that we find them, that we know what happened to them, that we know they're dead, that implies he has something that he wants to gain by doing this. Once we figure out what that is then we should find him." And hopefully before another young woman wound up dead.

Abe nodded approvingly. "Good job, Deputy. All right, we'll wait for forensics to see if they can find anything that might help us, although last time they couldn't so we won't bank on it. In the meantime, I want you to start retracing Elena's last steps. She went missing two days ago. See if you can find out what she was doing those last few days because chances are she came into contact with the killer."

That the sheriff was pleased with her initial assessment of the case and had given her a task straight off the bat bolstered her confidence. She could do this, it wasn't like she had never worked a crime before, and she had a bachelors in criminal psychology. This was kind of like jumping off the high board your first time diving, it was better to just jump on in and get started, it took away some of the nerves.

As she turned to walk away, Sydney caught sight of the burns on Elena Martinez's feet and couldn't help but shudder. The woman had suffered. A lot. And that thought left her feeling unsettled. Just what kind of man were they looking for? How could someone inflict that kind of pain and suffering on another human being? It was one thing to kill someone but to do that ... Sydney shuddered again.

"Sheriff?" she called after his retreating back, nervously wiping her still sweaty hands on her black pants. Them, and the white blouse she was wearing were really a little warm for the day, but she'd wanted to dress as professionally as she could.

"Abe," he reminded her as he stopped and turned back to face her.

"I'm not working this case alone, am I?" It was one thing to have worked patrol as an officer, she'd arrested her fair share of criminals, but working a potential serial killer case, that was something else, and she was beyond nervous that she would screw up somehow.

A small smile curved Abe's lips up. "No, I wouldn't do that to you, not on your first day here. Fletcher Harris will meet you in town and work with you, help you get the lay of the land, and get to know the locals since you only moved here yesterday."

Relief washed over her, this might not be how she expected things to turn out when she moved to River's End, but she was getting excited about working this case, bringing a serial killer down, getting justice for Naomi and Elena. The whole point of moving here was to build a new life, a life where she was stronger, and what better way to do it than this?

~

10:10 A.M.

. . .

Mission two accomplished.

He let out a relieved breath.

None of this was easy, in fact it was downright terrifying, but this was something he had to do, his entire future depended on it.

Quietly, he slipped through the shadows, content that no one was aware he had been watching the goings-on at the river and that no one was any the wiser that he was the one responsible for the young woman's death.

He was good at blending in, had spent an entire lifetime flying under the radar, being ignored or merely passed over because there was absolutely nothing about him that was noteworthy enough to attract attention. No one noticed him, no one even really saw him, and while there had been a time in his life where that had bothered him now he realized what a blessing in disguise it really was.

A blessing he was going to have to harness to see this through.

And he would see this through.

He had to.

Wasn't like he could let it go. If he did he'd be dead.

If he followed it through he might wind up dead anyway, but it was a chance he was willing to take, a risk he was willing to take, because if this worked out then he would finally be free.

Now that he had mission number one and mission number two completed it was time to move forward, he thought it was probably wise to try to lay low for a while, make sure the cops had no reason to suspect him, but he wasn't in control of this. This was bigger than him. This was bigger than anything he had ever imagined, and there were so many lives hanging in the balance.

Including the lives of people he cared about.

This was never a role he had seen himself in, and killing those poor girls wasn't something he had enjoyed or something that he had wanted to do. It was something he *had* to do. He didn't have a choice in this, he was merely a chess piece in a bigger game, and he had to do his part or suffer the consequences.

Whether he kept quiet for a few days or a few weeks wasn't up to him, he would know who was next when he saw them. There wasn't any way to know beforehand, no way he could be prepared, track the person down, follow them, find out as much as he could about them before he was called to take them and interrogate them.

Interrogate.

That was never a word he had thought he would be putting in a sentence with himself. He didn't interrogate people. He had no military or law enforcement background. He was just a guy who had been backed into a corner, all of his options stripped away, and left in a fight or flight situation, he'd had no choice but to take the fight option.

Helplessness stabbed at him along with a heavy dose of guilt. The screams of the women as the boiling water burned them echoed in his head. Would he ever forget the sound? He thought he probably wouldn't, would most likely have nightmares about it for years to come.

Assuming he lived that long.

He deserved to burn in hell for what he had done.

More guilt weighed down on him, crushing him until tears burned his eyes and his entire body shook.

He hated himself.

Hated what he had done.

Hated that he had been forced into hurting those women.

Hated that he had been forced into killing them.

Hated that he had been forced to dump their bodies in the river like they were nothing but discarded trash.

Why hadn't they just answered his questions?

If they had just told him what he needed to know, he would never have had to hurt them. He would never have had to kill them. He could have just let them go.

But they wouldn't.

They wouldn't answer.

"Please," he begged aloud, "please, next time just answer. Please," he pleaded with whoever was going to be next. He didn't think he could stand doing this again, but what choice did he have?

None.

And that sucked.

He fought back the tears and the constant ball of nausea that had been swirling in his stomach ever since he had been approached to take on this task. His life had all but ended that day, he was no longer the man he'd been before, he wasn't sure that even if he was able to get the answers he needed and he passed those answers on that he would be able to go back to his old life.

Ignoring the overwhelming sense of loss that realization brought with it, he shoved away his emotions, rubbed at his eyes, and drew in a deep, cleansing breath. He had to do this, that much was clear, and to do it, he would have to learn to get a better grasp of his emotions. They weren't letting him go until he gave them what they wanted, and he suspected that no matter how much he begged the next woman he was directed to take, she wouldn't be any more likely to give him answers than the first two had been, so he would have to torture them as well. Although he wasn't sure he could go through that again he knew he didn't have a choice so he would have to pull it together.

"You will do this. You will do this. You will do this," he chanted over and over. It was surprising what you would do when your back was against a wall. He was between a rock and a hard place, and as much as he was ashamed of himself he had chosen his life over the lives of others. If that made him a bad person then so be it, but in the end, it was better than being dead.

He was pretty sure that he didn't leave behind any forensics on the body, but it wasn't like he was a pro at this, he was acting on instinct and on what little he had gleaned from watching crime shows with his true-crime documentary loving wife.

Ex-wife.

Not that that was really pertinent at the moment. Still, he'd learned enough from her to keep the cops off his trail this far he only hoped that could continue because he didn't want to even contemplate what would happen if he failed this mission.

With the bodies in the cops' hands now he had to make sure that his place was cleaned. He hadn't had time earlier this morning, he'd had to make sure the body was positioned just the way he'd been told, and he'd had to time it just right, with summer approaching, people started their days earlier and the chances of someone finding him increased.

His luck had held this morning just like it had since this begun, but if he was going to continue to go undetected, he had to be smart. And the smart thing to do was go home, clean his house and car, and then wait for further instructions.

That was what he hated the most.

The waiting.

Waiting to be told what he had to do next.

Waiting to see if he would get the answers he had been ordered to retrieve.

Waiting to see if he was going to get caught.

As much as he hated it there was nothing he could do about it right now so he had to just keep moving. Become a robot, move on instinct, follow his instructions, go through the motions, and hope and pray that he would come out on the other side.

That was looking more and more unlikely with each passing hour.

He had been turned into a warrior in a war he was woefully inadequate to fight in. He had changed into a man he barely recognized anymore. He had committed unspeakable atrocities. He had taken lives that weren't his to claim.

He was a monster.

He was ... he was a soldier, whether he wanted to be or not, he was part of this, he had done what he'd been ordered, and he would see this through because it was his only chance. Maybe after he was finished there would be a way for him to make amends. It sounded ridiculous when he articulated it, even to himself, but he wasn't a bad guy, he wasn't a killer, he was just a man without any other options.

He made a vow here, and now, if by some miracle he was left standing at the end he would dedicate every single second of the rest of his life to do as many good deeds as he could to make up for all the bad deeds he had committed.

It would never be enough, but it would at least be a start.

~

5:37 P.M.

. . .

As soon as he stepped inside, he felt himself relax.

To Dr. Levi Black the diner held so many memories that it was almost like a second home. Chatting voices, laughing, the hustle and bustle of the combination of locals and the holidaymakers who were coming to make the most of the quaint town and activities in the river. The air was warm with the smell of coffee and pastries and mouthwatering burgers, he had long ago eaten his way through the entire menu, and now, over two decades later, he had only grown to love everything more.

His mouth already watered as he thought of the burger and fries he would devour as soon as he got them. He was starving having just left the hospital after a grueling shift where he'd stayed twelve hours extra after a particularly bad boating accident, and he needed some downtime before he headed home.

Levi hadn't gone more than three steps into the diner when someone crashed into him.

"Oof," the person grunted as they bounced off his much larger frame.

"Careful," he said, automatically reaching out to wrap his hands around the person's arms as they stumbled. "I got you. You okay?"

A pair of golden-brown eyes—the kind of unique and vibrant color you might expect to find on a cat—looked up at him through long, thick lashes.

Whoa.

She was beautiful.

Besides the stunning eyes, the woman had a light sprinkling of freckles across her cheeks and nose and silky-looking warm, brown locks that hung just past her shoulders. She was much shorter than his six foot three frame, maybe coming in around five two or five three. She was dressed in black pants that showed off a pair of sexy hips and a white blouse that highlighted every soft curve and a set of round breasts that he had to struggle not to stare at.

He'd lived in River's End since he was six, minus the two tours he'd spent as an army medic, and he'd been back here for the past three years, he knew everyone who lived here, but he'd never seen this woman before. Was she a tourist? Had she come to the quaint little town to enjoy water sports in the river or go hiking or camping in the surrounding forest?

For some reason that sent an unexplainable bolt of disappointment through him.

He didn't know her, but he'd definitely like to get to know her.

"Hi, I'm Levi, and you are?" he asked, letting his fingers trail lightly down her arms as he released his grip on her, confident she'd gotten her balance back.

Her gaze darted around the room, and her cheeks turned a cute shade of pink as she stammered, "I, uh, I'm, umm, Sydney. Sydney Clark."

"Well, nice to meet you, Sydney Clark." He grinned, knowing that flashing his dimples at a woman was a surefire way to get them intrigued, and since he was very much intrigued by Sydney he wanted her to feel the same way about him. It had been a long time since a woman had gotten him feeling this way, he liked to flirt, but things never went any further than that. Loss was like that, it took something beautiful and turned it into something painful. Something too painful to face.

And he hadn't faced it.

Not in three long years.

"Uh, nice to meet you too," Sydney said, her gaze lingering on him for a moment before flitting off, and Levi couldn't deny he felt a little smug knowing that he'd rattled her the same way she was rattling him.

"You in town for the summer?" he asked when it looked like Sydney was about ready to bolt. He wanted to get to know her, put her at ease.

"No, I just moved here. Yesterday," she added, finally meeting his gaze and holding it. A flare of awareness passed through her eyes, and they seemed to glow like shimmering gold, her tongue touched her bottom lip before disappearing. "I'm the new deputy," she said quickly, her gaze dropping to the floor.

Knowing that she wasn't just here on vacation made him feel happier than it probably should considering he'd known her for a whole thirty seconds now. Knowing that she would be working with his brother made him even happier because it gave him an in, a way to get to know her better.

"I'm Levi Black," he told her, "Abe's brother. I'm a doctor. I work in the emergency room at Sacred Heart Hospital, which's about five miles north of River's End, services the town and about five others in the area."

"I've only met your brother twice, once when I had my interview and then this morning at my first crime scene," Sydney said, looking a little less jumpy now that she had something to focus on.

"Yeah, I heard about that crime scene, the rumor mill has been in full swing about it all day."

"Oh, really?" she asked, looking surprised.

"Joys of small-town life, which you'll now get to experience first-hand," he said with a smile. If he wasn't mistaken, the fact he had been seen standing in the diner talking to the new deputy—the new *hot* deputy—would have made the rounds by the time the sun set this evening.

"I've never lived in a small town before," she said with a small smile of her own.

"You been a cop for long?"

"Four years now."

"You always wanted to be one?"

"For a while," Sydney replied. The tentative ease between them evaporated, and something crossed her face. "I better go," she mumbled, trying to make a run for it.

"Wait." Levi snapped out a hand and grabbed her wrist before she could bolt, he hadn't meant to upset her, and he didn't want her to leave just yet. "Sorry, I didn't realize that was a sensitive topic. You eat already?"

"Umm, no, I was just going to grab my phone from my car before I ordered."

"Why don't you come sit with me, we can eat together, I can tell you a little bit more about the town," he suggested. Levi didn't know what it was, but there was just something about Sydney that drew him in. Yes, she was gorgeous and sexy, but it wasn't that, it was just ... he didn't even know, but he wasn't going to examine it too closely.

"Well," she hesitated, clearly uncomfortable with the idea, and he wasn't going to force her, intrigued or not, he wasn't in the market for a girlfriend, flirting was one thing, but to open his heart again was something he wasn't sure he was ready for.

"Okay, then, enjoy your evening," he smiled again. Maybe once she settled into town she'd loosen up a bit, and they could get to know one another.

"Wait," she called as soon as he'd turned his back.

He faced her and watched as she dragged in a long breath, her nose was scrunched up, forehead furrowed, it looked like she was raging some sort of internal battle over something as simple as sitting and having a meal with someone in her new home in a crowded diner. That spoke volumes. It was obvious she was nervous, but she didn't have to be, he wasn't going to push her into anything. Interested in her or not he didn't hurt women. Well, except for ...

"Okay. Eating dinner with you would be nice, and I'd love to know more about River's End." She offered him a smile that hit him straight in the gut. Levi wasn't used to this, he didn't react to women this way. Women tended to be attracted to him, and he had no problem flirting while making it clear that he wasn't interested in a relationship, but Sydney made him want to throw that idea out the window.

"Perfect." Resting his hand on the small of her back, he felt an immediate rush of heat, like he'd been burned. What was it about this woman? He'd spent two minutes in her company and not only was he ready to take her home and do some serious making out, but he was ready to throw away three years of being single. Two minutes in her company and he was ready to forget the reason he had spent the last three years being single.

From the startled way Sydney turned her head and looked up at him he knew she had felt the same jolt of fire that he had. Levi put it down to the fact that his older brother had recently gotten married and his younger brother had started dating an old friend and things were getting serious between them. His subconscious obviously felt left out, and Sydney was the first new woman he had met in months, it was no wonder she had grabbed his attention.

"You have got to order a burger, Penny here makes the best you've ever had," he told Sydney as he steered her through the busy diner toward a quiet booth in the back. Subconscious reasons for this attraction he felt for Sydney or something more, Levi never turned down an opportunity to get to know a beautiful woman better.

~

6:21 P.M.

She was an idiot.

She'd made such a fool out of herself.

Levi must think she was stupid and probably wondered what kind of cop she was and why his brother had hired her.

Sydney wasn't usually so tongue-tied, it was just that the doctor was hot and when he'd touched her, she'd felt this kind of energy surge between them, it had been disconcerting. She had moved to River's End for a fresh start, a chance to finally set the past in the past and move on with her life, but she hadn't really thought any further ahead than a new job and a new place to live. She hadn't envisioned meeting a man, and she wasn't sure she wanted to.

She wasn't sure she was ready to.

Yet try as she might, Sydney couldn't get the image of Levi Black out of her head. Those bright hazel eyes, the smile that made his dimples show, that scruffy black hair, those muscles, the smell of his cologne, the way he laughed, and the sound of his voice as he told her all about the residents of River's End. The way his hand felt when it rested on the small of her back as he'd guided her through the busy diner.

It was like everything about him had been seared into her mind.

She didn't date, hadn't even as a teen, and yet as woefully inexperienced as she was, she had seen the attraction in his eyes as he looked at her. She felt it when he touched her. Knew it when he had stalled her attempts to leave and she had somehow found herself agreeing to stay and eat dinner with him.

It wasn't really a date though.

At least not in her mind.

This whole building a new life thing was new for her, and she wanted to take things slowly. Focus on her job, maybe make some friends—something else she was woefully inexperienced at—find out what it was like to be on her own, to be free to make her own choices, to live her own life.

Even if Levi was attracted to her and had been interested in asking her out, she was sure after spending half an hour in her company that he had dropped any such notion. Sydney knew she wasn't much to look at, too plain and too slim, no womanly curves on her body, she was awkward and shy, and the only time she truly felt like she knew what she was doing in life was when she was at work.

Being a cop meant everything to her, and this was her chance to show her new colleagues what she was capable of, she couldn't allow anything to mess that up. Certainly not daydreaming about a guy who was too sexy and good-looking to be with someone like her. Levi was way out of her league, and she better get that idea through her head and stop thinking about him. It wasn't like she wanted anything to happen between them anyway so she should just drop this whole train of thought.

"Sydney."

She looked up when she heard the door open and saw Abe standing there. "Hi, I'm just reading through the case files." Her boss had told her that with the possibility that they were looking for a serial killer, he was bringing them all in to go through the cases and get her up to speed, so after dinner at the diner with Levi, she had come right back to work.

"I heard you had dinner with my brother." Abe grinned at her as he took a seat at the small table in the conference room. The Sheriff's offices were small, the building had only five rooms, a foyer at the front, the conference room, Abe's office, another office she shared with the other deputies, a kitchen, plus a couple of cells they could put prisoners in.

"How did you hear about that?" she asked, face scrunching in surprise. She had only been back at work for ten minutes, she knew that small towns were renowned for their gossip mills, but boy did River's End move quickly.

"That's small-town life for you."

"Oh," she said in a small voice, not quite sure she was prepared for people to be all up in her business all the time. She was a private person, and while she had known life in a small town would be different, she hadn't realized it would be quite like this.

As if sensing her discomfort Abe sat beside her. "Hey, gossip aside, small-town life can be amazing. Nothing like knowing you have a whole town full of people who would drop anything and everything to be there for you. Here in River's End we look after our own, we have each other's backs. You're new here, but you show everyone you're here for the long haul, and it won't be long before you're welcomed into the fold. Don't be surprised to get a few catty looks from the single ladies in town though, my brother is a charmer and a flirt, and there are plenty of women who would die to have dinner with him."

"Does he date a lot?" As soon as she said the words she wished she could take them back. Why was she asking that? She didn't want to give anyone, especially her new boss, the idea that she was interested in hooking up. In reality, it was the furthest thing from her mind, despite her physical attraction to Levi. Her cheeks felt like they were on fire and she wished the floor would open up and swallow her whole to save her from herself.

Abe arched an eyebrow. "No. Levi doesn't date. At all. Flirt, yes. Charm the panties off of women, yes. Actually take them out on a date, nope."

"Oh," she said again, wishing she would stop blushing. Why was she disappointed at hearing that? She'd thought that he was interested and even though she wasn't, that had definitely made her feel ... she didn't even know. But apparently she had nothing to worry about in the dating department. She'd misread Levi—totally something she would do—and made assumptions when all he was doing was harmless flirting.

Well, noted.

Next time she saw him, she would keep that in mind.

Desperate to veer the conversation back into safe waters, Sydney picked up the files in front of her and shuffled them unnecessarily. "So while I was reading through the files on Naomi Franklin's murder, and from what I know about Elena Martinez's murder, the thing that stood out to me the most was the burns."

If he was surprised by her sudden change in topic Abe didn't show it, instead he ran a hand through his scruffy beard and studied her. "I agree. The burns mean something specific to him. You have any ideas on why that might be?"

Sydney nodded slowly. This was her first time working a case like this. Still, she had studied criminal psychology and she knew a lot about how the minds of monsters worked—she was related to one after all—plus Abe seemed sincere in wanting her opinion. Hence, she was comfortable voicing her ideas. "He might be scarred from a fire or burned some other way, if he asked them out and they turned him down he might feel it was because of his burn scars, and so he wanted to inflict the same damage on them."

Abe considered her words. "Why the feet though? If he had asked them out and they'd turned him down, and he believed that rejection was based on his scars, then why burn their feet? Why not something that would be more disfiguring?"

That made sense. If she was right in her theory that he was punishing them for their rejection then it would make more sense he might try to burn their faces, or possibly breasts or something womanly like that.

But the killer hadn't done that.

He'd burned his victims' feet.

From what it looked like he had submerged their feet up to their ankles in boiling water. That felt more like torture.

Why did you torture someone?

Because you were a sadist who got off on inflicting pain or because you wanted something from someone and they wouldn't give it to you.

Was that what this was?

Was the killer torturing his victims for information?

"I can see the wheels spinning in your head. What are you thinking?" Abe asked.

"I was wondering if the burns were him trying to get them to tell him something," she said a little warily, aware that sounded strange because what would the killer possibly want to know from two small-town girls. Suddenly, she was pleased that Abe had asked her this before Fletcher, Will, Julian, and Beau arrived, she didn't want to look stupid in front of all her colleagues in one shot. "But what?" she continued when Abe didn't say anything. "What would he want from them? It sounds crazy, right? That's probably not it at all." This was definitely a make a fool out of herself kind of day, and she wished she wasn't quite so good at doing that.

"Actually, it doesn't sound crazy," Abe told her. "I think you might be right."

Pride flushed through her. Stage one of building her new life by excelling at her job was well underway. Now she just had to figure out who this killer was and stop him before any more young women were kidnapped, horribly tortured, and murdered.

And that she had no idea how to do.

June 8th
7:49 A.M.

"Morning," Levi greeted his brother as he walked into Abe's office at the Sheriff's building.

Abe grunted in response, busy poring over a stack of files on his desk. Levi wasn't offended by his older brother's gruff ways, before Abe had met and fallen in love with Meadow, he used to be a whole lot more brisk with people. Letting go of the betrayal of his former fiancée and letting himself find happiness again had been good for him. Meadow was good for him. The woman was like a permanent ray of sunshine. She'd lived through a Hell that would destroy most people and yet she was constantly looking for reasons to be happy, reasons to enjoy life, instead of reasons to let the horror she had experienced rule her life. Any day now the recently married couple would be welcoming the arrival of Meadow's baby into the world. As soon as it was born, Abe would be signing the adoption papers to make the baby officially his, although he knew his brother already loved the little girl as though she were his own flesh and blood.

"I brought you breakfast," he announced, knowing that would capture Abe's attention. "Freshly baked cinnamon rolls from the bakery."

At that, his brother lifted his head, narrowing his eyes. "And why exactly are you in my office before eight in the morning with my favorite breakfast pastry?"

"So suspicious." Levi laughed, although his brother wasn't wrong in implying he had an ulterior motive for this early morning visit. "I brought coffee too."

"Okay, what's up? What did you do? You didn't get a speeding ticket, did you? Because if one of my deputies pulled you over and gave you a ticket, I'm not making it go away for you."

He laughed off his brother's warning, the deputies in River's End were his cousins Will and Julian, and his younger brother's best friend Fletcher Harris, none of them would give him a speeding ticket, not even Beau Caldwell who had moved to town just two months ago when he fell in love with River's End local, Sheriff's department office manager and receptionist, and honorary Black family member Poppy Deveraux. "I don't speed."

"Yeah, that's just what you tell Mom," Abe shot back. "Everyone in this town knows you've never followed a speed limit in your life. The only reason Mom believes you when you tell her everyone else is wrong is you give her that I'm you're sweet baby boy smile, and it makes her temporarily lose her mind."

Levi couldn't help but laugh at that. He had learned the perfect smile to shoot his mother whenever he had done something that would land him in trouble by the time he was about four years old. "That's because I'm Mom's favorite," he teased.

"You wish, little brother," Abe shot back with a smile. "Dahlia is the favorite, and you know it."

He couldn't argue with that. Not that their parents actually had favorites, but baby of the family and only girl Dahlia definitely held a special place in their parents' hearts, especially because of what she'd gone through as a teenager. "Have you spoken to her lately?"

"A couple of texts, but she never picks up when I call, never returns calls either," Abe said, his forehead creased with worry lines.

They were all concerned about Dahlia. She hadn't come back to River's End since she graduated high school, not even for holidays, and she rarely called any of them, it had probably been close to six months since he had last heard her voice. "We're going to have to do something about her, it's breaking Mom's heart, and Dahlia hasn't moved on."

"I'm not sure she can," Abe said quietly.

Levi hated knowing his baby sister was hurting, and there was nothing he could do to make it better. He'd do anything to help Dahlia, Abe and Theo would too, and their parents, and anyone in River's End for that matter. But Dahlia didn't see it that way, she was ashamed, and her solution was to just cut ties with everyone, including her family who loved her unconditionally.

"So to what do I owe the pleasure of this early morning visit and breakfast?" Abe asked, waving a hand to indicate he wanted the box of still warm cinnamon rolls.

"Well ..." he dragged the word out as he gave his brother the box and the cup of coffee.

"Well?" Abe prompted, taking a bite of one of the rolls.

"I wanted to ask you about your new deputy." Levi hadn't been able to get the pretty brunette out of his mind. All night he'd thought about her, about how nervous she had been and how much he'd wanted to put her at ease by wrapping an arm around her and dragging her up against him, kissing her until she forgot all about her anxiety.

"Sydney? Why do you want to know about her?" Abe arched a brow and brushed away a spot of icing that had stuck to his chin.

"I met her yesterday at the diner."

"I know, I heard about it before I even got back here for our meeting last night, and I don't think Syd was too happy to know she was the center of town gossip a day after arriving here."

"You know what this place is like." Levi shrugged, he'd lived here most of his life so he was used to the gossip mill, but Sydney was new to all of this, and it could be overwhelming.

"Seems like I should be asking you about Sydney, you're the one who ate dinner with her." Abe grinned at him.

"Yeah, but I could hardly get her to say anything, I mostly just told her about the town." Whenever he'd asked her a question she'd mostly deflected and countered with a question of her own. It had been a long time since he'd been intrigued by a woman like he was with Sydney, and he wanted to get to know her better. "So what do you know about her?"

"She has a bachelors in criminal psychology. She's been a cop for four years, she applied for the job because she wanted a change of scenery, wanted to move out of the city, see how small-town living suited her."

"I know all of that." That had been about all he'd managed to get out of her besides her name. "What else do you know?"

"I'm running a police force here not a dating service." Abe finished off his cinnamon roll and grinned at him, wiping his sticky fingers on a napkin. "You want to know more about her, then ask her."

"I tried," he said, frustrated. It was clear that Sydney was hiding from or running from something, and while he was sure it was nothing criminal—she wouldn't have gotten a job with Abe if it was—it was obviously something that had caused her to uproot herself and start a whole new life. There was nothing wrong with starting over, and it certainly didn't mean that the person was running away, but that coupled with the fact she wouldn't answer any personal questions got his gut tingling.

"Why the sudden interest in her?" Abe asked, head cocked to the side, gaze quizzical as though trying to figure out a puzzle. "It's not like you haven't had women throwing themselves at your feet since you got back, residents, tourists, patients or their families at the hospital. Why Sydney? Why now?"

"I don't know." He'd been standing, but now he dropped into a chair on the other side of Abe's desk. He didn't have a clear answer to that question. It just felt ... right. It felt like it was time.

"You're ready," Abe said. "You're ready to move on."

A no was automatically ready to come out. For the last three years he hadn't been ready to move forward, he'd thought that he never would be. It was why he flirted but never let anything go anywhere with anyone, he hadn't wanted to. Everything that had happened was still too raw, the pain was still too strong, the sense of still being connected to someone was there. But now, it just felt like maybe he *was* ready to move on.

"I can't explain it. When she bumped into me, I just felt this connection, it wasn't like love at first sight or anything, and yeah it's been three years since I was last with a woman, and Sydney is hot, so I wouldn't pass up the chance to get her into bed, but it's more than that. I want to get to know her, I think she could become someone really important to me. I can't stop thinking about her, and I want to get to know her better, but she's closed off, she doesn't want to let anyone in, I'm sure it's because of whatever motivated this change in her life. Anything you know about her at all, please tell me. I'm not asking you to break any confidences if she told you something she wouldn't want anyone else to know, I just need something, something that I can use to build a connection, show her that she can trust me."

Abe studied him a moment longer, then sighed. "Well, I guess since you brought me breakfast I'll give you something. Sydney said she can't cook, so chances are she's going to be eating a lot more meals at the diner."

That was exactly what he needed.

If Sydney would be frequenting the diner, then for the foreseeable future, he would be too.

Levi was determined to see if there was something between them. If there was then maybe he'd find someone who could finally help him heal from the loss he had suffered, and if not, then at least he'd end up with a new friend, and you could never have too many friends.

~

11:55 A.M.

Sydney was excited.

The longer she worked on this case and the more time she spent with her new colleagues the more her confidence grew. She was younger than the other deputies by a couple of years, and she had never been in the military like they had, but none of them had made her feel like she was inferior in any way. Last night they had sat around until late, discussing ideas and theories. Everyone had listened when she'd spoken and treated her like she was one of them, like she was every bit as good as they were at their jobs. While Sydney knew she wasn't quite as good as they were yet, she knew she would get there, she would learn everything she could from these men and become a better cop for it.

And she wanted to be a better cop.

She wanted to be the best cop she could be.

She wanted to be every bit as good a cop as the one who had saved her and her sister all those years ago.

This was what was important in her life right now, not worrying about sexy doctors who made her feel things she wasn't supposed to.

Too many years being told that her place in life was not to receive pleasure but to give it, made it hard for her to believe anything but. Although she knew that she had been brainwashed it still influenced her, still gave her anxiety when she thought about doing anything other than what she had been taught. And Levi Black made her want to do the opposite of what had been ingrained into her brain.

"Dale Jacoway's farm is just up ahead."

Sydney started at the words, realized she had been lost in thought, thinking about the past and the possibilities of the future, instead of focusing on her job. So much for her desire to be the best cop she could be.

Work.

This move was primarily about work.

Yes, it was about escaping the past and building a life that was all hers, but the main part of that was to excel at her job.

"Do you know Dale? Personally, I mean. Has he lived here long?" she asked Fletcher Harris who it seemed like she would be working with regularly since they'd spent the day before working together trying to pin down a timeline of Elena Martinez's final days. She liked Fletcher, he was quiet but smart, and yesterday they had worked well together, he'd taken the lead since he was the one with the knowledge of the town, but he hadn't just shoved her aside, he had included her in everything.

"He's a few years older than me, but the same age as Abe, since this is a small town, I knew him."

"What was he like?" As best as they could tell, Dale Jacoway had been the last person to see Elena alive which meant he was either the one who had abducted her or he might have seen the person who did. She wanted to know what to expect when they arrived, not because she was nervous but because she still felt the need to prove herself. Abe had taken a chance on her when he'd hired her to be the fifth deputy in his department, and she wanted him to know that he wouldn't regret it.

"His family was poor, and I remember that being a sore point for him. It wasn't like anyone in town was rich, but I know his family struggled, he didn't always have the things the other kids did, and it made him feel like he needed to prove himself."

"Was he ever violent? Into drugs or alcohol? Did he ever do anything that makes you think he might be the killer we're looking for?"

Fletcher briefly took his eyes off the road to shoot her a one-sided smile. "No, he never did anything that would make me think he could be the killer. Doesn't mean he's not, but I don't expect there to be any trouble today."

"I'm not worried if there is," she said a little defensively. "I've arrested my fair share of criminals, had some that wouldn't come quietly, I can hold my own."

"Wouldn't have you here with me if I thought you couldn't," Fletcher told her, and since his tone was sincere and not patronizing, she believed him.

"I hope it's him. I can't imagine what those women felt when he was torturing them, I don't want anyone else to go through that. I hope it's Dale and I hope we find something to prove it so we can arrest him."

"Can't argue with that. Here we are," Fletcher announced as he turned into a driveway.

They were out in the country, at the farm where Dale Jacoway had grown up. Apparently, his parents had died a couple of years ago and left him this place. Dale worked as a truck driver and grew a lot of his own food to help make ends meet. The man was still poor, and she wondered if that was still an issue for him. The farm was rundown, a complete mess, there were old cars dotted about through the overgrown yard along with piles of trash. The house was a small white farmhouse with a large veranda that could have been cute if it had been freshly painted and well maintained.

Fletcher parked the car, and they both got out. The temperature had risen today and was now unpleasantly hot, and again Sydney wished she could wear a cotton sundress or something besides her long black pants and blouse. But she was at work, she had to look professional, it was one thing for her colleagues to respect her, but she knew she still had to earn the respect of the town's other residents, and some of them might not be as willing to accept her as the new deputy.

Together they walked across the lawn and up the rickety steps where Fletcher rapped on a door that had been red at some point but was now more the color of dried blood and peeling to reveal the gray wood underneath.

It took almost two minutes but finally the door was thrown open by a man who looked surprisingly clean and well put together considering where he lived and the state of the property.

"Afternoon, Dale," Fletcher greeted the man.

"Fletcher? What're you doing here? And who's she?" Dale jerked his head in her direction.

"This is Sydney. Deputy Sydney Clark," he added.

Dale shot her a surprised look but then nodded. "Deputy Clark."

"Mr. Jacoway," she returned with a nod.

"So what can I do for you two?" Dale asked, leaning against the doorframe. "Can I assume this isn't a social call?"

"You can," Fletcher acknowledged. "May we come in?"

The man studied them from pale blue eyes that appeared larger behind his glasses. He seemed to be debating his options and Sydney wondered briefly if he would try to make a run for it. She would have moved her hand to rest on the butt of her gun, but Fletcher hadn't, and he knew Dale better than she did so she followed his lead.

"Why don't we talk here," Dale suggested finally.

"Any reason you don't want us in there?" she asked.

"So, why're you here?" Dale ignored her and turned to address Fletcher.

"You heard about Elena?" Fletcher asked.

"Heard she died, was found in the river."

"When was the last time you saw her?" Fletcher asked.

"Can't remember," Dale replied, but they both knew he was lying. Although she wanted to confront him on the lie she kept her mouth shut. It was clear he wasn't interested in including her so she let Fletcher take over.

"Oh?" Fletcher cocked a brow. "You don't remember seeing her three days ago? Word is that you approached her at the ice cream parlor around seven in the evening. From what we heard you asked her out on a date, and she rejected you. Told you she wasn't interested, and from the sounds of things, it wasn't the first time she'd told you that. You get angry with her, Dale? Angry that she didn't want to go out with you? Decide to teach her a lesson?"

Dale stiffened, standing straight and glaring at both of them. "I think you should leave. Now."

As much as she would like to stay, search his house and find the reason he hadn't wanted them to go inside, see if there was evidence that either Elena or Naomi had been here at some point, they didn't have a warrant so there was nothing they could do but what he'd asked.

"You have a nice day, Dale," Fletcher said with a tilt of his head, then turned and headed back toward their vehicle. Reluctant and frustrated, Sydney followed him.

"You think it could be him?" she asked when they got inside the SUV.

"I think he's definitely up to something," Fletcher said. "He lied about seeing Elena, and he didn't want us to go inside."

"His property is secluded, Elena and Naomi would have screamed when he burned them, but out here no one would have heard them."

"He was dressed nicely too. Those clothes were expensive. Dale drives trucks, not something I would have suspected that he'd be wearing. We discussed the possibility that the killer burned the victims' feet because he was trying to torture them into giving him information. What if Dale is into more than just driving trucks?"

"You think he might be trafficking drugs?" Sydney asked, eyes wide. A serial killer and a potential drug dealer, what a way to start her new job.

"Could be. Would explain why he's dressing nicely all of a sudden and why he didn't want us inside. It's possible that he was worried that Elena had seen or heard something that she shouldn't and that's why he had to torture her. It stopped her from turning him in to the cops, and it punished her for rejecting him."

"We need to get warrants for his house and truck, bank records too."

"We don't have enough for a warrant yet," Fletcher reminded her.

"Then we better find something to help us get it," she returned fiercely. She was not letting her first big case slip through her fingers, not when people's lives depended on it. There was no way to know how many other women Dale had asked out and who had rejected him, which meant there was no way to know if there were more potential victims.

As far as Sydney was concerned no one else was dying on her watch.

~

6:03 P.M.

If he sat in here all night he would draw attention to himself.

That was the last thing he needed right now, and yet he wasn't going to leave just because of the gossipmongers who had nothing better to do with their time than worry about what other people were doing.

Levi stretched and leaned back against the leather booth seat, the same booth he and Sydney had sat in last night when they'd had dinner. He knew that Sydney was uncomfortable with the attention she'd gotten because they'd eaten together, and he didn't want to make her more uncomfortable by approaching her here again, but it was the only option he had right now.

He'd come by here late morning, hoping to catch her if she stopped by for lunch, but she'd never come. Assuming that she was preoccupied with work, he knew all about the serial killer case that she had been thrown into the middle of, he'd eventually left.

Hoping that she'd at least be by for dinner, he'd parked himself here around five, ordering cup after cup of coffee and a few pastries to go along with it, while he pretended that he was busy working on his laptop.

He wasn't.

He was just scrolling away on social media, not really paying attention to anything that he was seeing, he was too busy thinking about Sydney.

What was it about her that had grabbed hold of him like this and refused to let him go?

She was pretty, but he'd met plenty of beautiful women, and none of them had ever done this to him.

She was smart, but he was a doctor, he knew plenty of smart women, and none of them had ever done this to him either.

So what was it about Sydney?

Maybe it was because she reminded him of Amy. Amy had been smart and pretty too, she'd also been vivacious, so full of life and energy that she seemed to have enough to impart to anyone she came into contact with. They'd met while they had both been serving, him as a doctor in the middle of a warzone and her as a helicopter pilot. There wasn't a single person on that base who hadn't been affected by Amy. She made people laugh, she made them smile, she made them feel like they weren't on a base in the middle of a warzone.

Amy was one of a kind.

Not a day had gone by since she had died that he hadn't thought about her, hadn't missed her, hadn't wished that things had worked out differently.

There wasn't a day that had gone by where he hadn't felt the deep weight of guilt.

He was responsible for Amy's death.

That wasn't something you got over.

Their relationship had been forbidden, and yet neither of them could deny the pull they felt. They were meant to be together, he'd known that from the first time he laid eyes on her. He'd seen their future, it had been marriage and children and growing old side by side, and no military rules were going to stand in the way of that.

They'd kept things quiet, and he hadn't minded when other men flirted with her, he was confident enough in their relationship. Amy loved him, she trusted him, and he had let her down.

Levi knew that as his first love he was never going to completely get over her death, she was always going to be a part of him, and he was good with that. He didn't want to let her go, he wanted to carry her around with him, his own personal ray of sunshine.

Over the last three years that pain and guilt had faded a little, it was still here, it would always be there, but he finally felt like he could breathe again.

As much as he knew time had made the difference, he couldn't help but feel that part of it was Sydney. She was quieter than Amy, more reserved, but he sensed her strength and determination, which reminded him so much of his Amy. Amy had come from a military family, her father had served, her mother had served, both her brothers and her sister served. She'd lost her mother, one brother, the other had been paralyzed in an attack and never been the same again, and yet nothing had deterred her from following in their footsteps and serving her country.

He respected Amy, and he respected Sydney, and ...

Speak of the devil. The diner door opened and Sydney walked in, looking impossibly sexy with her hair pulled into a neat bun, her light blue blouse drawing his attention to her breasts. Her heels clicked as she walked across the tiled floor. He loved a woman in heels. While most of their relationship he and Amy had been in the deserts of the Middle East, those times they had spent Stateside she'd always worn heels because she knew how it turned him on.

Clearing his throat, he lifted his gaze from what he knew were shapely calves beneath her simple black pants and as though sensing his eyes on her she looked right over at him.

Their eyes met and he felt it again.

It was like an invisible string had been tied one end around him, the other end around her and it was pulling the two of them together. He could fight against it, insist to himself that there was no way he could be this interested in a woman he'd only just met, but he didn't see the point. He had felt the same way when he met Amy, and that had worked out, if she hadn't died he'd been planning on proposing to her, starting their lives together.

There was no way he was missing out on another chance at having that same connection with another person. He'd missed it, when Amy had died it was like a piece of him had died with her, he wanted that piece back, he wanted someone to share his life with, he wanted to fall in love again.

Shooting Sydney his most winning smile, Levi stood and walked toward her. Sydney looked back at him uncertainly, she didn't smile and for a moment he thought she was going to bolt. She'd felt the connection between them, same as he had, he'd seen it in her face last night, but she was afraid of it. Had she had a bad experience with a man? Was she running from a toxic relationship, was that why she had decided to start over in River's End?

The idea of someone hurting Sydney stirred up that protective side of him. He was a doctor, and he's served to protect his country, feeling protective wasn't something new for him, but this was different. The only people who made him feel like this were his baby sister who had gone through a trauma that she still hadn't recovered from, Amy, the woman he had planned to spend his life with, and now Sydney.

He was taking that as a sign.

"Hey, Syd," he greeted her when he reached her side. He dipped his head and kissed her cheek, not where he wanted to kiss her, but they weren't a couple—yet—and so he couldn't go kissing her on the lips, especially not in the crowded diner.

"Uh, Levi, hi. I didn't expect to see you here," she stammered.

"I was waiting for you."

She started, then stared at him as though sure he was about to laugh like that had been a joke, but he wasn't joking, and he didn't play games. He was interested in her, he would back off if she asked him to, but until she did then he was going to be clear about his intentions, and his intentions were to get to know her better and then once he did, ask her out on a date.

"Dinner?" he asked.

"Umm, sure," Sydney agreed, her golden eyes still held a wary edge, but she was obviously willing to give him a chance despite her doubts and possible insecurities.

"Penny makes an amazing lasagna, homemade fries, and salad on the side," he told her.

"Sounds perfect, I'm starving, I skipped lunch."

"Something to drink?"

"Sparkling water is fine, it's hot today and I've been busy, haven't really had a chance to take a break, and I don't want to get dehydrated."

"You go sit down, I'll order and join you."

Sydney offered him a shy smile and tucked a stray lock of hair that escaped her bun behind her ear, then walked off to sit at the booth he'd been waiting for her in. Not wanting to waste a second of his time with her, Levi quickly ordered then went to join her.

"How was your day?" he asked as he slid into the booth to sit beside her. She looked surprised that he was sitting next to her instead of opposite her, but he wanted to be close, maybe put an arm around her shoulders once he got her to relax.

"Busy, but you know I can't talk about the case, right?"

"Of course," he assured her. "I hope you're making progress though. No one deserves what happened to Elena and Naomi, and I hope no one else winds up getting hurt."

"I'm going to do everything I can to stop that from happening," she said, voice strong and a fierce fire blazing in her eyes.

He believed her.

"I know you will," he said, reaching out to take her hand. Sydney was small but tougher than she looked, and he was positive that once she set her mind to something she didn't back down. Not for anything.

Sydney met his gaze squarely, and he saw gratefulness cross her features. That made him angry. Why should she be grateful that he believed her? For all her nervousness he knew that she was confident underneath, she was a cop after all, but did she also battle insecurities?

He knew all about that.

After he'd lost Amy, he doubted his abilities as a doctor for a long time.

But Sydney was competent enough that his brother had hired her which meant he would never doubt her abilities.

"Hey," he squeezed her hand to make sure she was focused on him. "You wouldn't have this job if my brother didn't think you could do it, and from knowing you all of a day I know that you take your job seriously and you give it everything you have. That means I know you're good at it. You never need to thank me for believing in you, you hear me? Never."

~

6:19 P.M.

Sydney didn't know what to say to that.

It was quite possibly the nicest thing anyone had ever said to her in her life.

No one had ever believed in her like that, and she hadn't even known Levi for more than twenty-four hours.

How could he know that she needed to hear that?

How could he know that she so desperately needed someone to believe in her?

Tears pricked the backs of her eyes, and she fought them back, not wanting to ruin the moment by crying, and without her even realizing it, she curled her fingers around his.

"Thank you," she whispered.

"What did I just tell you?" he teased, his eyes sparkling, giving her that grin that made his dimples come out.

"Sorry." She smiled back. She wasn't experienced with men, and she knew that he liked her, that was both nice and terrifying because she didn't know how she should respond. "But really, Levi," she said earnestly, "thank you. No one has ever believed in me like that before."

"You betcha." He grinned.

Sydney relaxed a little, maybe she didn't have to worry about things with Levi. Yes, she was wary of men, understandable given her past, but she didn't want to be afraid of them. Levi was a doctor, he was the sheriff's brother, there was no way he would hurt her.

"So, you up for a game?" Levi asked.

"Game? What kind of game?" She tried not to be suspicious but it was hard, she'd spent a lifetime expecting the worst.

"Kind of a get to know you game." From the look on his face he knew he was pushing his luck. She'd made it clear last night that she didn't want to talk about herself, but she had nothing to hide and intellectually speaking she knew she had nothing to be ashamed about. Moving here was about starting over so she would have to let people in at some point.

"Okay," she agreed.

"Really?" His eyes lit up like he hadn't been expecting a yes. "Okay, we each get to ask the other three questions, you can ask first."

"Any rules on the questions?" She had no idea what she wanted to ask but she kind of liked the idea of getting to know Levi better.

"Nope. That change your mind?"

She was no quitter. "Nope. Did you always want to be a doctor?"

"My high school sweetheart had cancer. She was first diagnosed when she was six, she beat it but it came back when she was thirteen, she beat it again, but when it came for her the third time it finally got her. She died just a couple of months before she would have graduated. I guess that's what inspired me to be a doctor."

"Oh, Levi, I'm so sorry." He still held her hand so she squeezed it. "Did you always intend to go into the military?"

"Yes. No question. My dad was, my uncle too, and my brothers and cousins and I always knew I would follow in their footsteps. One question to go."

"That was a two part one," she protested.

Levi laughed. She realized she liked the sound, it was so light and airy and yet very masculine. "Fine, two to go."

"What's your favorite animal?"

"Okay," Levi laughed again, "I wasn't expecting that. Giraffes."

"Giraffes? I wasn't expecting that," she parroted back his words. She'd been expecting to pick something more ... big and scary.

"Hey, they're cool," he told her. "Their eyes and those eyelashes, they're beautiful, and they were Missy's favorite."

"Aww, that's nice." She smiled, assuming that Missy was his high school girlfriend who had passed away. "Okay, last one, have you ever been married or engaged?" She wasn't even going to lie to herself and pretend she was asking this question for any other reason than that she was curious about Levi. If he was interested in her, she wanted to know as much about him to decide if she could take the risk of letting herself be interested in him too.

"No," Levi answered shortly and something passed across his face.

She'd overstepped.

Sydney knew it without him having to say it.

And this was why she avoided the whole dating scene, she was really —*really*—bad at it.

She tried to pull her hand back, her cheeks heating, but Levi tightened his hold on her. "I was almost engaged. Her name was Amy, but she died."

"Oh." Her eyes flew to his. How unlucky could the poor guy get? Two women that he had loved had passed away, she knew the pain of losing someone you loved, and she thought it was brave that he was still searching for love after having lost so much. "I'm so sorry, that's just awful."

"Thank you." He smiled, and this time the smile was more than just something flirty, this time it was more intimate, more personal, and she couldn't help but smile back.

"You're welcome. It's your turn to ask me questions now," she said, trying not to sound nervous and wondering how she would answer certain things he might ask her.

"What's your favorite color?"

Well, that was an easy one. "Pink."

"Pink?" he echoed, scrunching up his nose.

"Hey, pink is a great color," she protested. "But don't tell anyone it's my favorite, it might ruin my new deputy in town persona."

"Your secret is safe with me." Levi winked. "Just so you know my opinion of you has gone down now I know you love such an awful color."

"Hi, Levi." They both turned as a pretty young woman carried over a tray of food.

"Hi, Lynn," Levi said.

"How have you been?" Lynn, the waitress, asked as she batted her eyelashes at Levi, clearly flirting even though she was sitting right next to him.

"Fine," he replied tersely. "This is Sydney, she's the new deputy."

"Oh, yeah, hi." Lynn spared her only the briefest of glances as she set the plates and glasses on the table in front of them. "Let me know if you need anything," Lynn said. The smile she shot Levi clearly conveyed she didn't just mean if they needed anything else for their meal.

"Sorry about that," Levi said when she left.

"Not your fault. What are you like River's End's most eligible bachelor?" This wasn't the first time a woman had tried to openly flirt with Levi when they'd been together, there had been a couple last night.

"Kinda," Levi replied.

"Really?" If Levi was like the heartthrob of River's End what was he doing with her? There were definitely better catches out there than her. Lots of them.

"Hey." He reached out and cupped her cheek in his hand, his thumb brushing lightly across her cheekbone. "I don't sleep around, in fact I don't date at all, I think that's why there are a few women around who are interested in me."

That, and you're hot, Sydney thought but didn't say out loud.

"I like you, I'm not going to pretend otherwise, and I want to get to know you. If you aren't interested that's okay, we can still be friends. But if you are interested and we do get together then you don't have to worry about me cheating on you. I don't do that. And just because someone is interested in me doesn't make it mutual."

He was putting the ball firmly in her court.

She had never met a man who was so honest and straightforward, it kind of freaked her out because she hadn't moved to River's End with the intention of dating anyone. Sure, she'd known it might happen eventually but not on her second day here.

Since she didn't know what to say she just nodded.

That seemed to be enough and Levi smiled. "We should eat." Before he removed his hand he let his thumb trace slowly down her cheek to brush across her lips, a promise of what was to come if she said yes to the two of them getting together.

Heart thundering in her chest, Sydney couldn't help but suck in a nervous breath. She was so out of her element, and she wished she had even a little experience at dating.

When Levi let his hand drop she immediately missed it, and before she could jump into something she wasn't ready for she quickly picked up her knife and fork and tried the lasagne. "This is amazing." She practically drooled.

"Told you." Levi grinned as he took a huge mouthful of lasagna, his eyes falling closed in delight, and a vivid picture of his face just after sex flashed into her mind. She knew how to please a man, and she was sure she could make him come, but for once she wondered what it would be like to feel that kind of pleasure herself.

Quickly she brushed those thoughts away.

"You still have two questions left," she reminded him as she tried one of the homemade fries that tasted like little slices of heaven.

"You ever been married or engaged?" he tossed her own question back at her.

"Umm, no, neither." Dragging in a big breath, she admitted, "I've never been in a serious relationship."

Instead of looking surprised by her admission he merely nodded. Had he suspected that she wasn't very experienced? That he might have actually relaxed her rather than making her anxious, she didn't want him expecting things from her that she wasn't ready to give.

"Last one, do you have any family? Obviously you had parents, I mean you moved here to start over, so I was wondering how that impacted your relationship with your family."

"It didn't," she said simply. "I don't have family to impact. My parents are dead, my mom died when I was eleven, my dad and stepmother when I was fourteen, I have an older sister, but we don't have a relationship anymore." Walking away from her sister had been one of the hardest things she had ever had to do, but for the sake of her own sanity it had been a necessity.

"I'm sorry." Levi reached out and squeezed her shoulder, offering what comfort he could.

"Thanks."

"You definitely have a family here. River's End is a tight-knit community, we look out for our own, and you're one of us now.

Speaking of which, tomorrow we're having a community working bee at the Honeysuckle Hotel. It burned down a couple of months ago, and the owner is just the sweetest woman. Her name is Maggie Wilson, and she's dating my little brother Theo. Most of the structural work has been done and now it's just painting and laying floors and stuff so tomorrow the whole town is getting together to help out. I'd love it if you went with me."

Sydney froze, fork halfway to her mouth. Levi had said he was interested in her, but she hadn't expected him to ask her out so soon. "You mean like a date?"

"Kind of, most of the town will be there, and we'll be working, but yeah sort of a date. It would be a great way for you to meet everyone, and we'd get to spend some time together."

She could feel her pulse fluttering, and her hands suddenly got so sweaty the fork almost slid out, but she steeled herself.

This was her chance to finally build the new life she had dreamed of for so long.

There was no way she was throwing it away no matter how much it scared her.

"I'd love to go with you tomorrow."

~

9:23 P.M.

They were onto him.

They were onto him.

They were *onto* him.

They were onto *him*.

His hands clawed at his hair, he had no idea what he was supposed to do now.

Should he go to the cops and tell them everything?

Should he go to his superiors and tell them what was going on?

Should he abort his mission and hightail it out of here and disappear?

He had no idea.

Running probably wasn't the best of options, even if he did they would eventually find him. And if he was found his punishment would be much more severe than it had been last time.

No, he couldn't run.

And if he couldn't run, it meant his only choice was to keep going with what he had been tasked with doing. If he went to the cops he would have to put his life in their hands, and he knew he couldn't do that, so in the end that would result in running anyway.

He wouldn't put his life in anyone else's hands ever again.

He couldn't.

The only one he could depend on was himself.

Did people know who he was and what he was doing?

As he walked down Main Street it felt like everyone was looking at him. Their eyes followed his every move, probing deep down inside him and figuring out all of his secrets.

He hated it.

He didn't want them to see inside him.

He wanted to run away, hide, figure out a way to get out of the mess he had found himself in.

A mess of his own making.

That was the worst part, knowing that this could all have been avoided if he hadn't been so stupid. If he had thought things through better, then he wouldn't be stuck having to try to undo everything even though he knew it wasn't really possible. He felt like he was sitting on a boat in the middle of the ocean, only the boat had a hole in it, and although he had a bucket and was frantically bailing water out as fast as he could, it didn't do any good because water continued to leak in through the hole.

He would have to pull it together.

He couldn't fall apart now.

Focus on the plan. That was the way he could keep it together, if he had something to occupy his mind, and his time, then he would be able to keep going.

Okay.

The plan.

Focus.

Deep breath in.

Deep breath out.

Deep breath in.

Deep breath out.

Focus.

The plan.

Feeling calmer now, more in control, he was able to plan out his next move. He was out because he knew it was time, time to find the next one. He wished he knew who it was going to be ahead of time but he didn't, he only knew when he saw them.

Now that he was back in control he looked at everyone he walked past. He met their eyes, faked a smile he didn't feel, pretended he was just like them, out for a stroll through this quaint little town on this almost summer's evening. The sun had set, but it was a clear night and between the moon and the stars, the lights from the streetlights that lined either side of the road, and the fairy lights that were strung up around most of the stores, it was almost as bright as day out. That meant that he could get a good look at each person he walked past, searching their face, looking for the sign.

He was almost to the end of the street, and panic ebbed back through his calm mask. What if he was wrong? What if tonight wasn't the night? Just because he had gotten his instructions didn't mean that something couldn't have gone wrong. There was no way for them to contact him once he was off on a mission, they couldn't call him because someone might overhear, so if things had been called off he wouldn't know.

Had it been called off?

Should he abort?

Just as he was about to turn on his heel and head back the way he had come so he could go home, he saw her.

A woman, probably in her mid-twenties, she had long blonde hair that reached all the way down her back and shimmered like gold as it caught the light. She was laughing and talking to someone on her cell phone, and the smile on her face made her radiant. She was wearing high heels and a sexy red dress that barely came midway down her thighs.

She was the one.

The one he had been looking for.

He could tell by the dress.

She was the one he had been sent to find.

To find and question.

Just as he wasn't innocent in any of this they weren't either. They had brought this upon themselves just as he had brought this upon himself.

While that should ease his guilt it didn't.

He knew what he was doing was wrong.

But knowing it was wrong and having an alternate option that didn't end in his own death were two different things.

Shoving aside that guilt because it was only going to wind up getting him hurt or killed or arrested, he plastered on a wider smile and approached the woman.

"Excuse me," he said as he walked up to her.

Her momentary surprise when she saw him faded and she returned his smile with a hundred-watt one of her own. "May I help you?" she asked.

"I was wondering if you wanted to go grab a drink with me," he said smoothly. It had been a while since he'd had to be charming, but when he did have to be he could be.

"Oh, well, yeah, okay, I guess so. Hold on. Hey, Monica, some guy just asked me to go have a drink with him," she said into the phone. "Yeah, I guess he is," she giggled. "Yeah, I'll talk to you in the morning. I don't know what time. Okay. Love you too, bye. My sister," she said by way of explanation as she ended her call and slipped her phone into the red purse she had slung over her shoulder.

What was he supposed to say to that?

He wished he wasn't so nervous so he could think straight.

"She here in town too?" he asked, hoping he sounded a whole lot calmer than he felt.

"No, I'm just here passing through, thought I'd come into town tonight, see what was happening. This place is just the cutest," she gushed. "I'm Martha, by the way."

"Nice to meet you, Martha," he said, shaking the hand she held out.

She shot him a funny look when he didn't offer his name in return, and for a moment, he thought that he had tipped her off and that she would call this off and quickly retreat to a more populated place.

But she didn't.

Maybe because she was already tipsy enough that her defenses were lowered.

"Where do you want to go for a drink?" she asked.

"I know the perfect place," he replied. Reaching out, he gently grasped her elbow, nothing that could be deemed threatening in any way, but enough that as soon as he had her around the corner he would be able to dominate her.

"Is it far?"

"Nope, it's just in the next street. It's the perfect little place that only the locals know about."

"You live here?"

"All my life."

He led her around the corner, off Main Street where there were too many people milling about for him to do anything. The change was almost instantaneous, as soon as they were off the main street, it got quieter, darker, and for the first time, Martha appeared nervous.

"You sure it's not far?" she asked.

"Just two blocks that way." He pointed down away from the bustle behind them.

"You, uh, you never told me your name," she said as he continued to lead her away from any safety she might have been able to use to her advantage.

"No, I didn't."

He could feel her anxiety levels grow as she realized that she had made a mistake by trusting him and agreeing to come with him.

"Are you going to tell me your name?" Her voice shook as she asked the question and her entire body began to shake right along with it.

"No, I'm not."

The gravity of her mistake obviously now abundantly clear, she tried to yank herself out of his grasp. As she opened her mouth to scream he sprang into action. He moved her in front of himself and wrapped one arm around her waist to hold her close and the other he pressed across her neck.

He squeezed hard enough to cut off her air supply, effectively silencing her and preventing her from putting up much of a fight. Her fingers clawed at his arm in a desperate bid to dislodge him, but it was already too late.

As soon as she went limp in his grip he slunk into the shadows, his car wasn't far away, and he was confident that he could get there without anyone seeing him or Martha.

Then once he got her tucked away someplace where no one would hear her screams, he would find out if she had the answers that he sought.

June 9th
6:50 A.M.

She was early. It was still ten minutes until the time she had set with Levi to meet here at the diner before they went to the working bee at the hotel, and yet she couldn't stop fidgeting in nervous anticipation.

Sydney was new to this. In high school, she had been preoccupied with other things, she hadn't had time to date, it hadn't been a priority to her, and given what she had lived through she hadn't had any desire to date either. She didn't trust men, she knew what they were capable of, and she was wary of ever putting herself in a position where one would be able to hurt her.

That was where she and her sister differed.

While Victoria had allowed the brainwashing they had been subjected to, to shape the choices she made and the person she was, Sydney had rebelled against it, knowing that while some of it was too ingrained to break what they had been told was wrong. She didn't believe that her entire purpose in life was to please a man, she was worth more than that, she could live her own life. She could be her own person, have a job, friends, and if and when she was ready, a partner who treated her as an equal and not as a slave.

"Morning."

A hand landed on her shoulder and although she jumped, she managed to hold in the scream that almost escaped.

"Sorry, I thought you saw me come in," Levi said as he turned her to face him. He examined her face, searching her eyes, and then asked, "You okay?"

"Fine," she assured him, shoving away thoughts of her sister and her past. Today was about new beginnings, it was about her new life not her old life, and she was excited to meet more of the residents of River's End.

"You're sure?" He didn't quite look convinced.

"Positive."

"All right then, let's get going." His hand slid from her shoulder down her arm to her hand, which he clasped with his own before leading her out of the diner.

This was nice, holding hands, it was sweet and simple and gave her a chance to enjoy being with Levi without feeling pressured to do more. As determined as she was to build a new life, and as much as she liked Levi and was enjoying his company, she wasn't sure she was ready to do more. Sydney hoped he liked her enough to be patient with her. She believed him when he said he didn't sleep around, but he was still much more experienced than she was, and although he liked her that didn't mean he was prepared to wait until she was ready.

Too soon they reached Levi's car, and he let go of her hand to open the door for her, then took her elbow and helped her climb up into his truck.

"The hotel is only a few minutes' drive," he told her as he started the engine. "You already know Abe, of course, and my cousins, but you'll get to meet Abe's better half Meadow, and my younger brother Theo, and his girlfriend Maggie of course, since it's her hotel. My parents will be there too, and maybe my uncle."

So basically, she was meeting his entire family in one go.

Less than forty-eight hours after meeting him.

That felt like such a big step, and one that seemed to solidify the fact that they were now a couple, but this wasn't even really a date, and even though she'd had dinner with him twice she wasn't ready yet to think of them as a couple.

"Relax," he said as though he could feel her anxiety, and he reached out to take her hand and entwine their fingers. "There'll be lots of people there and other than Abe no one knows I'm interested in you. They only know that we've had dinner together a couple of times. No one needs to know any more than that, I don't want to make you uncomfortable."

That was sweet of him not to want to put her into a position that would make her uncomfortable, but ...

Wait.

What had he said?

Abe knew that he was interested in her?

"Relax," Levi said again, this time with a laugh. "Abe doesn't care, it's none of his business who I date or who you date, so don't worry about it. If and when you're ready I'll take you out for real. Today is just about letting you meet people, making you feel like you're part of the community. When I take you out on a real date, you'll know about it."

That prospect thrilled and terrified her.

His words also helped her relax. She wanted to be part of this community, she wanted River's End to become her home and the people here her extended family, she wanted to put down roots here.

Five minutes later they were parking in front of a huge stone building, there were at least two dozen other cars here, and there had to be over a hundred people that she could see milling about. This was amazing. That everyone in River's End loved Maggie Wilson and her hotel enough to turn out here at seven in the morning to help her get the place up and running again.

This was what she wanted.

She wanted there to be someone who loved and cared about her enough that they would do this for her. For as long as she could remember, it had felt like she was on her own. To have all of this was like a dream to her. She hoped Maggie knew what a lucky woman she was.

Levi came around and opened her door for her, and when she took his hand to help her climb down she felt a warm, fuzzy feeling wash through her. As nervous as she was to pursue anything with him she was equal parts excited. This was a whole new world to her, and she felt like Aladdin and Jasmine when they climbed onto that magic carpet to go flying through the air.

Sydney didn't let go of his hand as he led her toward a small group of people, aware of the prying eyes of the townsfolk on her but deciding not to care. She would have to get used to this, it was part of small-town life, and this place was her home now.

"Morning," Levi said when they reached the group. "Hi, Mom." He kissed a pretty woman in her late fifties with dark hair spotted with gray.

"My boy," Tatiana Black gushed as she dragged him in for a hug and kissed both his cheeks. "And who is this?" she asked, pointing straight at her.

"This is Sydney Clark," Levi replied.

"Oh, the new deputy," Tatiana grinned, grabbing her and hugging her fiercely. "You let me know if Abe is working you too hard, dear."

"Mom." Abe rolled his eyes at his mother.

Tatiana just waved him quiet and started making introductions. "This is my husband, Patrick," she said, pointing to a man who may have been Abe's identical double plus a couple of decades.

Patrick took her hand and kissed it. "Pleasure to meet you, Sydney."

"Likewise." She smiled, touched by how warmly the family was welcoming her.

"You know Abe, but this is his wife Meadow," Tatiana said, ushering a blonde woman who looked about ready to go into labor any second toward her.

"Hi, Sydney." Meadow beamed, grabbing her and pulling her into a hug. This family really liked to hug, hers hadn't been the touchy-feely kind, and it felt odd having strangers show her more affection than her family had.

"Nice to meet you." She smiled back.

"And this is my baby boy, Theo." Tatiana grabbed a man who looked just like Levi, and Sydney couldn't help but smile at such a large man being referred to as anyone's baby. "And the woman of the hour, Maggie." A pretty brunette with long, wavy locks smiled shyly, looking like she couldn't quite believe all these people were here for her.

"It's very nice to meet all of you, thank you for making me feel welcome," Sydney said. She'd never met such a lovely group of people, and she couldn't help but yearn for a family just like this one day.

"Of course, dear." Tatiana waved away her thanks like it wasn't necessary. "Plenty more people for you to meet today. Everyone wanted to come and help Maggie get this place ready to be open by July Fourth, everyone adores Maggie, and this place is like the center of the town."

"Well, I'm happy to be here to help and eager to get busy. What do you need me to do?" Sydney directed the question to Maggie.

Tatiana answered instead, "Meadow and I were going to do some painting, we'd love to have you join us."

She glanced over at Levi, she had anticipated spending the day with him, but she would enjoy getting to know his mother and sister-in-law.

"You go ahead, I'll check in with you later," Levi told her.

No sooner had he got the words out than Tatiana was ushering her over toward the front door, chattering away and completely putting Sydney at ease. This was nice, exactly what she had been seeking when she had left the city to come out here and start a new life. So far the move had worked out even better than she had anticipated. She liked her job, she liked the people, and she definitely liked Levi Black.

~

8:42 A.M.

She had been so stupid.

What had she been thinking?

Martha knew the answer to that, she *hadn't* been thinking.

Well, she had, but not about her safety.

She was never careless like this. Ever. She was perhaps the most cautious person on the planet. She thought through every single decision she made, including small ones that had no serious consequences.

She loved lists, she made them for everything, and whenever she had to make a decision she would write out a list of pros and cons to help her.

But last night was different.

This weekend was supposed to be different.

After breaking up with her boyfriend of two years when it finally became clear that he was using her and never actually intended to marry her or take their relationship any further, she had decided she needed to make some changes in her life. How many good things had she missed out on because she was so busy trying to be smart and logical instead of listening to her heart?

She knew one thing she had missed out on.

The love of her life.

She'd just graduated college, and he had asked her to marry him, but her logical brain had told her it wasn't the right time. They had both just graduated, they had student loans to pay off, careers to build, they shouldn't be getting distracted by having to put in all the work needed to build a successful marriage.

How stupid could she have been?

Trading love for a job had been stupid, but it was a mistake she could never take back.

She knew that because when she realized she had made a mistake and had looked up her old boyfriend, she'd found he was now happily married with a kid and another on the way.

And she was alone.

That had been the wake-up call she needed.

She was wasting her life.

So she had quit her job and decided to travel the country. She wanted to watch the sunrise and the sunset, she wanted to lie on her back in an open field and stare up at the stars, she wanted to see the great country she lived in, she wanted to meet new people and find out why she resisted happiness at every turn.

Now it was a moot point.

Because she had been pushing herself to let go of her rigidness and just live in the moment, she had agreed to go off with a stranger. A stranger who hadn't even told her his name. He had led her away from the busyness and safety of Main Street where most of the tourists and locals who had been out late had been, and as soon as he had got her alone where there was no one to see what he was going to do he had kidnapped her.

Instead of getting ready to go kayaking today, she was sitting in some rundown house, tied to a chair, her arms pulled behind her, each wrist tied to one side of the chair. Her ankles were also tied together, her feet sitting in a large metal bucket.

Martha had tried to get herself free, she had worked on loosening the ropes around her wrists, but all she had managed to achieve was rubbing herself raw until blood had dripped down her hands and puddled on the floorboards.

She was stuck.

Trapped.

And she had no idea what to expect.

She hadn't seen the man who had abducted her—didn't even know his name—since he had cut off her air supply until she passed out. He must have injected her with something after that because she didn't remember being brought here, wherever here was, or being tied up.

Already she had run a gamut of emotions. Pure undiluted panic when she had first woken up and found herself restrained, and she realized what a mistake she had made. Then anger, both at herself for being stupid and this man for abducting her. After that had come a deep-seated sadness at all the wasted opportunities that had passed her by in life, and all the things she would never get to do if she died in this room. Then the fear had come back, and she had sobbed and begged for her life, who she was begging to she wasn't quite sure, she had just wept and pleaded until her eyes stung and her throat was dry.

Now she was just resigned.

Resigned to her fate.

Resigned to her death.

Resigned to whatever would happen next.

Resigned to the idea that for once what happened next in her life was outside her control.

Voices.

Martha's head snapped up at the sound of voices. They were hushed, but from the tones it sounded like they were arguing. Was there more than one person involved in her kidnapping? Did one of them not want to go through with whatever they had planned for her?

Hope flooded through her at the thought that maybe her abductors were having second thoughts and might just let her go after all.

While she had seen the face of the man who had brought her here, she didn't know his name so if they let her go and she went to the cops there wasn't a whole lot she could tell them anyway.

"Please," she whispered aloud. "Please let me go."

A hard knot of anxiety settled in her stomach as she waited. This part was the worst, knowing that something bad was coming but not being able to stop it. For someone who had been a control freak since the time they learned how to talk, losing any power over herself and what happened to her was utterly terrifying.

Her heart thudded a heavy rhythm in her chest, her hands were sweaty, her chest felt like it heaved in each breath as though she had just run a marathon. Tears burned her eyes and as much as she wanted to give into them and sob out her fear she didn't give in to the urge.

She had to stay strong.

She had to fight.

She had to find a way to survive.

No one knew she was missing, at least not yet, although her big sister might get worried if she didn't hear from her in a couple of days. There was no way she could bank on the cops coming rushing in to save her. No, this was all on her.

"I said no," a loud voice shouted. She heard footsteps and then the sound of a door closing. Then more footsteps, coming closer this time, and then the man from last night appeared in the doorway of the room.

Martha stared at him.

He stared back at her.

She opened her mouth prepared to beg for her life like she had never begged for anything before, but before she could utter a word he stormed over to the chair, standing just in front of her, close enough for her to touch him if her hands had been free.

The man reached out and touched her cheek, his touch light, gentle even. "It doesn't have to be this way," he told her. "If you just tell me what I need to know then it can all be over."

Tell him what he needed to know?

What did that mean?

Panic hummed through her body. She could feel it, it was like the beat of a bass drum beating right on her chest, every reverberation echoing inside her.

"Wh-what do you want to know?" she stammered, trying to make herself sound strong and confident but failing miserably.

He leaned over, hands on his knees, so he was eye to eye with her. "You know what. I need to know what you saw, what you heard, what you know."

Saw? Heard?

She hadn't seen or heard anything that would get her abducted.

Had she?

"I don't know what you want me to tell you," she said desperately. If she knew what he wanted her to say she'd say it in a heartbeat. "Please, just tell me what to say. Tell me what you want to hear."

His face softened, and he touched the pad of his calloused thumb to her cheek, catching her tears as they fell. "It's okay, it's okay, I don't want to do this to you, but he insisted. I have to, you hear me?" His hands clasped her shoulders and shook her hard. "I don't want to do this, but I don't have a choice. If I don't they'll kill me. So please, just tell me what you know."

He sounded so sincere, and she believed him, but that still didn't help her because she still had no idea what he was talking about. She hadn't seen or heard or done anything that would put her on someone's hit list.

"If you don't tell me I can't help you," the man said. There were tears in his eyes too, and the hands that rested on her shoulders were shaking. "If you won't talk then you don't leave me any choice."

Abruptly he released her and disappeared out the door he had entered. Martha wanted to beg him to come back so she could plead with him not to do this, and yet at the same time, she hoped he never came back because she was sure she wasn't going to like whatever was coming next.

The man returned a minute later, a large electric kettle in his hands. She could see the steam pouring out of it. Her gaze dropped to the metal bucket her feet sat in, and her eyes grew round, her stomach swirled with a merciless twist of nausea that left her almost choking.

"Please," she begged. Tears streamed down her face, and her body shook so hard that it rattled the chair. "Please, I don't know what to tell you, you have the wrong person, I didn't see or hear anything, please, oh, please, don't do this."

"I have to," he said, unable to look at her as he stepped closer.

"No, no you don't, we'll go to the cops together, we'll tell them about the people who are making you do this, and they'll help us," she tried to reason with him.

"No one can help me," he said dully as he lifted the kettle so it hung above the bucket.

The man's face was devoid of color, and his eyes were scrunched closed, he had one hand pressed to an ear as though he hated what was coming as much as she did.

No.

No one could hate what was coming as much as she did.

Panic clawed inside her as her brain rebelled against the inevitable.

Desperately she tried to move her feet, but there was nowhere for them to go, tied to the chair as she was, the bucket was too high for her to lift her bound feet out of.

"Please, please, please," she babbled over and over again.

Her pleas did no good.

The kettle tipped further over.

A drop of boiling water hit her foot, and then another and another.

An inhuman scream filled the air.

Consumed with pain, Martha wasn't sure if it came from her or the man.

~

12:16 P.M.

Sydney looked so relaxed.

So happy.

Levi couldn't help but smile as she giggled at something his mom said to her, it was nice seeing her come out of her shell a little. He gathered she was nervous about this huge life change she had undertaken but that she'd had the guts to do it, to move somewhere new where she didn't know anyone impressed him. She was anxious about the changes and no doubt about whatever had caused her to run, but she was facing it head-on and doing it anyway. How could he not admire that?

He was attracted to her—especially today when she had ditched the workwear and was dressed in denim cut-offs that showed off her long, lean legs and a tank top that clung to her top half—he wanted to get to know her, and—once he was sure she would say yes—ask her out on a date. She might even be the one, but even if things didn't work out between them, he hoped she found what she was looking for in River's End. He hoped that she got the extended family support that she seemed to crave, and he was glad that his family and friends could give her that.

She giggled again when Meadow said something to her and wiped a hand at her face, leaving behind a trail of white paint that he could see even from where he stood. Meadow and his mom pointed at her face and laughed, and although he could see her cheeks turn pink, she laughed too.

Her smile touched him somewhere deep down inside. In a part of himself that he hadn't been sure he wanted to open up to anyone else again.

Losing someone you loved sucked.

Big time.

And he'd lost two people that meant a lot to him.

He had loved Dana as much as a teenage boy was capable of loving someone, and he had envisioned them sharing the rest of their lives together. Had she not died then they might be married right now, with a family of their own. His love for Amy had been different, he was older by the time they met, and he had a deeper understanding of what it meant to love someone and be in a relationship, even if it was a relationship that had to be kept mostly a secret.

Two loves of his lives, two shots at happiness, was he ready for a third?

The hardest part of moving on from Amy wasn't the hole in his heart he knew would never completely heal, nor was it the fear that he might lose another woman he loved, it was the guilt.

Death was a part of life.

It happened.

It was awful, it ripped you up inside, it made you want to give in to the grief and let it consume you, but it was inevitable, something you couldn't fight against no matter how hard you tried.

But guilt was something else.

Guilt was like a living thing that took up residence inside your body so it could destroy you from the inside out. It taunted you daily, reminding you of your failures, throwing them in your face, and telling you that they would forever define you. It made you lose sight of who you were, and it warped your view of the world around you. Guilt could kill you just as surely as any bullet.

It had nearly killed him.

After Amy's death, it had nearly convinced him to stick his gun in his mouth and pull the trigger.

Three years, a family who had been there for him unconditionally, and a lot of therapy had helped dull the wounds a little, and although he knew he would always have that little voice at the back of his mind taunting him about letting the woman he loved die, he had mostly learned how to silence it.

Silencing the guilt and moving on were two different things.

He was a flirter by nature, and he enjoyed bantering with a woman, but he always made it clear from the beginning that it wasn't going anywhere. Some women took that as a challenge and thought that if they tried hard enough to get to him, he would cave.

Sydney wasn't like that.

Just from looking at her, he knew she was battling her own demons and that whatever those demons were they had affected her deep down inside and changed the way she saw herself. Despite that, she had dedicated her life to a job where she could save others, and she was still living her life.

Her smile, the way her eyes dropped self-consciously to the floor, the blush that crept up her neck staining her cheeks an adorable shade of red, the uncertainty in her voice as though she wasn't aware of her own strength and beauty, Levi couldn't deny that all of it got to him.

It stirred something inside him.

She was beautiful, she was strong, she was sweet, she was—

"You got it bad."

He started at the voice and turned to see his younger brother standing beside him, a knowing grin on Theo's face. He was a straight shooter, and this wasn't a game to him, so he saw no reason to deny it. Instead he let his gaze wander back to Sydney who was wiping at the paint on her face with a towel someone had got for her. "Real bad."

"She's pretty, and she seems really sweet, and Abe hired her so you know she has to be good at her job," Theo said.

His family liking the woman he was with wasn't a requirement as far as he was concerned, he was thirty-one and his relationships were no one else's business, but that his family liked Sydney was a definite plus. Family was important to him, he was close with his, and he wanted his family to become Sydney's.

"You going for it with her?" Theo asked.

"If I thought she'd say yes I would have asked her out already."

"You don't think she's into you?"

"Oh no, she's into me all right." The heat in her gaze every time he touched her told him that while she might be uncertain about a relationship, maybe even uncertain about him, she was definitely attracted to him. "I think she moved here to escape something and whatever that something is has left her wary and maybe even afraid."

"You think she's running from an abusive ex?" Theo asked, a hint of controlled fury in his face as he no doubt thought about what had led Meadow into the life of their older brother Abe.

"Maybe. She is hesitant with the whole dating idea, I can tell, and she even hesitated to say yes to coming here today even though this could hardly be described as a date. Doesn't have to be an ex though, she might be trying to move on from a bad family situation." Sydney had nothing to fear from him, but it wasn't enough for him to tell her that, she had to learn it for herself. He had to show her, give her time, be patient, and not expect her to change overnight.

"And you? You got any hesitations about putting yourself in a relationship again after everything that happened with Amy?"

Levi looked up at his brother who had crouched beside him as he asked the question. He was supposed to be helping lay the floating floorboards in the hotel's foyer but knowing Sydney was in the next room, and watching her enjoy herself, he couldn't focus. With a sigh, he set his floorboards down and stood, running his hands through his hair.

Theo stood too. "You know it wasn't your fault. You followed procedure. Amy loved you, man, and she would want to see you happy. I think she'd like Sydney. Speaking from experience love hits you when you're not ready for it. Look at me and Maggie, if it wasn't for the fire we would never have hooked up, and now I get to spend the rest of my life with the woman I love. But if you really are interested in Sydney then you have to make sure that you've laid your ghosts to rest." His brother patted his shoulder and walked away.

He was right.

The only way to have a future was to make sure the ghosts of the past were laid to rest.

Sydney turned her head, noticed him watching her, and a tentative smile curled her lips up. The way his heart responded was all the confirmation he needed. He waved and headed toward her.

"You having fun with my mom and Meadow?" he asked when he reached her side, debating whether or not to put an arm around her shoulders and draw her close. Deciding against it since he didn't want to spook her when she seemed to be letting her guard down a little, he shoved his hands into his pockets.

"A *great* time." She beamed up at him, a hint of wistfulness passing through her eyes.

He wasn't surprised, both his mother and Meadow were bright, cheerful people who truly cared. His mom had been the glue that had held their family together for years, raising him and his brothers and sister on her own while their dad served overseas, and then supporting all of them as they followed in their father's footsteps. She never complained, she just took everything in stride and was always looking for the good in any and every situation.

"They're two of my favorite girls," he said, shooting the two other women a bright smile.

"They're lucky women," Sydney said softly, more than a hint of wistfulness in her tone. Levi was about to take it as his cue to ask her to have dinner with him tonight, but before he could, her phone rang. She pulled it out, glanced at it, then said apologetically, "Sorry, I have to take this."

She took a step away, and Levi hugged his mother. "Thanks for making her feel so at ease."

"It wasn't a hardship." His mother laughed. "Sydney is a lovely girl, so sweet, a little shy but I'd say it won't take her long to come out of her shell."

He hoped so.

He would wait as long as it took, but he hoped that she would realize he was someone she could trust, that she didn't have any reason to be afraid of him.

"I have to go," Sydney said, rejoining them. "Work. Another body."

The sadness in her voice told him that she took her job seriously, and while he respected that it sent a sudden shaft of fear through him. He had already loved and lost two women, and the one he was falling for now had a dangerous job. How would he cope if something happened to Sydney? Could his heart take another loss?

That was something he would have to figure out before he asked her out.

~

12:39 P.M.

She'd been having such a lovely time getting to know Levi's mother and sister-in-law that it was a shame to have to leave, but duty called. Her job was important to her so as much fun as she'd had getting to know some of her new neighbors, right now her place was at the latest crime scene.

"It was lovely getting to know you, Sydney," Tatiana Black said, giving her a firm hug.

"Lovely getting to know you too, Mrs. Black." She returned the woman's hug even though she wasn't one hundred percent comfortable with physical contact.

"Tatiana, dear," the older woman reprimanded with a light smack on her shoulder.

"Right, Tatiana." She nodded, never comfortable calling her elders by their first names.

"Will you be able to come back later?" Meadow asked, also hugging her, albeit a little awkwardly since the woman's stomach was so big.

"I'm not sure." Sydney cast what she hoped was a surreptitious glance in Levi's direction. The way he had been looking at her earlier—like she was some precious jewel—had made her insides go all gooey. She'd never been looked at like that by a man before, especially a sexy doctor. But now he was all intense, and she wasn't sure what the sudden change in his demeanor was about, but she was trying not to read too much into it. "It depends on what we find, how many witnesses there are to interview and stuff like that."

"I'll drive you," Levi offered, and that intense look was gone, his easy smile back in place.

"That's okay, Fletcher is coming to pick me up." If Levi had changed his mind about her spending time with his family then that was okay, they were *his* family after all.

"Then I'll walk you out and wait with you till Fletch arrives," he told her and rested his hand lightly in the small of her back and turned her, guiding her toward the front door.

"See you later, dear," Tatiana called out behind them.

Levi didn't remove his hand until they were out of the hotel and down at the end of the driveway. As soon as his hand was gone she missed it, despite the warmth of the day and the heat, she shivered as though cold. She'd never met a man who could affect her like this. She'd never even really looked at any man before. After what she'd lived through as a kid, her whole view of men had been warped, and this was the first time she had ever felt like overcoming that.

"Sydney," Levi said as he put his hands on her shoulders and turned her to face him, but before he could say more, a car horn honked, and then Fletcher was pulling up beside them. "Stay safe, okay?"

There was genuine concern in his eyes, and it hit her that his sudden change in demeanor back inside was because he was worried about her safety. It was clear that he was attracted to her, and he'd already told her in their game of questions last night that he had lost two women he had loved, so it made sense that if he was thinking of getting involved again that he would worry about losing her, especially when she had a potentially dangerous job.

"I'll be careful," she promised and couldn't not smile at him. How nice was it to have someone care enough about her to worry? Sydney couldn't even remember the last time anyone had cared about what happened to her beyond wanting to make sure she didn't get them in trouble.

"Good." He lifted a hand, hesitated, then brushed the backs of his knuckles across her cheek. The intimate gesture left a trail of fire where he touched, a fire that then seemed to spread through her body until it consumed her leaving her weak and shaky.

When he released her, she quickly climbed into Fletcher's car and tried to compose herself so he wouldn't see how Levi's touch had turned her into a quivering mess. She might not have any idea what she was doing when it came to men, but her body certainly knew how to react to a man's touch.

"Hey, Fletch." Levi bent over to look through the car window. "Stay safe, guys, and good luck."

"See ya, Levi, say hi to your mom for me," Fletcher said as he put the car in drive and started off.

Pushing aside all thoughts of Levi and romance for the time being, she asked, "So what do we know?"

"Some kids found a body," Fletcher muttered darkly.

Sydney shuddered, how awful for them. She knew exactly what it was like to see a dead body as a kid, it stuck with you for life. "Abe said she'd been killed the same way as the others. Do we have an ID yet?"

"No, she's not from around here."

Surprised when Fletcher turned off the road just past the end of the hotel's property line, she asked, "The body was found this close to the hotel? Where pretty much the whole town is today, do you think that's a coincidence?"

"What do you think?" he tossed the idea back at her.

"I think it's too big a coincidence to think he didn't do it on purpose, there are miles of river around here, plenty of places for him to leave the body, but he picks the spot where there are dozens of people. I think that means he's someone from town, someone who knows the goings-on here." It was the only thing that made sense, he was picking places where he knew people would be so he had to be knowledgeable about the area and the people, he couldn't be someone just hiding out near here.

"Agreed, it seems to be the most logical scenario," Fletcher said as he parked his car under a large tree.

There was crime scene tape strung up between two trees, and off to the side were a woman and her two crying children. The kids appeared to be about ten, only a little younger than she had been when she saw her first dead body.

They both got out, and as they strode toward the river where the body was waiting for them, she said, "It's only been two days since his last kill, it was almost a week between the first and second, he's escalating."

"Doesn't bode well for us," Fletcher said.

When they reached the river's edge, she got her first look at the body. The woman had long blonde hair, the ends of which reached into the water even though the woman's torso was out of it, the rope around her neck secured her to a tree. It was obviously important to the killer that they find the bodies, otherwise he would be weighing them down or hoping they floated far enough down river that no one would connect them to him.

The woman's neck had been sliced open like the others, and Sydney didn't have to see her feet to know that they had been horribly burned. She shuddered as a sickening wave of nausea rolled in her stomach.

She would not be sick.

Not here.

Not now.

Not with Fletcher standing beside her calmly surveying the scene.

Deep breaths, she coached herself, you got this.

Sydney turned to say something, but instead, her attention was drawn to something on the victim's neck. She took a step closer and crouched down so she could get a closer look.

"You see something?" Fletcher asked.

"This looks like bruising. What do you think?"

He crouched beside her. "Agreed."

"Doesn't look like a handprint, his arm maybe? Or something else? Why would he do that? He didn't with any of the other victims. Because she didn't know him," she quickly answered her own question. "If we're right and he really is a resident, Dale Jacoway or someone else, then he could have convinced Elena and Naomi to go with him because they knew him, but this woman didn't so he had to knock her out, possibly to transfer her someplace quieter where he could torture her."

But why?

That question continued to run through her head.

Why would he torture them?

Was it to get answers out of them like they thought?

Why dump the bodies in the water?

Why leave them tied up so they would be found?

How did he choose his victims?

Was it random?

Personal?

What was his end goal?

Sydney would take an answer to even one of those questions right now.

"We need to get her IDed so we can start making a timeline, figure out when she went missing and what she was doing her final hours. Maybe if we can find out where she was and what she was doing in town we'll find whether or not she met up with Dale in her final hours, or if she was seen with someone else." Sydney stood and stretched, her head might be swimming with a million questions, but there was determination there too.

She *would* find the answers she needed to find this man.

Anything else was completely unacceptable.

~

7:27 P.M.

It was quiet out here.

Peaceful too.

This spot was special to him. It held some of the best and most painful memories of his life.

Levi sighed as he leaned his forearms on the bridge's wooden railing and looked out at the river. It was still an hour at least until sunset, but thankfully the temperature had dropped a little, and there was a gentle breeze wafting across the water making it pleasant out. Dappled sunlight made the water sparkle and shimmer, and as the current kept it moving it felt almost like the river was alive. Birds twittered and chattered from the tree's branches lining either side of the river, butterflies and dragonflies flitted about, bees buzzed, flowers bloomed, this place was paradise.

The bridge that crossed the river was old and rarely used, the forest around it overgrown, and if you didn't know the bridge existed you would be unlikely to stumble upon it. He had found the spot back when he was a teenager, and it had quickly become a favorite of his. This was where he had spent the last hours he'd had with Dana before she had been rushed to the hospital, dying just seventy-two hours later. This was where he had first told Amy that he loved her. And this was where he had intended to bring Amy to propose.

Pulling the small black velvet box from his pocket, he opened it. The diamond ring immediately caught the light and began to shine like a rainbow in the sunlight. He could picture it gleaming on Amy's long, slender finger, she'd been tall for a woman, just over five foot ten, and skinny enough that she had been teased mercilessly about it when she'd been in middle school and high school, but to him she was perfection.

He could practically hear her squeal of delight as he got down on one knee and held out the box. She would have been clapping her hands and dancing from foot to foot in excitement. She would barely have let him get out all the words he had planned so carefully, wanting to convey just how much she meant to him before a yes would have been leaping from her lips. She would have thrown her arms around his neck and kissed him long and hard, then probably ripped off his clothes and insisted they go skinny dipping.

Levi made a sound that was a cross between a laugh and a sob as he held up the ring. "This is for you, Amy. I'll always love you, and I'll always be sorry that I didn't save you, but it's time. Time to move forward. Right?" he asked, needing a sign. Something that told him with concrete surety that it was okay to let go of the past and trust that the future could still hold everything he had dreamed about.

Between him and his three siblings, he had been the one who had always wanted love, marriage, and kids of his own ever since he could remember. He'd been a flirt since middle school, the first in his class to kiss a girl, the first to have a girlfriend, the first to embark on the journey of love.

But that journey hadn't been kind to him, and opening himself up again was hard.

A gust of wind washed across him, and what felt like a gentle caress against his cheek, right in the spot where Amy would always put her hand when they kissed, then the diamond caught the light again, glowing so brightly he had to squint.

His sign.

His sign that Amy was giving him permission to let another woman into his heart.

"I love you, sweetheart, this is yours." With that he lifted his arm and tossed the ring into the river, letting his past go with it. Levi didn't care if someone eventually found the ring and kept it. That ring was Amy's, he'd chosen it just for her, big and brighter than life, just like Amy, and he would never put it on another woman's finger.

If and when that time came he would choose a new ring, a ring that fit the personality of the woman he intended to give it to.

With a last look out at the river, he turned and headed for his car. He would never forget Amy, never forget that he could have saved her life, never forget that it was his fault that they weren't already happily married, but the pain and the guilt had loosened their hold on him.

He was ready.

Ready for a future.

A future he hoped might prominently feature a certain pretty cop with the most beautiful pair of golden-brown eyes he had ever seen.

Leaving a part of his heart behind at the river with Amy, Levi headed back into town, going straight to the diner. He might already be too late, she might have come and gone, but he would sit here until closing and hope that fate once again brought Sydney across his path.

Her job was always going to be something that concerned him, but he'd fallen for a girl battling cancer, and a woman who worked in a warzone, he could deal with Sydney's job as a cop. Could he deny that he was going to get a stab of worry in his heart every time he saw her walk out the door? No, he couldn't. But he knew that her job was important to her and he would never suggest or expect that she should give that up.

Besides, he knew his brother wouldn't have hired her if she wasn't good at her job. He had to trust in her because he knew that trust was the basis of every relationship.

As he stepped into the diner, he found it bustling and busy and assumed that everyone had finished up at the hotel and come on down for dinner. He scanned the crowds searching for Sydney, but he didn't see any sign of her.

"Hey, Penny," he greeted the woman who was only a couple of years older than him. She looked exhausted, she had four kids, two sets of twins five and under, so that wasn't unusual, but tonight she looked extra tired, and he assumed it was the crowd that had her run off her feet. "Sorry, won't take a moment of your time, but have you seen Sydney in here tonight?"

"Sydney? The new deputy?" she asked, a smile lighting her tired face. "The one who you've been hanging out with in here the last couple of days?"

"Yes, that's the one." He just managed to stop himself from rolling his eyes. He wasn't going to fuel local gossip by giving her any titbits that would quickly spread like wildfire. "So, you seen her tonight?"

"Nope, sorry, hon, I'm rushed off my feet, but I would have seen her if she'd come in ... speak of the devil." Her gaze moved to the door behind him, and when he turned he saw Sydney closing it behind her.

Like she felt his eyes on her, she met his gaze, and he saw the tight lines around her mouth relax, and the shadows in her eyes flitted away. She looked exhausted. She'd changed into work clothes since he'd last seen her at the hotel, her arms were wrapped around her middle, and she held herself stiffly like her muscles were tense. What he wouldn't give to take her back to his place, run her a hot bubble bath, then put her on his bed and massage every inch of her till she was so relaxed she couldn't help but drift off to sleep.

"You're staring," Penny singsonged behind him.

Throwing her a quick dirty look over his shoulder, he hurried to Sydney, dipping his head to kiss her cheek. Not where he wanted to be kissing her, but it was better than nothing. "You okay? You look tired."

"I'm fine," she said, straightening herself further.

"You don't have to do that with me," he rebuked gently. Immediately upon moving here she had been thrust into the middle of trying to solve a serial killer case, that couldn't have been easy on her. She should be trying to settle into a new place, get her feet beneath her, and instead she was working almost around the clock on a major case. Turning her around, he put his hands on her shoulders and began to knead her tight muscles. Sydney tried to tug away, but he didn't let her. "You can let your guard down around me," he whispered in her ear.

"People are watching us," she murmured back.

"So what? I don't care, let them watch." He hit a knot at the bottom of her neck and attended to it with his thumbs. Although he knew she was uncomfortable, she moaned despite herself and dropped her head to give him better access. "Better?"

"Mmhmm," she murmured. "You got magic fingers or something?"

"Something like that." He chuckled.

"You're incorrigible." She gave a small chuckle herself.

In less than a minute, he had felt her relax and the urge to ask her out on a date, a proper date this time not just hanging out together at the hotel along with most of the town, was strong, but something held him back.

Uncertainty.

Sydney was still unsure about him, unsure of what she wanted, and he sensed that if he asked her out now she would say no. And if she shut him down, then she might shut him out—for good. He didn't think that dating someone the second she moved to town had been on her agenda when she had planned this move, and he had to give her time to adjust.

When he turned her around to face him again, she kept her gaze fixed firmly on his chest, maybe sensing his desire to take their blossoming friendship and move it to the next level. She trembled slightly in his grasp, and he hoped that she wasn't afraid of him.

"Hey," he said softly, hooking a finger under her chin and nudging so she met his gaze. "You don't ever have to be afraid of me, I'd never hurt you, you know that, right?"

She studied him for a long moment, searching his eyes as though she needed to find something in them. Apparently she found it because she gave a small nod. "Dinner?"

"Thought you'd never ask." He grinned, the tightness inside him eased, and he realized maybe she wasn't as far away from saying yes when he asked her out as he'd thought. Slinging an arm around her shoulders, he eased her through the crowded restaurant. "Look at that, our table just opened up, it's like it was meant to be."

"Yeah, it is," she said, an edge to her voice that hinted she was currently struggling with something internally. Levi hoped she figured things out because she deserved to be happy, they both did, and right now the thing that made him happiest was Sydney. He hoped she felt the same way about him.

June 10th
6:24 A.M.

Running a brush through her hair, Sydney quickly divided it into three pieces and put it into a braid, so it wouldn't be too heavy on the back of her neck, making her hotter than she would already be as she and Fletcher tried to track down the final movements of the third victim, Martha Vilcow.

She set the brush down, intending to head back into her bedroom to put on her shoes, but she caught sight of her reflection and paused. She was pretty enough, Sydney supposed, if a little plain. Her nose was a little too pointy, but her lips were full and plump, her eyes were probably her best attribute. An unusual shade of golden-brown, it wasn't uncommon to find men who stared into them, but it was different when Levi looked at her.

It felt like he was looking through her eyes and into her very soul, managing to understand things about her that she never wanted another living soul to know about.

Should she put on a little mascara? Maybe some eyeliner? Eye shadow?

She didn't usually bother much with makeup, she was a cop, she spent her days dealing with suspects or victims, neither of whom cared much about her appearance. While she might work with five attractive guys one was married, and another two were in serious relationships, so there wasn't really anyone around to impress.

"Makeup really isn't necessary," she reminded herself as she turned from the mirror and switched off the bathroom light on the way out.

But she made it only three steps across her room before she spun around hurried back into the bathroom and pulled out a tube of mascara from her makeup drawer.

"A little mascara isn't a big deal," she assured herself.

With the mascara applied, the darker, thicker lashes framing her eyes seemed to make the color pop a little more. She decided against adding anything else because really there was no need to make an effort to impress him.

Levi had already made it clear that he was interested, she'd even thought he was going to ask her out on a real date last night when he'd given her that heavenly massage.

When he hadn't, she had been relieved and disappointed. It was really too soon to even be considering getting involved with someone, so it was probably for the best. Maybe after they'd done the friend thing a little more and she had grown to know him and trust him—not that he had given her any reason *not* to trust him besides his gender—then she could consider something more than friendship.

Leaving the bathroom, she slipped on a simple pair of black flats, then grabbed her purse and keys and headed out the front door.

She didn't really need to be up this early.

Sydney didn't need to be at work until eight, but since she wasn't much of a cook, she would stop by the diner first for breakfast. Her cooking skills weren't great. She could have managed cereal or toast, or even eggs—okay, well, maybe not eggs, she usually either under or over boiled eggs, or burned them if she tried to scramble them or make an omelet—what she wanted to go to the diner for wasn't food it was ...

Hesitant to admit it, even to herself, she had to gather her courage to admit that the real reason she was up early and going out for breakfast was that she hoped she might run into Levi again.

He did things to her.

Weird things, things that she had never experienced before, and she liked it just as much as she was scared of it.

She wanted to see him again, wanted to spend more time with him. He had become almost an addiction, hovering at the edges of her mind even when she was supposed to be occupied with other things. She had dreamed about him too. Levi was sweet, charming, easy to be around, and she wanted so badly to trust him but ...

He was a man.

Sydney sighed as she got into her car and pulled out of the driveway of the small cottage she was renting. She knew how ridiculous it was to lump all men together, she knew they weren't all the same, she knew it, she *knew* it.

So why didn't she know it?

She had met plenty of wonderful men in her life, good men, kind men, men who dedicated their lives to helping people, and yet all of that was overridden by the one man she should have been able to trust implicitly.

Her father.

Shaking off thoughts of the man, he was dead now, and this was her chance to finally move on. She wasn't going to blow it because he had tried to brainwash her to believe that men were bad and her job in life was to serve them. If Levi asked her out, she would suck it up, ignore her fears, and say yes.

With hands that trembled enough that someone would notice if they happened to look at them, she parked her car, locked it, and headed into the diner. It was much quieter this morning than it had been last night and as she scanned the room almost immediately she saw him. Her stomach made a funny little flipping motion, and a pleasant tingle rippled through her.

As soon as he saw her, he smiled, standing up, and walking over. He was wearing a pair of well-worn jeans that hung low on his hips and a green short-sleeved, button-down shirt that made his hazel eyes appear green. His smile made his dimples show and she felt herself melt at the sight of him.

"Morning," he greeted her as he leaned in, and for one moment, she thought he was going to put his lips on hers, but as he had last night he merely touched a kiss to her cheek.

"Morning," she returned with a shy smile. As much as she wanted to break free of the manacles her father had metaphorically placed on her it didn't mean it was easy. "I wasn't sure if you would be here this morning."

Levi arched a dark brow as he looked down at her. "But you hoped I would be?"

"Well, umm, uh, I, it ..." she stumbled helplessly. Did she admit that she *had* hoped to run into him here? Was it too soon to let on that she liked him? She was pretty sure that he liked her too, but what if she was wrong. What if he was just flirting with her because he flirted with everyone?

No.

He'd told her that he liked her.

Told her that he wanted to get to know her.

She could do this.

After all, she had packed up her entire life to move to a town where she didn't know anyone and start a new job. If she could manage all of that then she could answer a simple question.

"I hoped you might be here," she said, fixing her gaze on the floor and then chanced a quick glance up at him. She found him grinning down at her, a satisfied smile on his face, his eyes twinkling merrily, and despite her reservations she could actually imagine running her fingers through his hair as he kissed her until the whole world faded around her and it was just the two of them.

"Have dinner with me tonight," Levi said, reaching for her hand and entwining their fingers.

Dinner?

Tonight?

Admitting that she had been hoping to see him was one thing but going out on a date, a real live date, was totally another.

Butterflies in her stomach would be an understatement for what she was feeling right now. It was more like a herd of tyrannosaurs rexes fighting with a gang of velociraptors.

Wary of men or not, she was attracted to Levi, and he had been nothing but sweet with her, and the whole point of coming here was to be the new her. A her who wasn't afraid of men.

Her hesitation had his smile dipping, and that was enough to spur her into action. "Okay," she said on an exhale, then she repeated again, stronger this time, "okay. I'd like to have dinner with you tonight." There, that wasn't so hard.

"You would?" Levi's smile brightened again until it was almost blinding like the sun.

"Yeah, I would." She smiled herself, now that she'd said it she wasn't nervous anymore and she realized she was looking forward to their date.

Their date.

A date.

Her on a date.

She'd never been on one before. Her father had forbidden it and then she'd been too afraid.

What would she wear?

Would she make a fool of herself?

Would he finally kiss her?

Would she let him?

"Relax, I can hear you thinking." Levi laughed and wrapped an arm around her shoulder, pulling her close. "It will be fine, just trust me."

Trust him?

Could it really be that simple?

~

3:09 P.M.

Hiding in the shadows, he followed her.

This time he would have to be careful.

Really careful.

Things with Martha had been scary, and he was glad that he hadn't been told to go after another tourist in town. Well, he was partly glad about that. While it made it easier to get close to the women, it wasn't like he enjoyed questioning and killing people that he knew.

Why couldn't they only come to him when they had something concrete?

They were running scared, and he knew it. They were grabbing at straws, jumping on anything that looked like it could be what they were looking for instead of doing their homework. They were making him clean up their messes, and he hated that he had nothing he could use against them to get them to stop and leave him alone.

But he didn't.

And there was no use complaining about it.

Just get through this and maybe if he kept doing what they wanted he could earn his freedom.

With a sigh of relief, he saw Trina Liberty turn up her front path and hurry to the porch where she paused to shake off her umbrella before unlocking her door and heading inside.

This was it.

He wasn't going to get a better opportunity.

With a heavy heart, he ran a hand through his wet hair and walked across the street. The temperature today had dropped dramatically, gone was the sunshine and clear blue skies that said summer was only weeks away, the rain had been pouring down for hours, he was cold, drenched, and all he wanted was to go home, take a hot shower, climb into bed and try to sleep.

He couldn't remember the last time he had actually slept properly.

Weeks?

Months?

How could he sleep when he had the pressure of the world resting on his shoulders?

When he reached Trina's porch, he brushed away the raindrops dribbling down his forehead with a hand that was wet enough it didn't do a bit of good. He had no idea what he would say to her to convince her to let him inside her house, but he didn't have time to worry about that, the more time he spent standing out here the more chance someone might see him.

Knocking on the door, he shuffled from foot to foot as he waited, knowing that if anyone had noticed him he'd definitely stand out enough that they'd mention it to the cops and he didn't need that aggravation, he had enough to deal with.

"Oh, uh, hi," Trina said when she opened the door and saw him standing there.

If he'd had any doubt that she was the next woman he was to interrogate it evaporated the second he saw her.

He knew.

She was the one.

"Hey, Trina, I'm really sorry to bother you," he started, rubbing at the back of his neck where he's had a tight, aching pain that had been bothering him for weeks now.

"That's okay. What do you need?"

"My car broke down just down the block, and my cell phone is flat. I saw you walking down the street and wondered if I might use your phone?" The excuse sounded so lame to his ears, and he was sure that Trina wouldn't be stupid enough to fall for that, it was practically excuse number one in the creepy kidnappers guide to getting to a victim. He was considering whether he'd be able to shove the door further open and take her before she tried to shut it in his face, when she smiled at him.

"Sure thing, come on in." Trina held the door further open and then closed it behind him when he stepped inside her cozy house. "Can I get you a drink or something to eat while you wait for the mechanic?"

"Just water would be lovely," he replied, hardly daring to believe it was really going to be this easy. How lucky could he get? He was here in her home, and he was wondering whether it would be safer to just keep her here, question her, and then he could deliver whatever information she gave him on his way home where hopefully he could crash and fall into a deep and dreamless sleep.

"Sure thing. I'll be in the kitchen, my cell phone is in the living room," she told him as she disappeared down the hall.

Wanting to make sure he kept her at ease until he was ready to make his move, he went into the living room, picked up the phone, and dialed his own number—he would hate for her phone to ring in the middle of his fake call. His phone was in his pocket, but he'd turned it off so she had no idea that when he started talking, pretending he was explaining what had happened to his car to a mechanic, that he was in fact talking to no one.

Carefully, he adjusted the level of his voice and approached the kitchen. He needed to know what she was doing in there and if she might possibly have a weapon at her disposal if she was cooking, cutting up vegetables or something. He found her making cookies, a recipe book open in front of her as she went about putting ingredients into a mixer.

Confident that he would be able to get her subdued and tied up without any problems, he said into his phone, "Yes, I understand, the weather's terrible today, and there are meant to be storms later, but I'm waiting inside Trina Liberty's house." She had turned when she heard him speaking and nodded that that was fine. "Hey, Trina, can he call back on this number when he gets here?"

"Of course." She smiled and went back to her baking.

"She said it's fine. Call when you get here, and I'll come out to meet you. See you in an hour. Sorry, it's going to be about an hour before he can get here," he said apologetically when he ended the call and set her phone down on the table, careful it wasn't close enough for her to be able to reach. "Thanks again, you're a life saver."

"No problem. So you want to help me bake cookies for my niece's birthday?"

"Sure, I'm not much of a baker though," he said, trying to sound normal and not like his heart was beating a million miles a minute in nervous anticipation.

Timing was everything.

Especially if he was going to do this here rather than trying to get her back to his place.

He waited until she opened the fridge door to search for something and then he made his move.

Using his much larger body he shoved her into the fridge and threw her off balance.

Trine cried out and tried to spin around no doubt wanting to use some moves she had learned in a self-defense class to try to knock him down, but that wasn't happening. He kept his hold on her and shoved her sideways into the wall, slamming her once, twice, three times until she went limp in his arms.

There, it was done.

Dropping her, Trina bounced as she hit the floor and he turned his back on her to grab a chair and place it in the middle of the room. He didn't have rope or plastic zip ties on him so he would have to go scavenging through Trina's belongings to find something.

He searched her draws, found a ball of string, and decided that would have to do. If he made sure to wrap it around and around her wrists several times, it would probably be strong enough to hold her until he was done.

Just as he was turning to grab her, he caught a whir of motion out of the corner of his eyes, and then something was sprayed in his face.

Immediately his eyes began to burn, and his nose began to drip.

Mace.

She'd got him with pepper spray.

Trina let out an ear-piercing scream that would no doubt bring anyone within earshot running.

He couldn't let that happen.

If she got away, she would tell everyone that it was him who had attacked her.

Then he'd either be thrown in prison or the men he was working for would get to him because he had failed.

Prison was the better of those two options.

Ignoring the stinging and blurred vision that had him stumbling and almost losing his balance he took off after her.

Trina was halfway to the front door by then, thankfully he had knocked her about enough that she was also unsteady on her feet. He was able to get to her before she reached the door.

She let out another scream, but he launched at her and knocked them both to the ground. Any chance of an interrogation was over, whatever Trina knew would have to die with her.

Grabbing her by the shoulders, he slammed her head into the floor, over and over again until ...

Voices.

At the door.

It rattled, and he heard someone yell Trina's name.

It was time to get out of here.

Leaving Trina's now limp body behind, he jumped to his feet and ran through the house flinging open the back door and praying that everything wasn't about to come crashing down around him.

~

3:54 P.M.

This could be the break they had been praying for.

Sydney felt energized as she parked her car outside the latest crime scene. All the weariness that had been creeping inside her as she and Fletcher tried to piece together the last movements of their victims was gone now.

They had a live victim.

Trina Liberty had survived.

Just what condition the woman was in she didn't know yet, but she knew that Trina had been injured when she fought back and tried to escape. She hoped the woman could tell them who her attacker was because she wanted this case closed.

While she and Fletcher had been working victimology Will, Julian, and Beau had been looking closer into Dale Jacoway, looking for something that would either prove he was the killer or discount him as a suspect. As hard as they were all working they hadn't been able to catch a break.

Until now.

"Hey, Syd," Fletcher greeted her as he walked down the path of their victim's house and joined her on the sidewalk. They had split up after lunch. She had focused on tracking down Martha Vilcow's final hours while Fletcher had spoken with her family, trying to get an understanding of who she was and how she might have come into contact with the killer, given that she was the only one of the four victims who wasn't a resident of River's End.

"Hey." She grinned at him, that grin slowly fading when she saw he wasn't smiling back. Why wasn't he excited about this break in their case? "What's with you? This is what we needed, a surviving victim. She can tell us who tried to kill her."

"So far, Trina hasn't regained consciousness, she was in pretty bad shape when I got here," Fletcher told her. He had been first on the scene, responding to the 911 call that had come in from two men who had been out jogging when they'd heard screams for help. When he'd called her to tell her to get here, he hadn't mentioned that their victim was in such a serious condition.

"Is she going to be okay?" If she wasn't then how would they get their killer without her testimony?

"Too early to tell. Paramedics didn't appear overly optimistic, but hopefully once she gets to the hospital the news will be more optimistic."

Sydney blew out a frustrated breath. Her heart broke for the woman who had fought so valiantly for her life and might end up losing it anyway, but the cop side of her mourned the loss of the progress she'd thought they were making. "We need to know what she knows."

"Right now, we don't even know that this case is related to the murders," Fletcher said.

Her mouth dropped open. That this case wasn't related had never even occurred to her. "Of course it's related," she protested.

"Really?" He arched a blond brow. "The killer has never tried to attack a victim at their home before, he always takes them someplace else to torture and kill them. And Trina's house wouldn't have given him the privacy needed to torture her without someone hearing. The killer has also never messed up before. Right now, I just don't think we have enough to conclusively link this case to the others."

"None of what you just said proves this case *isn't* linked to the others either," she shot back. She knew this case was related, she *knew* it. Her gut told her that it was and she was going to listen to her gut until it was proved to be wrong.

"Right now, we have to keep our minds open, we need to look into Trina's life, see if there's anyone who might want to hurt her, and unless or until we get something concrete we can't assume it's the serial killer."

She bit her tongue to keep back another retort, partly because she wasn't as experienced as Fletcher so she didn't think she should be talking back to him, and partly because he was a man and she had been conditioned to believe she wasn't as good as a man.

Sydney hated that.

She hated that she couldn't break her father's hold on her. He was dead for goodness sake, she should be able to forget about the stupid things he tried to make her believe. She knew that it was lies and yet it was like he had planted something inside her and it had taken hold, even though some of it had been ripped out there were still roots there, roots that threatened to regrow what she had fought so hard to get rid of.

"Hey." Fletcher reached out and put a hand on her shoulder. "If this case is related then we'll prove it, and we'll get this guy, okay?"

"Okay." She nodded, appreciating his efforts to convince her.

"Why don't you go inside, do a walk-through, keep your mind open and just take in what you see, let the evidence speak to you, not the other way around."

She could do that.

Nodding at Fletcher, she headed up the garden path and took a step inside. Forcing herself not to look for reasons to link this case to the serial killer case and just take in everything she saw, Sydney scanned the room.

The first thing she saw was the broken front door. She assumed it had been broken when the two men who had come running to Trina's rescue because otherwise Trina would have just run outside. That alluded to the fact that Trina, like the first two victims, knew the man who had attacked her. Just like the way he had dumped the bodies, the fact that the victims seem to know him implied he was another town resident.

The second thing she saw was the blood on the carpet. That must have been where the killer got Trina, smashing her head into the ground over and over again until he had left her unconscious and fighting for her life.

Had the attack been focused just in here or had it started in another room?

Bypassing the blood, she headed through the living room and into a kitchen, the answer to her question was obvious when she walked through the door. The fridge door was open, some of the items inside had been knocked over, and a scattered pile of magnets was on the floor. A chair sat in the middle of the floor, away from the table where the rest of the chairs were tucked in neatly, and a ball of string lay over in a corner of the room.

There was something small on the floor under the chair. Unable to tell what it was from here, she walked over and crouched down, pulling a pen from her pocket to roll it over so she could see it better.

Mace.

Trina must have had it on her and used it on the man who attacked her, that had given her the time to run, but he'd obviously recovered quickly enough to get to her before she could get out the door.

So close.

Trina had been so close to getting away, but it hadn't been enough.

She knew all about that.

Someone had helped her and her sister get away, their job had been to bring back help, but they had been too slow and ...

Something slammed into her from behind.

Since she was still crouched down and off-balance, the force of the blow knocked her over, and she crashed down hard onto her wrists.

Whoever had knocked her down shoved his weight into her back and flattened her out, then tangled his fingers in her braid and slammed her head into the tiles.

Stars exploded behind her eyes, and she moaned in pain.

He lifted her head again, and she knew she had to make a move or she would die in here.

The back door had been open when the men who had come to Trina's rescue had come running in, and they had assumed that the attacker had run off, but obviously he had stayed behind, hidden, and now he wanted to kill her too.

Allowing the movement of him pulling her back to work to her advantage, she didn't fight him, pretended she was too stunned by the blow to fight back, then just when he was about to slam her head back down she rammed it back. It connected with his face, and she heard his pained grunt and knew she had scored a direct hit.

Instead of trying to shove his much larger weight off her, she rolled sideways and managed to break away.

The man had his face covered, but she saw the knife in his hand.

He swung it down toward her and instinct had her throwing an arm up to protect herself.

The feel of the blade slicing through her flesh made her cry out, and Sydney wasn't so proud to believe she was getting away on her own.

Opening her mouth, she screamed as loudly as she could. "Fletcher! He's in here!"

Her call for help startled the man, and she could see his indecision even though she couldn't see his face.

Obviously, deciding his freedom was more important, he let the knife clatter to the floor and ran out the still open back door.

A moment later Fletcher came running into the room.

"Syd," he said, running to her side.

"He was still here, he ran," she said quickly. She wrapped a hand around her bleeding arm, and Fletcher helped her sit up then dragged her back until she was propped up against the wall.

She'd nearly died.

She knew what it was like to live with the constant fear of death hanging over your head, but so much time had passed that the feeling had faded.

Now it was back, and there was only one thing she wanted right now, and that was Levi's arms around her, cradling her against that strong chest of his and making her feel safe.

Safe.

She should know better than to think that was possible.

The world wasn't a safe place.

4:29 P.M.

"She's stable, for now at least," Levi said as he looked down at Trina Liberty's unconscious form. The woman was a couple of years younger than his brother Theo but a few years older than baby of the family Dahlia, so he didn't know her as well as he otherwise might have, but he knew her enough to know that she didn't deserve this.

No one deserved this.

"We need to collect blood samples, then she needs to go for a CT scan and an MRI, and we'll run another EEG," he said to the nurses that were working with him in the ER. He'd been on shift at Sacred Heart Hospital, working the emergency room with two other doctors when Trina had been brought in. The hospital wasn't large, but it was well equipped to deal with most of the patients that came through the doors. If a patient needed treatment they weren't able to offer then they were sent to a larger hospital in the closest city.

He liked working here, it was the complete opposite of working in a warzone. The majority of his patients were victims of car accidents, river related accidents, or skiing related accidents. One thing about this job that never got any easier was dealing with people that he actually knew. River's End was a small town, as were the couple of other nearby towns that the hospital serviced, so chances were at least half of the patients he treated were people he knew well. The other half were usually tourists.

"What do you think her chances are?" nurse Tiffany Thomas asked, her gaze fixed on Trina's battered face. He knew that the two were friends and had gone to school together. He wished he could tell her what she wanted to hear, but he wasn't going to lie.

"There's a lot of swelling in her brain, so we won't know anything for sure until that reduces, but her first EEG wasn't promising. I'm sorry, Tiff."

"Me too," she said softly.

"You know we won't give up on her," he reminded the woman. That wasn't the way you did things in a small town. Yes, the constant gossiping and having people insert themselves into your personal life could be frustrating, but on the flip side, the sense of community was unparalleled. If you needed something then you had the support of every single person in town.

"I just can't believe she was attacked," Tiffany said as they prepared Trina to be taken down for tests that might help them determine whether she was likely to survive her injuries, and if she did, what shape she would be in if she woke up.

"She fought back though, she's strong," he reminded her. From what they knew Trina had been attacked in her home but had fought back, tried to run, and managed to alert passersby to the fact that she was in trouble. Levi had to wonder if it was related to the serial killer case. Trina was around the same age as the other victims, so it had to be a possibility, if it was, then Abe, Sydney, and the others were no doubt looking into it.

"An orderly will be by to get her soon, I'm going to wait with her unless you need me for something else," Tiffany said.

It was a quiet day so far so it was fine for Tiffany to stay with her friend. If something big happened and they had an influx of patients he could come and get her. "Talk to her, there's evidence that says patients who are in a coma might be able to hear the voices of those around them."

Tiffany nodded, and Levi pulled off his gloves and dropped them into the trash before he headed out the door. Just as he was walking back toward the nurses' station out of the corner of his eye he saw the doors open, and two people walk through, a blond man and a woman with brown locks.

Sydney.

Spinning around, he ran to her side. "What happened?"

"Suspect was hiding out in Trina's house, we assumed he ran because the backdoor was open and it wouldn't have made any sense for him to stay and hide. Apparently this guy doesn't care about what makes sense," Fletcher muttered, and from the look on his friend's face, it was clear he was beating himself up for not having cleared the house.

"He attacked you?" he asked Sydney. Her right arm was wrapped in a bandage that was already soaking through with her blood, and there was a bruise on her forehead.

Sydney's wide golden eyes looked up at him, it was clear she was shaken up, but she was holding it together. "He knocked me down, I got him off me, but he had a knife, I screamed for Fletcher, but he got me with it before he ran."

His heart was hammering a million miles a minute at the sight of

Sydney with blood on her, but he dragged his panic down and forced himself to remain calm. If she could do it then he could too. “Let’s go get you checked out, sweetheart,” he said as he gently took her elbow and guided her toward an exam room.

“I have to go back to the scene. You gonna be okay here, Syd?” Fletcher asked.

“I’ll be fine,” she assured him.

Fletcher turned and walked a couple of steps before returning to Sydney’s side. His blue eyes were a turbulent mess of guilt and self-recrimination. “I’m so sorry, Sydney.”

“It’s not your fault,” Sydney said firmly. “I didn't clear the house either. I thought he would be long gone. Stuff happens, at least no one else died.”

Fletcher nodded, not looking pacified, then stormed out of the hospital.

Levi led her into the small exam room, reassured by the feel of her arm beneath his hand. She could have died. Died. She would have been the third woman who he cared about to die.

Was he some sort of bad luck charm?

He didn't even believe in superstitious things like that, and yet he couldn’t deny that right now he certainly felt like he had to be to blame for the deaths.

Lifting his hand, he pressed it to her cheek, his thumb brushing lightly across her cheekbone as he stared into her eyes. She stared back at him, locking onto him as though he were her rock right now, and then she shuddered and he dragged her into his arms.

“It’s okay,” he soothed, one hand cupping the back of her head, the other stroking her back. “You’re okay. You're safe. You fought back and you survived.”

“I was scared,” she admitted in a whisper as she pressed her face into his chest and wrapped her uninjured arm tightly around his waist.

“I bet.” He was scared, and he hadn't even been there. Sydney was something special, he’d known it from the moment she had bumped into him at the diner, and he wanted them to get a chance to see what could grow between them, but that had nearly been cut abruptly short.

As scared as he was, he needed to pull it together and check her out, she was bleeding, would probably need stitches in her arm if the blood on the bandage was anything to go by, and she could have a concussion. Plus he hadn't even asked her yet if she had any injuries he couldn't see.

"Let me take a look at you." Reluctantly, he eased her back, then put his hands around her waist and lifted her up, setting her down on the bed and picking up her wrist to check her pulse. It was normal, and when he strapped a blood pressure cuff around her arm he found that was normal as well.

As though sensing his concern, Sydney put a hand on his arm. "I'm okay, Levi. Really."

"We'll see," he said noncommittally. "Let me look at your eyes." He shone a light in them and both her pupils reacted normally which ruled out the likelihood of a concussion.

"I'm not dizzy or nauseous," Sydney told him. "I don't think I have a concussion. Just a wicked headache."

"I'll grab you some painkillers once I check your arm." As carefully as he could, he unwound the bloody bandage to reveal a five-inch long gash. It was deep enough to still be oozing blood but not deep enough that she was in danger of losing too much blood. Thankfully the cut was on the outside of her forearm and not along the inside where the major arteries ran. Still, it was a serious enough injury and would require probably a dozen stitches to close.

"What's the verdict?" Sydney asked, her gaze fixed firmly on his face, avoiding looking at her bloody arm.

"You don't like blood, huh?" he asked.

"Not my own," she muttered.

"Just keep your eyes on me, honey. It's going to need stitches, but I don't think the damage is too bad. Can you feel this?" he asked as he brushed a fingertip across the palm of her injured hand and up and down each finger.

"Yeah, I can feel it," she replied.

"Can you squeeze my hand?" He put his hand in hers and although her face was pinched and she tensed in obvious pain she was able to squeeze his hand weakly. "Doesn't look like there's nerve or tendon damage, that's good. I'm going to numb your arm, and then I'll stitch you up. Are you hurt anywhere else?"

"No, just my head and my arm."

Now that he had checked her out and determined that she was mostly okay the tightness in his chest should have eased, but it hadn't. He knew her job was dangerous just like he knew that she had saved herself today, but still that fear was there. The fear of losing another woman that he cared about was strong. Strong enough that it made him want to give into it and walk away from Sydney before he got anymore invested.

Instead of giving in to that fear, he curled a hand around the back of her neck and rested his forehead lightly against hers, mindful of the lump. "I could have lost you today," he murmured, more to himself than to her.

"I'm not that easy to get rid of," she replied, and he sensed that had a deeper meaning than he realized right now.

"You know if you wanted to start our date early you didn't have to get yourself brought to the ER," he teased, needing to lighten the mood as he released her and prepared a syringe because if he didn't, he was going to kiss her and he didn't want their first kiss to be in a hospital.

"This wasn't really what I had in mind when you asked me to dinner," Sydney said.

"Oh no?" he asked as he swabbed a spot just above the gash. "Sharp prick," he warned as he injected the local anesthetic. "So, what did you have in mind for our date?"

Her cheeks reddened, and her gaze all of a sudden couldn't settle on anything. "Something more romantic than a hospital room and stitches," she said, her voice husky and he wondered what she was thinking about.

"Well, I can promise you that when I take you out to dinner tonight it is going to be a whole lot more romantic than this."

She sucked in a breath, and when her eyes met his, he saw a heat in them that he hadn't been expecting. Looked like his sweet, shy girl wasn't quite as shy as he'd thought.

~

6:46 P.M.

. . .

She drummed her fingers nervously on the table.

Sydney had always hated waiting. In many ways, she would rather just have the bad thing happen because the anticipation of wondering whether it was or wasn't going to happen twisted her stomach into knots.

Right now, she was anxiously waiting for her boss to show up. She liked Abe, and she knew he would never have given her this job if he didn't think she could do it, but she had messed up.

Big time.

She had done one of the worst things a cop could do, she'd made an assumption. In assuming that the killer would have left—no matter how logical an assumption—instead of hiding out there, she could have been killed. Fletcher could have been killed. And they had missed an opportunity to catch the killer.

If she'd done her job properly the killer would be in custody right now.

When Abe came in, she was expecting a reprimand. A reprimand she certainly deserved. Best case scenario, she might be allowed to keep working this case, maybe with a few days suspension, worst case scenario, she would be fired.

She prayed she wouldn't be.

Sydney was already starting to feel like River's End was her home, she liked the quaint town, she liked the people, and she liked Levi.

What would happen between them if she got fired?

If she did she certainly couldn't stay here, she'd moved here for the job, and without it, there was nothing to hold her here. She'd have to move because she'd have to look for another job, and if she got fired she couldn't count on a reference from Abe which meant she might not get another job in law enforcement.

What would she do then?

Her anxiety was growing, but there was nothing she could do about it. She was here at the Sheriff's offices for a meeting. She'd come straight from the hospital, and even spending time with Levi while he'd stitched her arm wasn't enough to bolster her spirits right now.

She didn't want to leave here and she didn't want to leave Levi, she didn't know where things were going between them, but even the fact that he was interested in her was enough to boost her self-confidence, and it definitely needed the boost.

Before she could work herself up anymore the door to Abe's office —where she had been told to wait for him—opened and her boss strode in.

Apparently not in any hurry to put her out of her misery and let her know what her punishment was for messing up, he didn't say anything, just walked around to his side of the table and sat down.

Realizing she was still drumming her fingers on his desk, she quickly snatched her hand back, wincing as she jostled her injured arm. Thankfully it was her left arm that had been cut, and she was right-handed so while the injury was inconvenient, it wasn't anything she was particularly concerned about.

"How's the arm?" Abe asked, his piercing hazel eyes assessing her.

"Fine," she replied in a small voice, hating that the anxiety she was feeling practically bled out of her every pore. If he didn't say something soon she would lose it. Unable to wait a second longer, she blurted out, "I'm sorry."

"For?" Abe prompted.

"For messing up today. I didn't clear the house. The witnesses who found Trina Liberty said they had found the back door open and we assumed the killer had left, because I mean, what would he have to gain by hanging around and maybe getting caught. I thought he was gone and I didn't even clear the house before I started walking through what happened. I'm sorry, I messed up," she finished forlornly. She didn't want to lose this job. She had fought so hard to get control of her life back, she loved being a cop because it gave her confidence she didn't have in her personal life, and now in one stupid moment she might have lost it all.

"Fletcher thinks it's his fault. He should have cleared the house before you went in, he was first officer on the scene."

Sydney didn't want anyone else getting in trouble for her mistakes. "I was the one who went in, it was my responsibility to make sure the house was empty."

Abe studied her again for what felt like an eternity, and then he nodded. "Mistakes happen, the important thing is that no one got hurt too badly. You get medical clearance to return to work?"

"Levi said I'm fine to go right back to work, but aren't I like in trouble or something?" she asked, confused about why he seemed to be letting her off the hook after she'd made such a disastrous mistake.

"I'm assuming you learned a lesson today?"

"Yes." She nodded her head emphatically.

"Then let's get back to work, the others are waiting in the conference room." Without another word, he stood and headed out of his office, leaving her staring open-mouthed after him.

That was it?

She wasn't going to be reprimanded?

Unable to quite believe her luck, she stood and followed the sheriff through to the conference room.

As soon as she stepped through the door, Fletcher jumped out of his chair and pulled one out for her. "How're you feeling?"

"I'm fine," she replied firmly. She already felt like she had an uphill battle to earn these former soldiers' respect—more so than ever after what had happened today—and she didn't want them fussing over her like she was some poor helpless girl.

Because she wasn't.

Not anymore.

And she had promised herself that she never would be again.

"I know you've already told us what happened this afternoon, but I want you to go through it again, try to focus on the details," Abe told her.

Fighting back a shudder as she remembered the fear that had coursed through her when her head was slammed into the floor and she realized she was fighting for her life—and might lose—she focused her mind. "I found a can of mace on the floor in the kitchen and was thinking that Trina must have used it to get away. Someone knocked me over, he grabbed my head and slammed it into the floor." Absently she lifted a hand to touch the lump on her forehead, she was lucky he hadn't hit her harder and knocked her out or she would never have walked out of that house alive.

"What do you remember about that moment?" Beau asked her.

Sydney was about to say nothing specific, but then she paused. "His hand was really big, much bigger than my head." She hadn't realized that until she focused on the details. "I guess that means he's a big guy."

"Big but you got away from him," Will said.

"When he went to slam my head into the floor again I moved with him, then caught him off guard and managed to slam my head into his face. When he was distracted, I rolled sideways and managed to get away from him. He swung the knife, and that's when I called Fletcher, he must have realized it was time to go otherwise he'd get caught because he ran. I didn't see his face, he'd covered it with a dish towel."

"You said he was white," Abe said, and she nodded even though she didn't think it was a question. "What else did you notice about him? Was his skin smooth? Wrinkled? Were there tattoos, or scars, or freckles, moles? What color was his hair?"

"His skin was smooth so he wasn't old. I didn't see any tattoos or scars, there were no moles but maybe a few freckles, and the hairs on his arm were brown," she rattled off, able to remember more with his pointed questions. "It could have been Dale Jacoway."

"We have another suspect," Julian told her.

"Oh, who?" She hadn't heard that there was another suspect on the table. She wondered when they had added him to the suspect list.

"Will and I were going through our victim's last days, and we found that all four of them had been to the bookstore the day they went missing," Julian explained.

She hadn't been to the bookstore yet, but she'd walked past, it was a charming little store that looked like it was about a hundred years old. "Who owns the bookstore?"

"His name is Alan Dunkin. He's forty, recently divorced, wife and two kids moved a couple of hours away so his wife could move in with her parents. He doesn't get to see them much anymore," Will recapped.

"Fletcher and Sydney, you two can interview him first thing in the morning," Abe ordered. "Okay, let's call it quits for today, we have a couple of things to add to our killer's profile, and we'll see where it takes us."

Everyone was standing up ready to leave when a memory slipped into the forefront of her mind. "I remember something else," she blurted out.

The others stopped and looked at her.

"He said something to me. I didn't even remember that he did until just then. When he was swinging the knife down, he said, 'Is it you? Are you the one?' But what one? I've only been in River's End for five days, and Martha Vilcow had only been here for a few days. So who is he looking for? What does he think they did? And why is he burning their feet in his quest to get those answers?"

~

9:52 P.M.

The diner was quiet tonight, probably because it closed in a little over half an hour, and although he'd been here for two hours already, he hadn't eaten anything, just drunk cup after cup of coffee until he was sure Penny was tired of bringing him refills.

All he could think about was Sydney.

Levi hoped she wasn't overdoing things. Yes, he'd given her medical clearance to go back to work because he knew the others would be looking out for her, but she still had a five-inch gash in her arm with a dozen stitches holding it together and a lump on her head that was no doubt going to be a mess of black and blue by morning.

In short, she should be at home resting, especially at almost ten at night.

Since she'd been attacked, they'd postponed their date, the idea being when she finished at work she could make it an early night, as much as he knew it was best for her if she was at home in bed right now, he couldn't help but hope she'd stop by here first.

It probably wasn't going to happen, he had accepted that, it was almost ten, she had no doubt finished her meeting and gone home to get some sleep, and yet he would sit here until Penny kicked him out just in case.

Four days.

That was all the time he'd known her, but it felt so much longer. He'd always been the Black brother to follow his heart. Oldest brother Abe was the serious one, the distant one, the one who was hard to get close to. Youngest brother Theo was the fun-loving, easy-going one. He'd been the sensitive one, probably the reason why he had headed into medicine, he was a carer, a nurturer, he wanted to help those around him.

He might be the only one of his brothers who was still single, but it was because he had lost the first two loves of his life not because he had been the last to fall in love. Now he was staring chance number three in the face, and he was excited to see how it went.

Movement at the diner door caught his attention, and a moment later, it swung open, and Sydney stood there.

Her eyes immediately swung over to what had become their table, and she smiled when she saw him sitting there.

"I thought I told you to go home early, get some rest," he told her as she walked over.

"A girl's gotta eat," Sydney shot back.

He couldn't help but smile at her easy tone. There was such a change in how she interacted with him after just a few days. Gone was the shy, awkward girl, in her place was a sweet woman who wasn't afraid to say what she was thinking. He sensed the wariness was still lurking underneath and that it would take time to earn her trust and get her to relax completely, but he was up for the challenge.

"What are you smiling about?" she asked.

"I know we decided to postpone our date, but you're here, and I'm here, and how about we have dinner?"

"Sure." She smiled up at him like she had hoped he would say that but wasn't going to be the one to initiate dinner.

"Let's go." He grabbed her hand as she went to move toward the table.

"We're not eating here?"

"Nope." He led her back to the counter where he said to Penny, "Thanks for putting up with me tonight." He handed her some cash because she'd tolerated him sitting here all night without eating anything.

"Not necessary, Levi," she said, handing it back.

"Course it is." He winked, and she rolled her eyes at him but took the money.

Still holding Sydney's hand, they headed out into the crisp night. The rain had stopped around the time he finished his shift at the hospital, but there were still puddles everywhere. The sky however had cleared, and a million twinkling stars looked down on them.

Sydney paused to stare up at them. "This is my favorite part about living in the country," she said on a dreamy sigh. "In the city you hardly see any stars because there is too much light, but this is gorgeous."

"Not as gorgeous as you," he said with a slight teasing lilt to his voice even though he meant every word. He got that this was new to her and he didn't want her to feel pressured, he had the feeling she would spook easily.

Her cheeks turned an adorable shade of pink, but she gave him a smile. "Thanks."

"For telling you you're beautiful? Only speaking the truth," he told her as they started walking toward his house which was only a five-minute walk away.

She went another shade of red. "You're such a charmer."

"Guilty as charged, it's still a fact though. So you ever traveled out to the desert?"

"No, before I moved here I'd only ever lived in one place, and we never really went on vacations when I was a kid."

He heard the sadness in her voice and hated it. Levi decided then and there that as soon as he earned her trust and she was comfortable with the idea that the two of them were a couple, he would book them a vacation someplace where she could see what an expanse of dark sky filled with stars could really be like. "My family didn't travel a lot either, my dad was in the military, and since he was stationed overseas and we were here, my mom didn't have time to take four kids on vacation."

"You served too though, so you've traveled."

"I have." Amy loved to travel so whenever they were on leave they always split their time between his family, her family, and visiting a new country.

"What's your favorite place you've ever been?"

"Finland," he replied immediately. "Amy and I stayed in these amazing igloos with glass roofs, and lying in bed watching the northern lights light up the skies was an experience I'll never forget."

"Sounds magical," Sydney said with another dreamy sigh.

"It was really something else," he agreed as he steered her off the sidewalk and onto the garden path that led to his front door.

"We're eating dinner at your house?" Sydney said. All her calm and relaxed demeanor vanished, and she was suddenly tense and wary.

"Unless you don't want to, we can walk back to the diner if you're more comfortable."

Sydney seemed to debate the idea, but then she said, "No, it's okay, we can have dinner here."

She was still tense, and that was the last thing he wanted. "Just dinner, Syd, nothing more. And if you feel uncomfortable you can leave whenever you want, although I'll be walking you back to the diner to get your car," he said firmly. River's End was usually a safe town, and Sydney was a cop, but there was a serial killer on the loose, and she'd already been attacked once today, so no way was he letting her make the short walk alone.

"You're one of those, huh?" she asked as she relaxed again and a teasing quality came into her tone. "One of those tough alphas who like to be in control, you just hide it under your charm."

Levi laughed at her very apt depiction of him. "Come on, let's go eat."

She came willingly as he led her up to his front door and he hoped that meant she realized she had no reason to fear him. Whatever had happened to her in the past had touched her deeply, and he hoped he was able to help her move forward.

Inside he switched on the lights. "Kitchen is down the hall and take a left," he told her. "Anything you don't eat?"

"Nope, I'm easy. I wouldn't have minded eating at the diner though, you didn't have to go to all this trouble."

"It's no trouble, and I wanted to do something special for you to make up for our date getting rescheduled." Although he considered this a date of sorts he would have organized something a lot more special than a rushed dinner at ten at night.

"This is kind of a date," Sydney said hesitantly as she followed him down to the kitchen.

That was exactly what he wanted to hear. "I might have a few candles for a candlelight dinner."

"Very romantic." She nodded approvingly.

"I aim to please." He winked at her then opened the fridge door, grabbing a few vegetables and a jar of homemade tomato sauce he had made the week before. He'd cook up some pasta, add the sauce and vegetables, and he had ice cream for dessert. He could have done better if he'd been more prepared, but he'd intended to take her out to a fancy restaurant in the next town over for their date.

"What can I do to help?" Sydney asked, standing in the middle of his kitchen.

"Not a thing, you're my guest."

"I can still do something," she protested, her hands moving a little at her sides like the idea of sitting back and not helping was foreign to her.

"No way, you just sit your pretty little behind down and relax." He motioned to the breakfast bar where there were two stools.

Her cheeks flaming red again, Sydney somewhat reluctantly did as he told her to and took a seat.

"You want anything to drink?" he asked.

"I'm good, I'll wait for dinner."

Levi nodded and grabbed a knife from the block on the counter and began to chop a green pepper.

"Huh."

He glanced over his shoulder at Sydney who had her head cocked to the side. "Huh, what?"

"You're really good at that."

"You're surprised?" he asked with a grin. He loved to cook, as a kid he had always been the one in the kitchen helping his mom make dinner.

"A little. Why are you always at the diner if you're such a great cook?"

"To see you," he answered honestly.

"Oh," she said like the idea had never occurred to her. "That's really sweet. I assumed it was because you're like me and not that great at cooking so eating out is just easier."

Her golden-brown eyes had softened, opening a little to let him see inside to the real her, and she was smiling up at him like he'd just given her a precious gift. Their eyes met, heat fizzed between them even though there was five feet and a counter between them.

His gut said the timing was perfect.

Levi set the knife down and closed the space between them, taking hold of the back of the stool Sydney sat on and spinning it around so she was facing him. Her eyes immediately met his, and her lips parted, the tip of her tongue darting out to wet her bottom lip.

He bit back a groan, what he wouldn't give to yank her off that stool and into his arms, kissing her until she couldn't breathe, couldn't think of anything but him. But Sydney was tentative about being alone with him, and he didn't want to do anything to fray the fragile trust he'd built, she was special and should be treated as such.

Taking things slowly, he curled a hand around the back of her neck, then dipped his head and lightly whispered his lips across hers. She tasted sweet, like honey, and her lips were so soft he couldn't help but imagine what they would feel like against his skin.

When he straightened, she gave the softest little sigh, and if he hadn't already been hooked that would have done it.

Sydney was worth the wait, she was worth the work it would take to get her to believe in him—in them.

June 11th
7:57 A.M.

She couldn't wipe the smile off her face.

Sydney couldn't even remember a time she had smiled this much.

It was all thanks to Levi.

Last night had been amazing, he'd cooked the most delicious dinner for her, and after the kiss they had shared, they had sat around for hours talking. True to his word, he'd walked her back to the diner when they finally realized it was nearly one in the morning and they both had to be at work early and had reluctantly called it a night.

The more time she spent with him the more the walls that had been built around her began to crumble.

He made her happy, he made her glad that she had shrugged off the shackles of her family and fought to build her own life, he made her believe that she could have a normal future and everything that she had ever wanted.

How could she not smile about that?

With a minute to spare, she grabbed her purse and stepped outside. Fletcher would be here at eight to pick her up so they could interview Alan Dunkin. She was keyed up about the interview, wondering if she would recognize him when she saw him as the man she had tussled with yesterday.

Absently, she touched her fingers to the bandage on her arm as she locked up and walked down to the sidewalk as she saw Fletcher's car pull to a stop outside her house. Levi had checked the wound and rebandaged it last night before she went home, and while it hurt with a kind of distant pain, it wasn't any worse than some of the punishments she had been subjected to as a child.

"Morning," she said as she slid into the car, wondering if Fletcher was still going to be beating himself up about what happened yesterday. In her mind it was done and over with. They both should have been more careful, and although she knew it was always something she would regret she had learned from it and it was a mistake she would never repeat.

"Morning. Sleep okay?" Fletcher asked. If she hadn't caught his arched brow she would have thought he was implying she might have had nightmares or something about being attacked, but the eyebrow suggested he was actually digging for details on her private life.

"Let me guess, you heard that I went to Levi's house last night?" she asked. She still wasn't used to this small-town life gossip mill, it was like someone was always watching.

Fletcher laughed, and she felt her anxiety melt away. "You got life in River's End all figured out already I see."

"I get that people like to get all up in everyone's business, but I don't see what's so interesting about the fact that Levi and I have had dinner together a couple of times."

"It's because you don't know that Levi has literally been the object of pretty much every girl's crush since middle school. He can flirt the socks off anyone without even trying, flash those dimples at a girl and she can no longer think straight. But as much of a charmer as he is, he only ever takes things further if he's serious. He's only ever been serious about three women. Missy, Amy, and now you. In the three years since he moved back here he's never shown any interest in a woman, then you

—the new girl—get his attention so quickly, it's no wonder that everyone is interested. There are a lot of disappointed women in River's End right now."

Maybe that should make her feel special, and in a way it did, but it also made her nervous.

She was about as inexperienced as possible, and it sounded like Levi could have anyone he wanted. So why did he seem to want her?

Before she could work herself into a neurotic panic attack about what possible reason Levi could have found to show an interest in her and convince herself that he must have an angle that he was trying to work because that was what she had been taught about the way men behaved, Fletcher parked the car.

Work.

There was time to be paranoid about her budding relationship later, but for now she had to focus on this case. The need to prove herself was still there, all the more after yesterday's events and she wanted to be the one to find something that would crack this case open. Not because she wanted the ego boost or anything, just because she wanted Abe and her new colleagues to be proud of her, she wanted to pull her weight, she didn't want them ever to regret that Abe had hired her because they felt she was a liability.

"What's Alan like?" she asked as they both exited the car into the already muggy morning. There hadn't been any more rain since yesterday evening, but it was still cloudy, and the air was humid, hinting that there might be more rain coming later.

"Odd," Fletcher replied.

"Odd how?"

"He's ..." Fletcher trailed off as though trying to summarize how best to describe the man. "I don't know, he's just odd. He loves books, especially old books, and he doesn't always do well in social situations, he speaks really fast so it can be hard to follow what he's saying, and his IQ is off the charts. I always get the feeling whenever I'm around him that he looks down on everyone else because they aren't as smart as he is."

On the porch, she knocked on the front door. The house was small, the blinds were drawn so she couldn't peek through and get a hint of what Alan's home would be like. The yard was tidy, and the house looked freshly painted. It was right in the middle of town so if Alan was the killer this wasn't where he was torturing and killing his victims.

Around thirty seconds after she'd knocked the door was opened by a man who was the epitome of the nerdy, borderline crazy professor. His hair was long and a wild brown-streaked-with-gray mess, his brown eyes were hidden behind a pair of wire-rimmed glasses, he was wearing a pair of light brown trousers and a gray shirt that was buttoned wrong and half tucked in.

"Oh, Fletcher, hi." The man sounded confused to see them even though they'd made an appointment with him the day before. "And you're Sydney, right? The new deputy."

"Deputy Clark," she corrected. She didn't want to be too chummy with the man when they were here on official business.

"Yes, yes, yes, of course," he mumbled. "What can I do for you?"

"We talked to you yesterday, Alan," Fletcher reminded him. "We needed to talk to you about the murders?"

"The murders?" the man echoed, one finger pushing his glasses up his nose.

"Yes, there have been four so far. All of the women were in your bookstore the day they went missing," Sydney informed Alan.

"Oh no, that's terrible, just terrible," Alan said. "Come in, come in, of course I'll tell you whatever I can to help."

He ushered them into a house that looked more like a junk bookstore than a home. There were piles of books everywhere. Literally everywhere. They had to edge around them, and when they got into the living room, Alan had to move several large hardback books to clear space for them to sit on the couch.

"Sit, sit." He gestured at the sofa. "Drinks? Do you want something to drink?"

"No, thank you," she replied quickly. It was hard enough keeping the man focused without distracting him with anything else.

"You say I saw the women on the day they died?"

"Naomi Franklin, Elena Martinez, and Trina Liberty, along with a tourist Martha Vilcow," Fletcher said, and they both watched to see Alan's reactions.

He stared blankly at them for a moment before nodding slowly. "Yes, yes, I know Naomi, lovely girl. I'm afraid I can't remember Elena or Trina though."

Sydney thought that was odd. According to Fletcher, Elena had been coming to River's End every summer for the last two decades to visit her grandparents and Trina had lived here all her life, Alan should know them. The man was flighty at best, and although all four victims had been in his store the day they disappeared, she was having a hard time picturing this man committing the murders. She just wasn't sure he had it in him to be as controlled and careful when he abducted them or when he dumped their bodies. And as much as she had hoped when she met him she would know for certain one way or the other if he was the one who had attacked her, she honestly wasn't sure.

"What were they doing in your store, Alan?" Fletcher asked the man.

"Buying books," the man shot back, his tone bordering on condescending. "What else would they be doing in there?"

"Do you remember seeing them? Maybe noticing someone watching them or following them?" she asked.

"I don't remember seeing them let alone anyone watching them." Alan shrugged like the entire thing bored him. "I don't pay much attention to anything but my books. I'm sorry those women are dead, but I don't have the answers that you're seeking."

His lack of empathy and his inability to focus on anything but his books explained his recent divorce, it was no wonder his ex had finally had enough and had taken their kids and left. But was he focused enough to have committed the murders? Of that she wasn't so sure. She couldn't say she liked the man, but that didn't mean he was a killer.

Didn't mean he wasn't though.

~

11:39 A.M.

. . .

"Hey, Trina," Levi said softly as he walked into her hospital room. While the woman was no longer a patient of his having left the ER to be moved to ICU, he'd known her since she was a kid and he wanted to check in with her.

Especially this morning.

"Levi," came the whispered reply, and the woman in the hospital bed cracked open her eyes and offered him a small half-smile.

"How're you feeling?" He kept the lights off as he let the door close behind him and walked over to the bed. The woman had regained consciousness overnight, and there didn't appear to be any lasting brain damage. When she'd been brought to the ER yesterday, he hadn't even been sure she would make it let alone wake up so quickly. Trina Liberty was one lucky woman.

Being attacked in her own home aside.

"Other than the mother of all headaches, I'm okay, just tired," Trina replied.

He wished that he could let her rest, but Sydney and Fletcher were on the way here to question Trina about what she remembered from the attack. "Fletch and the new deputy are on their way here to talk with you so you might have to postpone that nap," he said lightly as he sat on the chair beside her bed.

Panic filled her face, the resulting spike in her blood pressure set off the machines standing around her bed.

"It's okay, Trina," he said soothingly, reaching over to rest a hand on hers. "You're safe here, he won't get to you again, and you know Abe and those guys, they're not going to stop until they get this guy. Plus, the new deputy is amazing," he said dreamily, hoping to distract her and help her calm down.

"Sydney, right? You got yourself a crush on her?" Trina managed a smile, and although her blood pressure was still too high, it was dropping back down into normal range.

"Teeny tiny one," he said, holding up his thumb and forefinger about half an inch apart.

"Teeny tiny, huh?" Trina gave a small chuckle then winced.

"Okay, maybe more than a teeny tiny crush." He grinned, pleased to see that his distraction had worked and she was calming down further.

"So sexy, charming Dr. Black is off the market now, that's too bad, there's going to be a lot of disappointed ladies in River's End." Trina sighed.

"Hey, you're gonna blow my ego out of control if you keep saying things like that," he joked.

Trina gave another small chuckle, then her face clouded over. "Levi …"

Whatever she had been going to say was cut off when there was a knock on her hospital room door before it opened, and Fletcher and Sydney walked through it.

Immediately his gaze swung to Sydney, neither of them had gotten much sleep last night because their date had lasted well into today, and they'd had to skip breakfast together because she'd had an early morning interview with a suspect. He immediately noted the shadows under her eyes, and her injured arm was tucked protectively against her stomach, but his gaze lingered on her smile.

Sydney was a beautiful woman but when she smiled … it was like something shifted inside him. He got this feeling like something warm and tingly had taken hold in his stomach, it touched every part of him, including his heart, and when he looked at Sydney his heart did strange things, things he couldn't even put into words.

"Hi, Fletcher," Trina said, mustering another smile even though tension pretty much radiated off her. "And you must be Sydney. Levi and I were just talking about you."

Sydney did her cute blushing thing again, and as much as he wanted to walk over and give her a kiss, she was here for work, and he didn't think she would appreciate that. He'd wait until she and Fletcher were finished here and then he'd sneak a couple of minutes alone with her under the guise of checking on her arm.

"Morning, Syd, I had fun last night," he greeted her.

"Yeah, me too." She shot him another one of those winning smiles.

He couldn't take his eyes off her and might have just sat there drinking in the sight of her, but Fletcher cleared his throat. "Hi, Fletcher," he said sheepishly.

"Morning," his friend drawled, an amused expression on his face. "So, Trina, how are you feeling?"

"Headache and tired, but otherwise I'm okay, lucky," she added.

"We'll make this as quick as we can," Fletcher promised. "We know that you've got some retrograde amnesia, but we wondered if there was anything you remember about the attack."

Retrograde amnesia was common after a head injury. Sometimes those memories of just before the injury came back and sometimes they didn't, but Levi understood how frustrating it must be for Sydney and Fletcher. They wanted to get this killer off the streets, and Trina was the only one who had seen him and survived.

Besides Sydney who hadn't gotten a look at his face.

That she had come face to face with a serial killer still made him want to throw up, but he quickly shoved the thought aside. She had fought back and saved herself, she was a tough one, and he couldn't be more impressed with her.

"It's all a blank, sorry." Trina sounded upset like she was letting them down.

"Nothing to be sorry about, it's not your fault," Fletcher assured her. "What is the last thing you remember?"

Trina's brow creased as she thought. "Yesterday morning I went to the bookstore first thing to pick up a book ... but I can't remember who it was for. I just remember being in the store and then nothing."

Fletcher and Sydney shared a look at that, but he knew better than to ask what it was about. He was here because he was a doctor and given Trina's current state, Fletcher had asked him to hang around while they spoke with her.

"Your memories might come back," Levi told Trina to reassure her.

"Or they might not. It's so frustrating to have a piece of my life missing, even if it is just a day."

Given what she had survived maybe it was for the best if those memories never returned.

"Do you remember anything unusual in the days leading up to yesterday?" Sydney asked. "Anyone watching you, anyone following you, anything that made you uncomfortable?"

Trina shook her head slowly. "I can't think of anything. Everything was just the same as always and then ... this ..." she waved a hand at the hospital room. "I'm sorry, I wish I could help." Her eyes were starting to droop, and she looked exhausted. Time to call it quits.

"I think that's enough for today," he told Sydney and Fletcher.

"One more question?" Sydney asked.

"Sure," Trina answered before he could.

"Did you talk to Alan Dunkin at the bookstore?"

"Yeah, I think I did, he was helping me look for a book."

"How did he seem?" Sydney asked.

"Flighty, talking too much, same as usual."

"Okay, thanks." Sydney smiled at the woman.

"Get some rest, Trina, I'll come visit you later on in my shift." He gave her hand a squeeze and followed the cops out the door. "Syd, I want to check your arm before you go."

"Oh, uh, okay," she agreed.

"I'll meet you in the car in fifteen," Fletcher told her as he headed off down the quiet hospital corridor, obviously wanting to give them a few minutes together.

"Let's go down to the ER," he said, his hand on the small of her back as he guided her to the lifts. "You get any sleep last night?"

"A couple of hours. You?"

"A couple of hours," he said, leaving out the part where he'd taken a cold shower because after one chaste kiss in his kitchen and then another when he'd left her at her car he'd been turned on like he had never been before.

The lift dinged, and they stepped inside. "So are we still on for dinner tonight?" Sydney asked.

"Definitely, my shift finishes at seven. Do you know what time you'll be done?"

"Unless anything major happens I can be done by then," she replied. Since the *anything major* was another murder, he sincerely hoped that there wouldn't be anything major happening today.

"Tonight is a proper date so I'll pick you up at your place at seven-thirty." Tonight he was going all out, romance central, this was their first real date, and he wanted to make it special. The lift beeped, and the doors opened, and he returned his hand to the small of her back as he led her down to an empty exam room.

"I can't wait to see what you have planned." Sydney smiled at him. Most of the wariness was gone from her eyes now, and she just looked excited and a little shy. He hoped the shyness would fade once she realized just how much he truly liked her.

"Let's take a look at this arm." He was sure it was doing fine, and it wasn't really necessary that he check it out again, but he wanted a reason to snatch a few minutes alone with her. Sydney sat on the edge of the bed, and he took her hand and unwound the bandages, the edges of her wound were red but not enflamed, and it hadn't bled any since he looked at it last night. "How does it feel?"

"A little sore, but it's nothing I can't handle."

That he could believe. He was pretty sure there wasn't much that Deputy Sydney Clark couldn't handle. He still held her hand, and his thumb rubbed lightly across the sensitive skin on the inside of her wrist making her shiver and suck in a breath.

"I wish we weren't in the hospital right now," he told her.

"Oh," the word tumbled from her lips, her eyes locked onto his.

Maybe one little kiss could hold him over until tonight.

Keeping hold of her hand, he stood, moving between her knees, he curled a hand around the back of her neck, his fingers threading through her silky brown locks. Her eyes never left his as he dipped his head and claimed her mouth.

This kiss was deeper than their other two had been, it held more passion, more intimacy, more of a connection.

He'd been wrong.

One kiss couldn't hold him over.

One million kisses would never be enough.

He was falling hard and fast.

~

4:22 P.M.

Being pregnant was awful.

Well, no not completely, Meadow Black rebuked herself. Her pregnancy had been full of ups and downs, the lowest times of her life along with the highest. Finding out she was having a baby was what had convinced her that it was time to flee her abusive ex, leading her right to Abe.

Her husband.

She'd been married most of her adult life, but there was something special associating that with the man who loved and cherished her instead of the man who beat and belittled her.

If it hadn't been for this baby, she never would have run, might even be dead by now. She had always known it was only a matter of time, but when it was no longer just her life at stake, she'd known that she couldn't play Russian roulette with her life anymore, hoping her luck held and he didn't kill her.

Now everything was perfect.

With a husband who adored her and a family who were as much hers and her baby's as they were Abe's, her life was finally the fairytale she had always dreamed of having ... if this baby would finally come out.

She was already several days past her due date and being this big was starting to get to her. She'd forgotten what her toes looked like, her back ached, just getting in and out of bed or up and down out of a chair was almost impossible, and she had to pee all the time. She wanted her daughter to hurry up and make her appearance in the world.

"Come on, baby girl," she rubbed her stomach, "Daddy and I really want to meet you."

At first, she worried that Abe might not be able to love this baby, not so much because he wasn't the biological father, but because the biological father was her abusive ex-husband. But he had been not only supportive but excited about this pregnancy from the moment they became a couple.

Meadow knew he would be an amazing dad. If you didn't know him he was this big, tough guy with tattoos and a beard, he was intimidating —almost downright terrifying—but underneath, he had a heart of gold. He was her own personal big, squishy teddy bear.

Tears brimmed in her eyes, she loved him so much, so much that sometimes it hurt, and she couldn't wait to bring their daughter into the world and then add a whole mess more children to their family. Her tears trickled out, darn pregnancy hormones had her so emotional all the time. More times than she could count over these last few months, Abe had held her in his arms, soothing her, offering her ice cream, or anything else he could think of to get her to stop crying.

She giggled at the thought of her tough-guy husband in a panic over some tears. What was he going to be like when their kids threw tantrums to get their way? Big softie would probably hand over whatever they wanted just to see them smile.

With a sigh, she realized she had to pee again and did not relish the idea of dragging herself out of the swing on the front deck of the house she shared with her husband. It was a sweet little cottage out in the forest, and she remembered the first time she had come here. Back then she'd been scared and alone, unsure who to trust, but now this place was her happy place.

Sweat trickled down her back as she managed to get to her feet. The heat was another reason she couldn't wait for this baby girl to make her grand entrance.

Meadow was just stepping through the front door and preparing for the mammoth task of climbing the stairs to get to the bathroom when she felt a rush of something wet between her legs.

Did she just pee on the floor?

No.

Her water just broke.

With a squeal of excitement that it was finally time to get this baby out of her, she pulled her cell phone—which Abe had insisted she keep on her at all times—from her pocket and called her husband.

"Hey, Med," his voice came down the line a moment later. "You hot, tired, and cranky, baby?" he clucked sympathetically.

Fighting back a giggle because she *had* called Abe multiple times a day these last couple of weeks hot and tired and frustrated and ready to not be pregnant any longer. "Nope, not this time. It's time."

"Time?" he repeated.

"Baby time," she elaborated.

"Are you? Did you? It's time for the baby to come?" Her calm, cool, always in control former marine turned sheriff husband sounded panicked.

"My water just broke, I'm in labor." She couldn't keep the excitement out of her voice. She wasn't like most women, she wasn't afraid of the pain she was about to experience giving birth, she had been beaten every day for years on end, sometimes so badly her husband was forced to bring in a doctor to check her over, so no matter how bad this was she knew she could take it. Besides excitement to meet her daughter overrode everything else, she couldn't wait to hold her baby in her arms.

"Okay, sweetheart, I'm on my way, I'll be there in ten minutes."

"I'll be waiting, I'll grab the bag and—"

"No," Abe said firmly, "you just sit your pretty little butt down and wait for me to get there."

"All right, Mr. Bossy," she harrumphed. She knew Abe fussed because he cared but four long months of him fussing over her like a mother hen was more than enough for a lifetime.

"See you in ten," he repeated, "and I better find you sitting waiting for me when I get there."

"Love you."

"Love you back."

When Abe hung up, she put the phone back in her pocket and then debated climbing the stairs to grab the hospital bag anyway, but a contraction suddenly hit her, and she leaned against the wall for support.

Okay, maybe she'd do as Abe said and sit down and wait for him.

When the contraction passed, she headed back out to the porch and dropped down onto the swing. While she wasn't afraid of the pain that would come with childbirth, she *was* afraid of something going wrong. Four months ago she had been beaten badly by her ex, and although her doctors had said that everything was okay with the baby that lingering fear that they were wrong hadn't left her.

What if the baby wasn't okay?

What if something went wrong during the delivery?

What if she hadn't done her job and protected her baby?

The sound of an engine ripped her from her fears, and she looked up to see Abe's truck skidding to a stop at the end of the driveway. He practically threw the door open and jumped out, running over to her.

"Hey, baby, you okay? You in pain?"

"I'm good," she assured him, but the fear that something would happen to the baby was starting to weigh on her.

"Everything's going to be fine, babe, I promise." He pressed his lips to her forehead. "I'll grab the bag, and we'll get you to the hospital."

He left her for a moment to run upstairs, retrieve the bag she had packed when she hit the eight-month mark just in case their baby was an early bird, and then he locked up and came back to her side. Without a word, he scooped her up into his strong arms and carried her toward his truck.

"I can walk, Abe," she told him.

Her husband merely huffed. "You *can*, you just won't be, not for a few days at least."

She rolled her eyes at him but stifled a laugh. Alpha males, you couldn't live with them, but she couldn't live without them. Hers anyway.

Abe set her in the passenger seat, buckled her in, then tossed the bag in the backseat and hopped back into the driver's seat. He'd left the engine running and immediately began to drive them to the hospital.

The closer they got the more afraid she got.

She'd had one job with this pregnancy, to protect this baby and keep it safe, and instead she'd gotten herself nearly killed. If anything happened to her daughter she would never forgive herself.

As if sensing her fears—something she shouldn't be surprised at because Abe always knew what she was feeling—her husband reached for her hand. "The baby is fine, Meadow, every scan we've had she's been as healthy as it's possible for a baby to be. Everything is going to be fine, we're in this together, okay? You and me, a team, you got this."

A team.

For all his alpha maleness, Abe always treated her like an equal. While her ex had constantly told her how pathetic and weak she was, saying it so often she grew to believe it, Abe always built her up. He believed in her, in her strength and determination, and that had helped her so many times these last four months as she had battled to leave the past behind.

"Hey." Abe squeezed her hand until she looked at him. "This little girl is as strong as her mama. You don't have to worry about her."

Holding onto those words, Meadow prepared herself to meet her daughter.

~

6:41 P.M.

Sydney gave herself an assessing once over.

She'd added a few curls to her hair and left it hanging loose around her shoulders even though she knew the weight of it on her neck would make her hot later. She'd put on more makeup than she usually wore when she went to work, partly because she wanted to look her best, and partly to cover the bruise on her forehead from her scuffle with the killer the other day, but not too much because she didn't want to look like she was trying too hard.

Even though she was.

She wanted tonight to go perfectly. Not just well but *perfect*.

Scrutinizing her outfit, she very nearly decided to change—for the fifth time—but decided that the soft lilac silk of the sundress clung to her body, showing off her small curves without being too revealing, and was nice enough if he was taking her to a fancy restaurant while not being too dressy if he had something more casual in mind.

Sydney's gaze fell to the bandage wrapped around her left forearm. She wished there was something she could do about it, but for the time being she was stuck with it, so she may as well just pretend it wasn't there.

She added a little bit of lip gloss and then smoothed her hands down her dress and decided that primping in the bathroom was only going to make her more nervous. And really there was nothing to be nervous about. What was the worst that could happen tonight? She'd already kissed him, and she knew he wouldn't pressure her for more than she was ready to give.

Levi Black was the opposite of what her father had told her men were like.

Okay, so he was charming and sexy, and he liked to flirt, but he was deeper than that. He didn't just want her for her body because he could have any number of women who were a lot more willing to fall into bed with him than she was. He liked her, he wanted to get to know her, he'd been nothing but sweet and fun, and she knew that she'd been right and that her father had tried to brainwash her into believing lies.

She might not know what Levi saw in her, but so far he had given her no reason to doubt him, and as her years of therapy had taught her, she wasn't going to overanalyze things because that only led her to a bad place. When she stayed too long inside her own head all her doubts started to creep back in, and before she knew it, she was back to being the quivering, terrified teenager who had been brainwashed and abused.

But she wasn't that girl any longer.

Now she was a strong, confident, independent woman.

Yes, she was shy in new situations, especially around men she didn't know, but she was a cop now, and she had worked hard to get to a place in her life when she was ready to metaphorically and physically leave her past behind and start over.

She'd been given a chance to be happy, to be normal, and she wasn't going to waste it.

Grabbing her purse, she headed through to the kitchen, intending to make herself some tea to try to calm her nerves while she waited.

As she stood in her kitchen waiting for the electric kettle to boil, no microwaving tea for her, she looked down at her feet. She was wearing a pair of slinky white stilettos that were no doubt going to have her feet in agony by the end of the evening, but she'd bought them when she was planning her move, hoping she might one day have cause to use them, and now she did.

This was it.

Her first real date, since last night's impromptu dinner at Levi's didn't really count.

Her stomach was churning and her hands shaking so much that she splashed hot water over the counter when she tried to make her tea. She was so nervous but just as excited, it was like she was about to become a real woman.

Sydney was just putting a tea bag in her mug when her phone began to ring. Levi's name popped up on the screen—he'd put his number in her phone last night—and she couldn't stop the huge grin that spread over her face.

How lucky was she that a guy like him was interested in a girl like her?

Snatching up her phone, she touched accept and held the phone to her ear. "Hey."

"Hey, Syd."

There was something in his voice that immediately had warning bells going off in her head. "Is something wrong?"

"No," he said quickly. *Too* quickly. "Well, not *wrong* exactly, but I'm really sorry, Syd, I have to break our date for tonight."

The room drained of oxygen.

Her heart stopped beating.

Her entire body turned numb.

Levi was breaking their date.

He didn't want to go out with her.

She'd been wrong.

Her father was right.

The worst part was she had no one to blame but herself for this relationship—which she was now wondering if it had been anything more than her own fantasy and imagination concocting something that didn't exist—ending before it had ever really gotten off the ground. Levi was a man, he had needs, needs she hadn't fulfilled.

"Syd?" Levi's voice snapped her out of her panicked haze.

"Yeah, sure, no problem," she tried to sound nonchalant, like she couldn't have cared less one way or the other, but was sure she had failed miserably. "I'll let you get back to whatever you're doing. Bye." She hung up then tossed the phone down on the counter like it still possessed the power to hurt her even though the phone call was over.

How many times had her father told her what her job was?

She was a woman.

Her sole purpose in life was to please the man in her life.

She should have given him sex last night at his house. Or if he didn't want that she was adept with both her hands and her mouth at giving a man what he wanted.

Why hadn't she done it?

She knew it was the only way to keep a man.

Her father had drilled that into her from the time she was eleven years old.

If Levi had changed his mind about her, she had no one to blame but herself.

"No, Sydney," she rebuked herself aloud. "Dad lied. You know that. Because of Mom, his view of women was warped. He's wrong. It's not my job to provide sexual favors for men. How many times did your therapist tell you that? I thought you believed it. It's why you left your sister and everything behind. You're here to build a new life, to leave the past where it belongs. If Levi doesn't want you then you'll be fine. You didn't come here to find a man you came here for you. Suck it up, buttercup."

Resting both hands against the countertop, she let her head hang down and dragged in a slow breath, counting to ten as she did so to make sure she got enough oxygen in her lungs. She repeated the process ten times. Ten lots of ten, enough time to refill her lungs with oxygen and clear her mind.

Her pep talk did the trick, her panic was receding, along with it her hope and dreams for the future.

Okay, so she didn't have a man in her life, it wasn't the end of the world. She had a life, she had a job, and she was starting to make this place her home. She'd avoid Levi for the next few days, or weeks, or months, or however long it took until she could look him in the eye without feeling a stab of pain in her chest.

"You got this, girl, you've bounced back from worse, you can handle a little rejection from a man you just met."

That was true.

She'd known Levi not even a week yet, that wasn't enough time to have developed feelings any deeper than interest and a passion that ignited like a spark whenever his hazel eyes looked at her.

"Can't miss what you never had, Syd," she said. She straightened and gave herself a brisk shake, moping over what had never been hers wasn't going to serve any purpose. Better to just brush off the disappointment and move on. Starting with returning the dress and the ridiculous heels to her closet, then washing her face, then she could put on her PJs, and maybe she'd eat a bowl of ice cream for dinner, comfort food was exactly what she needed right now.

With her spine as straight as steel, she headed back to her bedroom. Her mother's death hadn't broken her, her father's abuse hadn't broken her, being left an orphan at fourteen hadn't broken her, her sister falling into a relationship with a man like their father and making the devastating decision to walk away from Adelaide after several failed attempts to help her hadn't broken her, so Dr. Levi Black, a man she'd known for only a few days certainly wasn't going to break her.

As she slipped the heels off, Sydney had to admit it certainly felt like a piece of herself was broken.

CHAPTER *Six*

June 12th
8:03 A.M.

He was officially an uncle.

Levi hadn't been able to wipe the smile off his face since little Dawn had entered the world at thirty-two minutes past two this morning. Things had gotten a little scary there for a while, the baby's heartbeat had dropped, and Meadow had started bleeding badly, and in the end, she'd been rushed in for an emergency cesarean.

Mother and baby were both doing well and would be going home in a couple of days. That little girl was already loved more than she could know, she might not be a Black by blood, but she was a part of their family in every way that mattered. Every one of them was smitten with the tiny baby girl, even his little sister Dahlia who had made a very brief visit to the hospital to meet her new niece before leaving again.

That Dahlia had come meant a lot to all of them, but that she had left so quickly only reinforced their concerns.

But worries about his sister weren't for today.

Today was a day about celebrating the beginning of the next generation of Blacks, and to make matters better, his little brother Theo had announced that he and his girlfriend Maggie were now engaged and expecting a baby.

His family was growing.

The absolute joy on his parents' faces when they had held their first grandchild in their arms had stoked something deep inside him. He'd always thought he'd have kids by now and yet he was thirty-one and wasn't even married.

Yet.

But there was Sydney.

What he felt for her echoed what he had felt for Amy, and he could see her in his future, but last night's phone call had him concerned.

Something in her voice, she'd been trying too hard to make it sound like she hadn't really cared one way or the other if their date had gone ahead, then she'd abruptly ended the call and refused to answer or reply to any of the other calls or texts he'd sent.

Originally, when he'd learned Meadow had gone into labor he'd intended to go to Sydney's pick her up and ask her if she minded having dinner in the hospital cafeteria so he could be there for his family, but then everything had gone downhill, and he hadn't wanted to leave, even just to go and pick her up. He would have explained all of that if she had just given him half a chance.

In hindsight, maybe he should have seen this coming. He'd known that she was wary of the whole dating thing, and it didn't take a genius to figure out that it probably had something to do with whatever her reasons were for moving here. He knew that both her parents were deceased and that she had an older sister, but other than that, he didn't know much about her life before she arrived in River's End.

Levi wished he had some clue as to what had upset her and what was running through her head right now so he knew how to proceed.

With a weary sigh, he dragged his hands through his hair and scrubbed them down his face. He was tired, and he would have loved to head straight home after leaving the hospital, take a shower and fall into bed because he'd been up since six yesterday morning, but he needed to sort things out with Sydney first.

So he was sitting at the diner, in their booth, hoping that she would stop by for breakfast like she usually did. She might not want to let him talk, but he *was* going to explain things to her. He knew that even though he'd hurt her having to call the date off last minute she was a smart and logical woman, and she'd realize it wasn't because he hadn't wanted to go out with her just that circumstances had gotten in the way.

He wasn't angry with Sydney for being upset. He knew she wasn't some drama queen looking for attention and wanting to manipulate him into coming running after her for some sort of power trip. She was genuinely hurting and obviously battling some pretty heavy demons, and he wanted to help her with those. He wanted to prove to her that whatever it was that had hurt her in the past she didn't have to be afraid with him, he would never hurt her or betray her.

Taking a long drink of his coffee, he stared at the diner door as though he could conjure Sydney out of thin air if he focused hard enough.

What was he going to do if she didn't show?

He'd already called her a dozen times, sent a dozen texts, and it was pretty clear that she had no intention of replying or answering. He could turn up at her house, but he wasn't sure she would let him in the door. There was always the option of going down to the station and cornering her there, but he was wary of doing that because he knew that she was self-conscious at work and felt like she had to prove herself. He got that, his brother and his cousins could be intimidating guys, and she was the youngest and the newest.

"Argh," he groaned quietly. He felt like he was messing things up somehow, but he had no idea why or what he would do to fix it.

One thing was clear.

He would have to convince Sydney that she was safe enough with him that she could open up, tell him what she was running from and who had hurt her, and what he could do to make things better.

Because that was what he did.

He made things better.

He fixed things.

Except when it came to the women he loved.

Missy had died of cancer, and he hadn't been able to save her or even do anything to ease her suffering except for hold her hand which had made him feel woefully inadequate.

Amy had died because when her chopper went down he was the one who had triaged the injured, tagging the love of his life as the least injured and therefore the one who had to wait while everyone else was attended to first. She had thrown a blood clot that had gone to her lung and killed her before there was anything he could do to stop it.

Now Sydney was hurting, and he didn't know what to do.

"Hey, hon." He looked up to meet Penny's sympathetic smile. "Your girl hasn't stopped by this morning?"

"No, she hasn't."

"You didn't have a fight with her, did you?" she asked.

"No, not exactly. More like a misunderstanding I want to fix if she'll give me a chance."

Penny tutted, then patted his shoulder. "I'm sure you'll work it out, after all, she's a lucky girl to have you, she'll realize that."

That was just it.

It was *him* that felt like the lucky one to have a chance with her. It felt like Sydney didn't give her trust to many people, and he was honored that she had given it to him. He was pretty sure that in her mind he had taken advantage of that and blown up whatever fragile bond they had built.

There was no way he was letting her go.

Definitely not like this.

"She's pretty special, huh?" Penny asked.

"Yeah." Levi smiled as he pictured her pretty smile, the way her cheeks went pink when she was embarrassed, the way she'd stuttered nervously when they'd first met, the way her lips felt when he kissed her, the way she tasted, the way she fitted so perfectly in his arms. "She's pretty special."

"You're going to fight for her, right?"

"Absolutely. I just have to figure out a plan." Not that he would give up, but Levi knew that would be easier said than done. Whatever had happened to Sydney it had left her with deep scars that were probably barely healed. She thought that she was in this alone, but she was wrong, he was there, and he would support her in any way she needed.

He was tired of being alone, he wanted to start his life, he wanted someone to share it with, and he wanted that someone to be Sydney.

Now he just had to convince Syd of that.

"You let me know if you need anything," Penny offered. "I like Sydney, and it's good to see you so happy again, it's been a while."

Three years in fact.

Three years, seven months, and twenty-four days.

When Amy had died, he wasn't sure he would ever want to move on, which was why he had never initiated any relationships, believing that if the right woman crossed his path he would know it.

And he did.

Sydney was the right woman for him, the one to finally give him the forever that had been denied him twice already.

Now he just had to hope and pray that Sydney would give him a chance, that she wouldn't let her demons destroy her and their chance to be happy.

~

1:09 P.M.

It was such a beautiful day.

Wednesday Adams had the car windows rolled down, the breeze sent her wild red curls whipping around her face, she had music blaring, and she was singing along at the top of her lungs, the sun was shining making patterns with the dappled light through the tall trees that lined the road.

She was buzzing with excitement.

The kind of excitement that said she was quickly heading toward what could be the rest of her life. She was heading across the country to meet her boyfriend, and she was hoping that he would propose.

They'd been dating for a little over a year now and although she lived on the east coast and he lived on the west coast, things had gotten pretty serious. They video called every day, texted dozens of times throughout the day, and visited each other whenever they could. They had talked about the possibility of her maybe moving to live closer to him. She owned her own business which she ran online so she didn't have to worry about her job, and while leaving her family behind would be hard she'd be able to see the love of her life every day.

This could be it.

She was driving out to spend the entire summer with him, and if he did propose, then she wouldn't be going back other than to pack up her stuff and organize to have it transported to her new home.

Her stomach grumbled loudly as she turned onto another quiet country road and she debated stopping at the next town. According to her GPS, there was a small town called River's End just another couple of miles down the road. Maybe she could stop for lunch and take a little break before continuing on. Or if the town was a quaint one, she might even see if there was a hotel or something and spend the night. She was a sucker for a cute little town which was part of the reason she had decided to drive rather than fly. It would take her a couple of weeks, but she was kind of looking forward to the solitude, and she had the most amazing man waiting for her when she did arrive.

Deciding that she would take a little detour to River's End, Wednesday was keeping an eye out for a sign telling her when she should turn off to whatever road led to the town when she saw a man standing at the side of the road, next to a car with the hood up, waving madly at her.

Should she pull over to see if she could help?

She wanted to, but she was a twenty-six-year-old woman, traveling alone, and there was always the possibility that the man could be using a broken down car as a way to lure her into a trap.

But ...

She couldn't turn away someone who might be in need.

Wednesday had always been that way, she was the kid in school who had sought out the lonely and bullied kids and made friends with them, she brought home stray animals, and she made friends with the lonely old lady who lived next door and never had any visitors.

She pulled her car in behind his, grabbed her cell phone, turned off the music, and got out. Her plan had been not to get too close in case she needed to make a quick getaway to her car, but the man immediately ran over, his eyes zeroing in on her phone.

"Thank you so much for stopping," he gushed, a huge smile on his face. "I lost my cell phone about a week ago and haven't had a chance to replace it yet, and wouldn't you know it's now that my car chooses to break down. Could I just call a tow truck, then you can be on your way. Unless you're a mechanic?" He teased, an easy smile still in place.

Relaxing at the man's relaxed and friendly nature, she smiled back. "Not a mechanic, sorry, but you can use my cell phone."

"You are a lifesaver." He grinned.

"It's no problem, really," she assured him and handed him her phone.

While he took it and presumably made his phone call, Wednesday took a few steps off the road and into the surrounding forest. It was beautiful out here. The dappled light, the gentle breeze, it was hot but not unbearably so, and she could hear the sound of the river rushing somewhere nearby.

It was gorgeous.

Her dream was to live in a quaint little town just like this, preferably in a cute little log cabin with a view of a river or a lake. She wanted wildlife around, wanted fresh air, and wanted a relaxed pace of life. She wanted to live in a place where everyone knew everyone and stuck their nose in everyone's business because they were like your extended family. She wanted to sit on her porch and watch sunrises and sunsets, she wanted to hike on bright summer days, and curl up in front of a roaring fire in the winter.

She wanted this.

Footsteps followed her as she wandered further into the forest, and she assumed it was the man from the car coming to give her phone back. She realized that she hadn't asked his name, that was stupid, she should have asked that first thing, and she probably shouldn't wander any further from the road.

Wednesday turned around a split second too late.

A body slammed into her, knocking her to the ground.

She landed on her wrist and arrows of pain shot through her body, but she didn't hear any crunching sounds so she was taking that as a good sign and assuming she hadn't broken it.

The man was trying to flip her onto her stomach, no doubt to bind her hands behind her back.

That wasn't happening.

Unfortunately for this man, she was not only a black belt in Taekwondo but also taught self-defense classes weekly.

Throwing her body weight back she managed to dislodge the man enough to get him off her. She followed up with a kick to the groin, as he was still on his hands and knees and she was just beside him. He yelped in surprised anger and pain, and she took advantage of that opportunity to run.

She'd wandered further away from the safety of her car and the road than she'd realized so she took off as fast as she could, stumbling over the terrain as she went in her panic.

"No," the man yelled behind her. "I can't let you go. It's you, I know it's you, I can see it, I know I've got the right one this time. You see it too, don't you?" he asked.

There were two of them?

That wasn't good for her.

The road was only twenty yards or so away when something slammed into her.

Not a person this time, and not a bullet either, but pain zinged about her body, radiating out from a spot on her back.

Wednesday stumbled again as something else hit her.

When the third hit came, she cried out and went down to her knees.

A rock slammed into the ground beside her and then another hit her leg.

He was throwing rocks at her, and not teeny tiny ones.

Another hit her and then another.

The force of each blow increased as the man got closer.

She would have tried to get back up, keep running, but the rocks kept coming, one after another, hitting her legs and her arms, and she had to cover her face to protect it.

At last the man was standing beside her. He looked down at her, and she cowered. Gone was the smile and easygoing nature he had projected at their cars. Now the man's eyes were wild, and he looked at her with a mixture of guilt and determination.

"Are you sure this time?" he asked, only he wasn't looking at her. He was looking beside him, but when she looked where he was looking she didn't see anyone.

Was he mentally unstable?

Did he really think someone else besides the two of them was here?

"I don't want to make a mistake again," he said to the empty space. "You have to be sure. Are you sure that it's her?" Apparently, the figment of his imagination replied because the man nodded and looked relieved. "Okay, if you're sure that she has the answers that we need then I'll take her."

She wanted to keep fighting, get back on her feet, run, hopefully make it to her car, but her entire body was aching with throbbing pain, and the man held another rock in his hand. He held it up, and she hated that she cowered from him. "Please, let me go," she begged.

"I want to but I can't," he said and sounded genuinely apologetic. "I need answers, and you're the only one who can give them to me. If I don't get them they won't leave me alone." As he said that he had gestured at the empty space and the person he obviously saw there.

This was not good for her.

The man was crazy, and she suspected that the questions he wanted answers to really didn't have any answers.

She opened her mouth to beg again because she sensed he truly didn't want to be doing this, but before she could he slammed the rock into the side of her head, and a swirling vortex of black pain swallowed her up.

6:12 P.M.

All day she had been struggling to concentrate.

Sydney kept replaying the situation with Levi in her mind, trying to figure out if there was a way she could have kept him.

She knew playing the what-if game wasn't productive, sometimes in life bad stuff just happened, there was no way to avoid it, and your time was better spent finding a way to deal with it than wondering what might have happened if things were different.

So she was trying to move on.

It was what it was, and there was no point in wasting time working herself up over it. She'd only known Levi for six days now so that wasn't enough time to have become overly attached. Moving on shouldn't be too hard.

And yet it was.

Something about him had stirred up feelings inside her that she'd never felt before. She'd had crushes in high school, but she'd been the weird girl with no friends so she'd never acted on them. What she felt for Levi went deeper than that, he made her feel safe, and he made her feel special, and she'd been excited—albeit nervous—to see where things went with him.

Obviously, she had read more into the situation than there was, that was her mistake, and while she'd love to say it wouldn't make it harder for her to take this step next time it was too early to say that. She'd worked so hard to get to this place, and Levi's rejection hurt. It made her want to curl up inside her house and never let anyone get close to her, she didn't want to live her life that way. She wanted to be normal, wanted her job, wanted friends, and wanted someone to share her life with.

It obviously wasn't going to be Levi, but she wasn't giving up.

She couldn't.

She had worked too long and too hard to get to this place to do that.

Her phone rang, and when she saw Fletcher's name instead of Levi's, she answered the call. "Hey," she gave a listless greeting.

"You sound beat, Syd. You should call it quits for the day, we don't have anything new on the serial killer, and you've been there since six this morning. Go home, get some rest, and we'll attack this case again tomorrow."

He was right. She hadn't slept well and had come in early, working a few hours on the serial killer case before dealing with an incident in a bar in the next town, and then a domestic at a farm on the outskirts of town before coming back here to work on the case some more. She'd avoided her colleagues as best as she could because she didn't want to see anyone, and she was definitely ready to head home and chill for the evening before trying to make it an early night.

"Yeah, maybe you're right, I'll talk to you tomorrow."

"Night."

"Night," she echoed, wondering what Fletcher did for fun. Besides Abe and Beau, none of her colleagues appeared to have significant others, and she had to wonder why. They were all former military turned cops, they were all sexy as sin, and they were all nice guys if a little more alpha than she liked in a guy. Women should be practically knocking down their doors—and for all she knew they were—and yet they were all single.

Restacking the files she'd been looking through, reports from the coroner on their victims, and forensics reports, she grabbed her purse and her phone and headed out of the station. The place was empty, Poppy left at six, and if anyone needed anything after hours they called Abe directly.

Dragging her feet to her car, Sydney gave herself permission to wallow just for tonight, and then she'd commit to working on moving forward. Her therapist had always told her not to run from her feelings, feel them, accept them, process them, and then find a way to deal with them. So that's what she'd do. She'd accept that Levi had hurt her feelings, then make herself believe he didn't owe her anything, and then she'd just go back to focusing on work and enter the dating scene when she was ready.

No rush.

She was twenty-six, she had the rest of her life before her. There was no need to jump into something too quickly.

Maybe this break up with Levi was actually for the best. Things had moved quickly, much quicker than she had intended, and that wasn't a smart thing. She needed to be sure before she got in too deep, and that took time.

So time it was.

Sydney had parked at the diner before she even thought about what she was doing, but as soon as she turned the engine off, she realized that this was probably a mistake. Levi could be here, and she wasn't ready to face him yet. Maybe she should just go home, she probably didn't have much in her fridge, but she was sure she could scrounge up something.

No.

Moving here was about owning her life, and in her new life she didn't run away from anyone or anything.

Determinedly, she got out of her car and walked over to the diner's door, she could do this. If Levi was there she would just avoid him, and if luck was on her side, he would still be at work. She wanted to build a future here, and that meant forming bonds with the other people in town. She wasn't going to let Levi scare her away from doing that. This was her home too.

Her resolve to be strong lasted until she opened the door and saw Levi sitting at the counter—not in the booth they had shared several times over the last few days—a woman beside him, her hand resting on his thigh as she laughed at something Levi had just said.

Levi was shooting the woman that gorgeous grin that showed off his to die for dimples, and it was enough to make tears sting the backs of her eyes.

She shouldn't have come here.

Sydney quickly backed up and hurried toward her car.

Halfway there she heard him.

"Sydney, wait."

Of course she didn't, she couldn't handle talking to him right now, seeing him flirting with another woman, knowing that she hadn't been anything special to him and once he realized she wasn't going to put out on the first date, he had decided to cut his losses and move on was too much for her right now.

"Sydney," he called again, and she could hear him running after her. His legs were longer than hers, and he caught up to her before she got to her car, moving around her so he was in front of her, blocking her escape. "Are you okay?"

"Fine," she said, knowing he could see on her face that she was anything but.

His brows formed a V, and it was clear he didn't believe her. "I'm so sorry about having to break our date, I want to make it up to you. I have to stop by the hospital soon to see my new little niece, but we could do a late dinner, around nine?"

New little niece?

Meadow must have had her baby.

Was that why he'd broken their date last night?

Mortification hit her hard as she realized what a stupid mistake she had made.

What was wrong with her?

She had a great guy, sweet, sexy, thoughtful, he was genuinely interested in her, and she let her past cloud her vision, making her see things that weren't there.

That was the very thing she had promised herself she would never do.

"Sydney?" Levi took a step toward her, concern written all over his face, and he reached out for her.

Quickly she backed up, holding a hand up to ward him off. Tears were threatening to burst out, and she had already made enough of a fool of herself in front of him without blubbering like a baby.

Running around him, praying he wouldn't follow, she jumped into her car and sped off, needing desperately to be safe and sound and alone in her own home. As soon as she had parked her car in the garage and locked her front door behind her, she let her tears fall.

Dropping to the floor, she pulled her knees to her chest, wrapped her arms around her legs, and buried her head as she sobbed her heart out.

What was wrong with her?

Why couldn't she let it go?

She should have known better than to think a man like Levi would callously use her like that, and yet she had believed he had. She hadn't thought he'd had a good reason for breaking their date but obviously she had been wrong, his sister-in-law had been in labor bringing his first niece into the world.

She felt like an idiot for believing the worse. So many years spent learning that everything her father had taught her was wrong, and in one moment she had reverted into that old mode of thinking. She was so angry with herself and yet at the same time she had to remind herself that it was hard to change a lifetime of belief.

Exhausted and cried out, Sydney pushed herself to her feet. There was no point crying over spilled milk, best to shake off the embarrassment, learn her lesson, and not repeat the mistake again.

As she dragged heavy feet into her kitchen to scrounge up some dinner she heard her phone ring. As much as she wanted to ignore it, it could be a work call, so she pulled it out and saw Levi's name on the screen.

She ignored the call.

She had humiliated herself in front of him, and while she fully intended to own her mistake and apologize to him, she couldn't do that tonight.

The phone stopped ringing, and about thirty seconds later, it dinged announcing a voice message. She ignored that, and when the phone dinged a minute later with a text message she ignored that too. She got that Levi was worried because she'd been acting like an idiot, but she just really couldn't handle anything else tonight.

Tomorrow.

She'd deal with all of this tomorrow. She'd get up and put her metaphorical big girl panties on and go and explain things to him. Sydney was positive that she had ruined any chance of them becoming a couple, but she would still do the right thing and say she was sorry.

But tonight she would eat more ice cream and cry because as much as she wanted to believe she had moved on the events of the last twenty-four hours showed that she was still much more under the thumb of her father than she had realized.

Obviously, she hadn't made as much progress as she'd thought, and that hurt.

June 13th
5:48 A.M.

"On your knees."

"No, Daddy, no, please don't," Sydney begged.

"Never disobey an order from a man," her father yelled, backhanding her across the face so hard she fell to the floor.

Her father reached down and grabbed her by the hair, yanking her up onto her knees. One hand remained tangled in her hair as he unzipped his pants.

"You will learn, child. I won't raise a whore like your mother." His face was twisted with fury, the same way it always was when he talked about her mother. Her life had changed forever that day her mom had died.

"Daddy, please, I don't want to," she cried, tears streaming down her cheeks.

"What you want is irrelevant, you are a woman, it's your job to please

the man in your life." With that, he shoved his boxers down his legs and forced her head forwards until ...

Sydney woke with a start.

Her heart hammered, and when she touched a shaking hand to her forehead she found it coated in a sheen of sweat.

It had been a long time since she'd had nightmares about that time in her life and it didn't take a genius to figure out what had triggered them.

Levi.

She'd been such an idiot, and she hated that she had thought the worst of him. Realizing that she had made a lot less progress getting over what her father had done to her and her sister had been a huge blow, and now she felt stuck. Unsure where to go next. Did she need more therapy? She didn't want to have to go that route again but she would if she had to, she was committed to moving forward no matter how hard it was.

And it had been hard.

The hardest thing she had ever done in her life.

But if she wanted to have a life then she didn't have any choice.

Ignoring that sickening swirling in her stomach and the headache pounding at her temples, both of which had been a constant in those days when she had been her father's prisoner, so she was used to dealing with them. Shoving the covers away, suddenly claustrophobic by their presence, she climbed out of bed, and the instant light-headedness told her she would have to eat some breakfast.

Actual breakfast.

Not ice cream.

The thought of eating made her feel sick, but she had learned long ago that you did what had to be done, and that included eating regular meals, keeping hydrated, and getting to bed at a reasonable hour. She'd failed with two of the three the last two days, barely eating, and even though she had gone to bed at a reasonable hour last night she had tossed and turned for hours berating herself for being stupid.

She would have to rectify that.

Rushing through her shower, she stuck a couple of pieces of bread into the toaster and ate them with a little bit of peanut butter. She had to force them down, but she did it, and it actually helped the nausea to have something in her stomach.

Not wanting to hang around her house, she decided to head to work early. Sydney was torn between being glad that there had been no more victims of the serial killer and knowing they didn't have enough to get him yet, they needed another victim, and they needed him to make a mistake.

Just as she was heading out the front door, her phone rang. It was Abe. "Morning," she said as she answered. "And congratulations on becoming a daddy."

"Thanks. It was a rough ride, but Meadow was amazing, and Dawn is perfect, just perfect."

She could hear the pride in her boss' voice, and it made her smile. Abe would be a great dad, the kind of dad any kid would be lucky to have, and nothing like her own father. "I'm so happy for you, I bet you can't wait to get them home."

"I can't. I'll be in later today, but we got a couple of reports of what appears to be an abandoned car on River Road, just north of town. Can you go check it out?"

"Of course," she said, pleased to have something to do that would occupy her mind. She just had to get through today, and then tonight she would go and find Levi and apologize.

"Check-in when you're done," Abe said, and then he was gone.

Sydney had expected him to tell her to be careful, or something along those lines, and that he hadn't bolstered her confidence because it felt like he trusted her. Jumping in her car, she headed off toward River Road. When she'd taken the job here she had spent a few days studying her GPS, so she knew all the streets in and around the town, as well as where the more secluded farms were located.

As soon as she turned into the road she saw the car, it was stopped at the side of the road like the occupant had parked it there and then disappeared.

Immediately her gut said there was more to it than that.

Scanning the area to look for anything out of place, she parked behind the abandoned car. Why would someone just leave their car here? If it had broken down, surely they would have called for help or waited for someone to drive past. But if that was what had happened then the person who owned the car would still be here.

Maybe they had stopped to go for a walk through the forest and gotten lost?

That didn't seem particularly likely given that they were close to the town so there were a lot of properties around. Surely the person would have wandered close to one of them at some point.

Climbing out into the already warm morning, she noted the car's license plate and circled around it to make sure no one was inside. There wasn't, neither was there any visible reason why the car had stopped, the hood wasn't up, and there were no flat tires or signs of an accident.

She'd take a short walk around just in case the driver was around here sick or hurt, then she'd find out who the owner of the car was, what they were doing here, and see if that helped figure out what might be going on.

"Hello?" she called out as she walked a few steps into the forest. "I'm Deputy Clark, is anyone out here? If someone is here, call out." She paused and waited to see if there would be an answer.

There wasn't.

Not wanting to venture too far just in case there was something nefarious going on around here, Sydney walked about fifty yards into the woods, turned left and walked another fifty yards, then back to the middle and fifty yards in the other direction, pausing every so often to call out.

When she didn't find anyone she went back to her car. There was something out here that gave her an uneasy feeling, like whoever belonged to the car hadn't disappeared of their own free will.

Something was going on here.

Grabbing her phone, she ran the license plate and learned the car belonged to twenty-six-year-old Wednesday Adams. As soon as she got back to the station, she'd make some calls to see if she could find out why Wednesday was near River's End, hopefully that would give them the answers they needed.

Sydney was steps away from her vehicle when she saw another car coming down the road.

It took her only a second to realize it was coming too fast.

And heading straight for her.

Was the driver aiming for her?

Was it whoever had made Wednesday Adams disappear come back to try to make sure they covered their tracks?

As it got closer, she saw that the driver of the car was hunched over the wheel. Injured maybe? Heart attack? Stroke?

All of that flew through her mind in the few seconds it took her to fling herself out of the way.

Pain flashed through her body as she landed hard on the ground, but thankfully she got out of the car's path before it hit her, and a moment later she heard a crash as it plowed into a tree.

Ignoring her minor aches and pains, she ran toward the accident, already grabbing her phone to call for an ambulance. This was not how she had envisioned her day turning out, but it seemed like she might be seeing Levi sooner than she had thought.

~

7:20 A.M.

"Hey, buddy, how's that arm feeling?" Levi asked his young patient as he entered the small exam room in the emergency room where nine-year-old Ryder Thomas and his mother were waiting for him.

"It's okay." The kid shrugged nonchalantly like a broken arm was no big deal.

"You're going to have to wear the cast for at least four weeks," he warned the boy.

"No big deal."

"I hate to break this to you, Ryder, but the cast means no swimming."

His mouth fell open, his eyes widened, from the look on the boy's face, he may as well have just been told that school was going to be twenty-four hours a day, seven days a week, fifty-two weeks of the year and he'd never get to play again. "No swimming? Like at all?"

"Like at all," he confirmed.

"Not in the pool?"

"No pools."

"And the river?"

"No rivers either. Mom will have to put a bag over the cast when you take a bath or a shower," Levi informed the kid.

"Mom's going to have to help me take a bath?" Ryder curled his nose up at the thought.

"She's going to have to help you with a few things for the first few days at least. Then when your arm doesn't hurt so much anymore, and you get more used to the cast you'll be able to do more things on your own, and by the end of the month, you'll hardly remember you have it on."

"A month is a really long time," Ryder whined, the first sign of tears in his little face since he and his mom had arrived in the ER two hours ago.

"It is, buddy, but it'll go fast, I promise you that." Levi remembered how slow time seemed to move when he was a kid, whereas now it was like he blinked and another year flew by. "You know if you don't want to miss out on a month of swimming maybe next time don't let your brother dare you into seeing who can climb the highest in the tree."

"Amen to that," Ryder's mother said with a tired smile. "Getting woken up by screams at five in the morning is not how I like to start my day."

"RJ's littler than me, I couldn't let him get higher," Ryder immediately protested, a smug smile replacing the teary eyes. "And I beat him, I got all the way near the top, and he was only in the middle."

Levi laughed, he knew all about sibling rivalry, and as the middle boy he knew he was always stuck between wanting to emulate everything his big brother did while hating that his little brother was always shadowing him. "Come here, and I'll sign this thing for you." Pulling out a blue marker, he signed the cast.

"Oh, cool," Ryder gushed when he saw what he'd written.

"You can give him Tylenol every few hours if he needs it, keep him quiet and resting as much as possible for the next couple of days. He needs to come back in forty-eight hours to have another x-ray done just to make sure everything is healing well," he told Ryder's mother.

"Thank you so much for taking such good care of him," she said.

"Of course." He smiled back. "And you, no more falling out of trees," he said to Ryder, giving the boy's hair a tousle as he headed out of the room to check on his next patient.

The hospital was quiet at seven in the morning, he'd taken an extra shift to fill in for a colleague whose kid was sick, and the distraction was just what he needed. Levi was worried about Sydney. He'd waited for her at the diner again last night, and this time she'd shown up. Her timing couldn't have been worse. She'd come in just as Brianna Martin had been flirting with him, he'd already rebuffed the woman a dozen times, but she wouldn't take no for an answer. Of course Sydney would have to choose that moment to walk in, and the look on her face as she'd fled had almost gutted him.

Pain and betrayal had been evident on her face, and he hated that he was the cause.

Of course he'd gone after her. He'd wanted to explain about baby Dawn and why he'd had to break their date but as soon as he'd told her the betrayal had morphed into guilt and self-recrimination.

He'd tried to comfort her, but she'd warded him off and then fled.

Levi had been torn between wanting to give her the space she obviously needed and following her back to her place and forcing her to tell him what was going on. He'd never do that though, just like he wouldn't push her into anything she wasn't ready for. If she had second thoughts about them, he'd take a step back and wait until she was ready. He could be patient when he had to be, he just hated that she was hurting and he couldn't fix it.

Picking up another chart from the desk, he headed for the next room. Work would occupy him for the time being, and he'd give Sydney a couple of days then he'd track her down. While he was willing to be patient with her, what was growing between them felt too special to just let it go without a fight, and Sydney was worth the fight whether she knew it or not.

Inside the next room was seventy-four-year-old Matthew Hampton. The man had been brought in late last night after he'd become badly dehydrated and passed out. Despite his age, Matthew was fit and healthy and sharp as a tack. Mr. Hampton had been his high school chemistry teacher and the football coach, and it was hard seeing him like this, lying in a bed, unable to get about and not cracking jokes.

The cause of his dehydration hadn't been determined yet, but they were worried about his kidneys, and they were just waiting to transfer him up to a room. Levi moved quietly about the room, not wanting to wake the man when he was finally getting some rest. He checked his vitals, jotted some notes on his chart, then headed back out.

As soon as he stepped into the corridor one of the nurses came running over. "Levi, we have a car accident victim coming in. Male in his forties drove into a tree. A witness said it looked like the man was passed out before he hit the tree. She received some minor injuries when she had to jump out of the car's path."

Even though he was happy to be out of the high-stress world of being a doctor in a military hospital in the middle of a warzone, he couldn't deny that he sometimes missed the adrenalin rush. River's End and the other towns in the area were small, sleepy towns. Most of the time it was car accidents and minor injuries like Ryder's broken arm. In the winter they had broken bones from skiers, and in the summer there were water sport or heat related injuries, but nothing like what it had been when he was serving.

Adrenalin buzzing through his system, he began to give instructions to his team. They were a well-oiled machine, and by the time the ambulance pulled up to deliver their patient everyone was ready and waiting.

"This is Spencer Wu, forty-six years old, single-vehicle car accident. Unconscious on the scene, hasn't regained consciousness, obvious head injury, witness said that he was already passed out before the crash, so possible heart attack, stroke or seizure," the EMT said as they wheeled the gurney into the trauma room.

As he'd said the word 'witness', the medic had nodded his head at someone following along behind the EMTs and their patient, and Levi's eyes automatically followed.

His heart tried to jump out of his chest when he saw who was standing there.

Sydney.

She was dressed in her usual black pants and white blouse. Her pants were dusty and dirty, her blouse was torn, and he saw blood on her arms and a fresh bruise on her cheek.

Her eyes met his, and he saw her composure crack, emotions flashed across her face, most prominent was guilt, and she quickly broke eye contact.

His instincts were to go to her, sit her down, check her vitals, find out where she was hurt, and make it better.

But he couldn't do that.

His job was to treat the most seriously injured person first, and while he knew there was no getting around that, memories flooded his mind of the day Amy had died, he knew he didn't have a choice That day he had ignored his instincts and left the woman he loved to treat the others, only to find out later that unbeknownst to him she had been more seriously hurt than he'd realized.

That day he had lost her and a piece of his heart along with her.

That wasn't going to happen today though.

Sydney looked okay, she'd likely just split the stitches in her arm when she'd jumped out of the way of the car. Spencer Wu was unconscious, had possibly suffered a heart attack or something even before the accident.

Still, he had to ask. "Syd, you okay?"

"Fine, take care of him," she said, her brief gaze meeting his.

Praying she was telling him the truth because Amy had spoken those exact same words to him that fateful day, he went to work on his patient.

~

7:54 A.M.

"You didn't have to come and check on me," Sydney told Abe as he joined her outside the hospital. She'd come out here because she needed a little time on her own to calm down as adrenalin left her system making her shaky, and she hadn't wanted to let anyone know.

"Wanted to make sure you were doing okay," Abe replied, leaning against the side of the building beside her.

She didn't know what to say to that.

It was odd to have anyone worry about her, it had been so long since anyone cared about anything that happened to her. While she'd been standing out here, letting the balmy air warm her, the adrenalin crash leaving her chilled, she'd been contemplating how she had no one to call about what had happened. Her family consisted only of a sister who had been so deeply affected by what their father had done to them that she was married to a man who beat her daily, and no matter how hard Sydney had tried she couldn't convince her to leave. Both her parents and her stepmother were dead. She didn't have any extended family and no real friends.

She was on her own.

Really and truly on her own.

There was no one to call when something happened, no one to talk things through with, no one to hug her and give her a multitude of platitudes to make her feel better, no one she could just let go in front of and have a cleansing cry.

Just her.

"Syd, if you want to take some time off, that's okay. You've been through a lot in the last few days."

That was the last thing she wanted right now. She needed her job, it was the only place where she actually felt in control of her life. "I don't need to take time off. I'm fine, really I am, just needed a moment."

Abe was silent for a moment, and she knew he was examining her to decide whether or not she was telling the truth. "Before you go, come up to the maternity ward and meet baby Dawn," he said, pushing off the wall.

"I'd love to." She smiled, relieved to be off the hook.

Her boss was halfway back to the door when he paused and looked over his shoulder at her. "You have blood all over you. Make sure Levi takes a look at you before you leave. And, Sydney?"

"Yeah?"

"If you don't go in and let him tend to your injuries, I'll send him out here to find you." The way Abe said it made it sound like he was trying to play matchmaker as much as he wanted to make sure that her injuries were looked at.

Not waiting for her to reply, he headed inside, leaving her staring after him. Nervous butterflies fluttered in her stomach, she knew she had to talk to Levi, apologize to him, and it was certainly better to get it over and done with rather than obsessing over it, but that didn't mean she was looking forward to it.

The way he had looked at her in the ER had almost had her knees buckling. How was it possible for one look to affect her so deeply? His gaze was like a warm caress, it was tender, and it soothed her, made her want to forget about everything but the two of them.

But she couldn't do that.

Obviously, given her reaction to Levi canceling their date, she was in no position to be in a relationship right now, she still had a lot of growing to do, and it wouldn't be fair to Levi to ask him to wait until she could be a good partner especially since that might never happen.

Rubbing her temples where a headache was trying to make itself known, Sydney decided there was no time like the present. She may as well head inside and get the whole uncomfortable conversation with Levi over and done with.

Resolutely, she headed through the ER's doors, and like they were programmed to do so, her eyes immediately found Levi. He was at the desk, a pretty young nurse was batting her eyelashes at him and leaning in toward him so she was all but plastered across him.

Jealousy immediately flooded through her just like it had last night at the dinner.

Following the jealousy came a slice of pain.

Which annoyed her.

She and Levi had eaten together at the diner a few times and had dinner once at his house, they weren't a couple, and he was free to date or flirt with anyone he wanted to.

Before she even registered what she was doing, her feet had spun around and were walking her back outside.

No, she commanded herself. *Go back there and face him, you're no coward.*

Levi had told her that she was special, he had told her that he wanted to reschedule their date, he hadn't given up on her so she couldn't just go prancing off like some overly dramatic teenager.

Summing reserves of strength that were quickly dwindling away, she straightened her spine and spun around again, heading straight over to the desk.

Levi noticed her before she was even halfway there and immediately headed toward her. "Syd, I wondered where you were, come on, let's go take a look at you."

Cupping a hand under her elbow, he led her over to the same exam room he'd taken her to, to check on her arm after they'd interviewed Trina the other day.

The room he had kissed her in.

The feel of his hand on her skin was enough to have it sparking like he was a match and she was a candle. It made her want so much more, but she was no longer comfortable with her own judgment or the place her head was in.

Inside the exam room, he guided her over to the bed and helped her onto it. His fingertips brushed lightly across her cheek where it had hit the ground when she'd dived out of the way of the car.

Like it did every time he touched her, heat flooded her body then pooled in her stomach. Their gazes met, and awareness flashed through his eyes. He knew how he was affecting her and by the looks of things he was affected the same way.

"I don't think you broke a bone, but you'll have another bruise to go with the one on your forehead," Levi said, his voice husky, his fingers trailing lazily down her cheek and along her jaw before whispering across her bottom lip.

When he removed his hand she felt the loss deeply, but then he took her arm and very gently peeled her ripped blouse away from the now mangled bandage, then began to unwind it. Sydney couldn't help but wince as it ripped away from the dried blood.

"Sorry." Levi stopped, his gaze on her face.

When he looked at her, she seemed to lose the ability to think. He was such a great guy, sexy, good-looking, smart, and funny. He obviously could have any woman he wanted, so why was he interested in her?

"I hate that you think that," he said.

"Think what?"

"That you're not good enough. It's written all over your face."

Her eyes dropped to the floor, embarrassed. He'd been through a lot, lost a lot, and yet he seemed to have it together. So why couldn't she get it together?

Hooking his thumb under her chin, he nudged her face back up so she looked at him again. "Sydney, you're a beautiful woman, you're smart and sweet, any guy would think you are a great catch."

"I'm sorry," she blurted out before he could make her feel worse by uttering more compliments. "About getting so upset that you canceled our date and for running away from you last night."

"You don't need to apologize to me," Levi told her. "I'm not angry with you about either of those things, I'm just concerned about you. I can see that you're hurting and I want to help you."

He sounded so sincere, and he was being so nice to her, especially after she'd thought the worst of him not once but twice and it only made her more agitated. "I know that I owe you an explanation and I'll give you one." As much as she didn't want to go into the details of her past, she owed Levi that much at least.

"No." Levi shook his head firmly, his grip on her chin tightened. "You don't owe me anything. If you don't want to tell me what's bothering you, that's okay. I hope you will open up to me, I hope you know you're safe with me and can tell me anything, I think you're special, and I want to help you, but what happens next is up to you."

She was so nervous.

She had wanted this for so long, a normal life, putting her demons behind her, moving on, it all sounded so simple in her head, but it was so much harder to actually accomplish.

"I want to give you an explanation," she said firmly, meeting his gaze squarely without blinking to add emphasis to her words.

The smile he gave her almost had her melting into a puddle. "I'm glad to hear that. Can I have dinner with you tonight? Maybe cook something and bring it around to your place?"

Peace settled over her. Maybe she still had a shot with Levi after all. Maybe he'd understand about her past and be willing to be patient with her while she continued to work on herself. Levi was everything she had ever dreamed about and that he seemed to be really and truly interested in her was as exhilarating as it was confusing.

Buoyed by his insistence to fight for her and the confidence it gave her, she reached out with her good arm and wrapped it around his neck, drawing him in and kissing him.

Without breaking the kiss he sat beside her and slid her onto his lap, his arm wrapped around her waist while his other hand cupped her cheek. The kiss became hungry, and she wanted so much more, physically as well as emotionally. She wanted to trust in him and build a life with him, she wanted the two of them naked and in bed together. She wanted to see what it would feel like when he was inside her when just his lips on hers was enough to make her combust.

"Is that a yes?" Levi asked against her lips.

"Oh yeah, I'd love to have dinner with you tonight, and then we can talk." She'd be nervous about it all day, but it was better to just get this conversation over with and let the chips fall where they fell.

~

11:13 A.M.

His head was pounding.

It was like there was a colicky baby in there, screaming its poor little lungs out, the sound reverberated around his brain, growing exponentially until it felt like his very own body was trying to kill him.

Why wouldn't it stop?

What he wouldn't give for just five minutes of silence, of peace, of not feeling like he was being ripped apart from the inside out.

But that didn't seem to be in the cards for him.

He had done everything that they'd asked of him, but it wasn't enough. It was never enough. He just wanted this to be over, he wanted his life back, he wanted to be free.

If he wanted that then his only choice was to keep forging forward.

To that end, he dragged in a mouthful of muggy air, stretched, then with feet that felt like they had been encased in concrete, he headed back inside the house where the others were waiting for him.

The woman he'd tricked into pulling her car over was sitting tied to a chair in the middle of the room. Her bare feet were sitting in the metal bucket, and just the sight of it was enough to have his stomach turning as it remembered the smell of burning flesh. The woman had told him that her name was Wednesday Adams and he assumed her parents had thought that would be an amusing and quirky thing to do. He wondered briefly if she had felt the same way. Right now, her head hung limply, chin against her chest, she was quiet, and for that he was blissfully grateful.

The room's other occupants looked over at him when he walked in, and the looks on their faces filled him with dread.

It was time.

"Can't we wait a little longer?" he asked. He was no psychopath, he didn't enjoy inflicting pain on others, he didn't want to torture Wednesday just like he hadn't wanted to torture any of the other women, and he hated that he had been backed into a corner and not given a choice. Not that he had really been *backed* into a corner, more like violently shoved into the corner then forced to stay there and do as he was told or face the consequences.

"This needs to be done now, you know it does," the man who was in charge told him, the other man—his bodyguard—stood watchfully at his side. He knew that he would never succeed if he tried to take his boss out, the bodyguard would shoot him before he got close enough to do anything.

Unless ...

What if he threw the boiling water at the bodyguard instead of pouring it into the metal bucket?

If he aimed for the man's face surely he would be incapacitated enough by excruciating pain to be able to fire off a shot. If he was really lucky, the bodyguard would drop his weapon, and he could get to it before his boss, and then for once he would be the one in charge.

"Who are you talking to? There's no one there."

He turned at the voice to see Wednesday had opened her eyes and lifted her head and was watching with a mixture of concern and apprehension.

His brow furrowed. What did she mean? Had he hit her harder on the head than he'd realized? There was quite obviously two other men here besides him. One was sitting in a chair, his legs crossed, his hands folded neatly in his lap, a calm, almost bored expression on his face. The other was standing beside the chair, black sunglasses covering his eyes, his arms crossed over his chest, his gun prominently displayed in a halter at his hip.

"What do you mean?" he asked Wednesday, casting a look at his boss to find the man staring silently back at him. "This is my boss, he's sitting right there, wearing a black Armani suit, and his bodyguard is right beside him."

"There's no one there," Wednesday insisted, a hint of panic in her voice. "Do you really think there's someone there?"

"Come on, I don't have all day." His boss lifted a finger and tapped it to the face of his Rolex.

"Don't you hear him?" He looked to Wednesday then back to his boss.

"I don't hear anyone, and I don't see anyone. I think you're hallucinating."

That was ridiculous.

In fact he would *rather* be hallucinating than stuck in this vicious circle of trying to find answers to questions that he was beginning to think didn't have any answers.

But this wasn't a hallucination.

It was all too horrifyingly real.

"Start the interrogation," his boss ordered.

With a heavy heart, he stepped closer to the chair. "I'm sorry," he whispered quietly, not wanting his boss or the bodyguard to overhear because if they did, he was likely going to find himself tied to a chair about to be tortured. "I must have hit you too hard, I didn't mean to, I didn't want to." He hoped she believed that. He didn't mean her any harm, he was just doing what he had to do to stay alive. Self-preservation was a master that wasn't easy to conquer, and he had well and truly submitted to it.

"If you don't want to hurt me, then don't," Wednesday implored. "I promise you that there's no one here, I think you might be sick, maybe you have a brain tumor or a mental illness, I'm not sure, but there's something wrong with you. If you let me go I'll take you to the hospital. The doctors there will be able to help you get better. Please."

If only life was that simple.

"If you answer the questions truthfully I won't have to hurt you," he told her, silently begging her to do just that. "Just tell me what you know."

"What I know? About what?"

"About *it*," he replied.

"I don't know what *it* is," Wednesday said on a sob. Tears trailed down her dirty cheeks, and on her exposed skin he could see the dark black and blue bruises from where he'd thrown the rocks at her to prevent her from fleeing. He hated looking at those marks, hated even more knowing that he was the one who had caused them.

"You do, you have to, he said you're the one, I've been wrong before, and I don't want to be wrong again. You were there, you know what's going to happen, I know it's you, you have the sign, the same as the others but it's brighter."

"Brighter? What does that mean? I don't know what you mean," she wailed.

She was lying.

She had the halo, the same one that all the others had, only hers was ten times brighter.

That meant she was the one.

The one who would destroy them all.

"If you just tell us when it's going to happen then I can convince them to go easy on you, but you have to speak up. No one is coming to save you, and if you don't tell me what they want to know then they're going to make me torture you, I don't want to do that, so please, please, just tell us what you know."

"I don't know anything. I was just taking a cross-country drive on my way to see my boyfriend, that's it. I don't know anything because there's nothing to know. Whatever you think is happening here it's not." Desperation was pouring off her, and for a second a flicker of doubt lit inside him.

Was she right?

Was he sick?

No.

He didn't think that could be true.

He was perfectly healthy, and there was nothing wrong with him beyond the fact he had accidentally gotten himself caught up in this mess by being careless. He'd hit Wednesday Adams over the head in order to get her here, he'd obviously caused her some serious damage, and now she was the one hallucinating.

"I have other things to attend to today. She's not going to give it up, get the water," his boss ordered.

Knowing better than to disobey a direct order, he turned and walked through to the kitchen to prepare the water.

"No," Wednesday screeched. "No, please, don't do this. You don't have to, you really don't, I promise you this isn't really happening. No one is making you do this, it's all in your head, please believe that. Please."

Blocking out her terrified pleas, he waited for the water to boil then carried the kettle back in with him. Casting a glance over at the armchair where his boss was reclining.

The man nodded.

This was it.

Make it or break it time.

Was he man enough to try to take out the bodyguard and his boss to spare this woman?

One glance at the man in the armchair and he knew he couldn't do it.

The eyes that looked back at him were as black as night and as cold as a block of ice.

Doing anything but what he'd been told was suicide.

With a heavy heart, he walked up to Wednesday Adams.

Steam billowed from the top of the kettle and Wednesday fixated on it. Her whole body trembled, hard enough to shake the chair, and she whipped her head from side to side as she wept. "No, no, no, no, no, please, please, please, please, please, no, no, no, no, no. Don't do this.

Please, don't do this."

"You didn't leave me any choice," he said quietly, more to himself than to the woman.

Wednesday's feet strained against the ropes restraining her ankles as she continued to babble hysterically.

With an agonized growl, he poured the water.

Inhuman shrieks filled the air.

He was going to Hell for this.

~

2:34 P.M.

Nervous anticipation coursed through her body.

Sydney was both looking forward to and dreading her date with Levi tonight. It would be one thing if they were doing something fun, but they weren't, she needed to tell him about her past. While she knew she had nothing to be ashamed of, she'd been a child, not able to do anything to change her circumstances, that didn't mean that it was easy to talk about.

But it was the right thing to do, and she knew it had to be done.

She didn't back down from things no matter how hard they were, and if she and Levi were going to have anything meaningful—assuming she hadn't already turned him off with her multiple freak-outs—then he had to know the truth. She couldn't expect him to understand where she was coming from and that she was sensitive about certain things, if he didn't know about her past.

Glancing up from the file she was supposed to be reading when Fletcher put his phone down, she asked, "What did you find out?"

"Parents told me the same thing the boyfriend told you," Fletcher replied. "Wednesday loved being outdoors, and she loved small towns. They think it's possible she might have pulled over to the side of the road with the intention of getting out and going for a walk."

Wednesday Adams was the owner of the car that had been left at the side of the road. After leaving the hospital this morning with her arm freshly stitched and bandaged, she'd run the license plate, identified the owner, then began looking into the woman. From what they had learned, Wednesday had been traveling across country to spend the summer with her boyfriend. According to the boyfriend, he'd wanted Wednesday to fly over, but she'd liked the idea of enjoying some alone time and visiting as many small towns as she could.

"What did the parents have to say about the boyfriend?" she asked. "Do they like him? Do they think he might have something to do with her disappearance?"

"Parents love him, said he treats their daughter like a queen, he encourages her in her business, he showers her with love and attention, and he had already asked them for their daughter's hand in marriage because he wanted them to be okay with her moving to the other side of the country."

"Yeah, I got the same story from him. I guess so long as his alibi checks out then we can cross him off as a suspect."

"We still don't know that anything nefarious went down," Fletcher reminded her. "Which is why I've asked Mia to get her team together."

"Mia runs the search and rescue team, right?" She was new to town and still trying to get everyone straight in her head.

"Right. If both the boyfriend and the parents think it's a possibility that she got out of her car and walked off on her own, then it's possible she got lost and managed to wander past all the farms in the area and is lost somewhere on the mountain. Or it's possible she fell and was injured and unable to get help. If she's out there, Mia and her team will find her."

"Unless Wednesday fell into the river," Sydney added. "If she fell, hit her head, and was taken downstream it might be days before her body washes up somewhere."

"True," Fletcher agreed, "but sooner or later she will turn up."

"Wednesday's a young woman, around the same age as Naomi, Elena, Martha, and Trina. What if she's the serial killer's next victim?"

Fletcher was quiet for a moment, considering the possibility. When his blue eyes met hers, she knew the idea had crossed his mind as well. "No way to prove she is without a body, but no way to prove she isn't. I got a call from Alan's ex-wife, she said that when he came up to visit their kids last he was acting peculiar. She said he spoke about being followed, and warned her that she and the children could be in danger. When she pressed him on why he thought that he was vague but seemed to be serious about the idea that something was going on."

"You think whatever he's paranoid about might have something to do with the murders?"

"We speculated that the killer was burning them as a method of torture to try to get them to give up some information. Given that the killer has gone after residents of River's End and at least one, possibly two, women just visiting or passing through, then it's a possibility that whatever he thinks they know is all in his head."

"Makes sense," Sydney agreed. "If he thought they had seen something or heard something that might get him in trouble you'd expect he'd focus only on residents. Martha had only been here a couple of days so it's unlikely she had time to get involved in any of the killer's business. And if Wednesday is also a victim, then all she did was drive through town."

"We should start speaking with everyone who's had any contact with Alan the last few weeks. The man keeps to himself, but his shop is always busy, and he buys groceries, has bad asthma so he picks up medication at the pharmacy, he goes to enough places that people will have seen him, spoken to him, maybe we can find someone who can corroborate this paranoia, and maybe have some information on what started it."

"We also know that Dale Jacoway was in contact with every single one of the victims, and that he asked at least three of them out on dates, it's possible he asked Martha out too, so we should keep looking into him, especially with what I found out today."

"What did you find?" Fletcher asked.

"You know how we were wondering if Dale was involved in something to do with drugs? Well, the owner of the trucking company Dale works for was just arrested for drug trafficking. If his boss was trafficking then there's a good chance that Dale is somehow mixed up in it."

"Any evidence to suggest he is?"

"Nothing concrete yet, but the arrest was only just made early this morning, they're still going through everything, trying to figure out how many employees might be involved. I asked that they let us know if anything turns up implicating Dale. To go along with the idea that perhaps whatever the killer thinks the victims saw or heard is only a figment of his delusions, several drugs can induce paranoia. If he's trafficking he might also be using. Could even be sneaking it out from under his boss' nose, maybe he was high when he asked out the victims, maybe he thought they realized it and might tell someone, word would get back to his boss, so he tries to find out what they know then takes them out."

"Both of those scenarios are possibilities," Fletcher agreed. "So we're no closer to figuring out which of our suspects is more likely to be the killer, and to be honest, we don't even have enough to prove that it's one of them and not someone else entirely."

"So we have to keep all avenues open. I wish he would make a mistake, slip up, but so far even when things don't go to plan like what happened with Trina Liberty, he was still able to adapt and get away."

"He'll slip up sooner or later, they always do," Fletcher assured her. "I'm going to go check in with Mia on the search so that Julian doesn't have to." He paused when he realized what he'd said like that wasn't supposed to slip out. "Julian and Mia have a rocky history. They were together, some bad stuff went down a couple of years back, and it broke them up. Things between them since have been majorly awkward and whenever we work with search and rescue, Abe, Will, and I try to run point."

"Okay," she said, curious and wanting details, but knowing it was none of her business, she kept her mouth shut. "I'll start making my way around town, see what people have to say about Alan, and if anyone else is aware of his recent paranoia."

"Check in with you later," Fletcher said as he headed out.

Sydney couldn't help but smile as she watched him go. She was already feeling a part of this department, the guys had been great, they all treated her respectfully like she was one of them and a valuable member of the team, and it was the first time she had ever really felt like she was part of something. She'd loved her old job, but she'd just been one of dozens of cops, this was different, they were a small team which meant she was working more closely with others, and that made her feel like they were a little family.

If she and Levi ended up together, then some of them really would be her family, Abe would be her brother-in-law, and Julian and Will would be her cousins-in-law if that was a thing.

Just like that the nervous anticipation about tonight was back.

After tonight, would Levi still see her the same way? Would he still want to date her? Would he still think she was special?

Or would he think she was too big a mess to take on and walk away?

~

6:47 P.M.

They'd arranged for him to be at her place at seven, but Levi couldn't wait any longer. It was only fifteen minutes to go, and the desire to see her was so overwhelming that his body was almost aching with need.

Grabbing the box where he'd packed their dinner, he got out of his car, locked it behind him, and walked down the garden path. The little cottage Sydney was renting was adorable. It had a wide porch with a swing, a pretty little garden full of a bright array of flowers, and a stone fireplace that would be wonderful to curl up in front of in the wintertime. The house used to be owned by a lovely elderly couple. When he was about twelve, he'd done the garden for them to earn a little extra money, and when he was done they'd always bring him inside for a piece of freshly baked homemade pie.

Sydney's car was in the driveway, and there was a light on inside, when he knocked on the front door, it was opened almost immediately. She stood there, gone were the black pants and white blouse, in their place was a pair of bright green yoga pants and a pink t-shirt that perfectly highlighted her breasts.

"Hi." She smiled nervously, picking at an imaginary thread at the hem of her t-shirt. "I thought since we were just eating here there was no need to get dressed up."

She said it like she thought she might have made a mistake and he couldn't help but frown. "Syd, you can wear whatever you want whenever you want. I think you'd look beautiful in a sack, and right now it's pretty much all I can do not to just stare at you and drool."

That drew a tentative chuckle out of her, and she opened the door wider to let him in. She must have rented the cottage with the furniture in it because it was the same as he remembered from when the Elderways owned the place.

"You renting this from Matilda Elderway?" he asked. Matilda was the couple's only child and was one of those people who had hated small-town life and fled to the city as soon as she could, never to return.

"Yep. I didn't own much, and nothing I loved enough to bring with me, so I thought this would make things easier until I had time to go house hunting, buy my own place, then I can furnish it with all new things," Sydney said as she led him over to the kitchen.

Since he had promised himself he wouldn't do anything to pressure her, Levi didn't mention that he hoped once they were serious she'd move in with him, he kept his mouth shut and followed her. "Since it's so warm today and I didn't get back from the hospital until late I just made us a pasta salad."

"Yum." Sydney bent over to pull dishes out of a cupboard giving him a mouthwatering view of her backside, and he had to quickly think of something unsexy so that he wasn't sporting blatant evidence of just how beautiful he thought she was when she turned back around. He had to tread lightly here because as much as he knew Sydney was trying to put her issues behind her, they obviously still had the ability to impact her.

"I also brought a bottle of sparkling water, and my mom is already getting excited about having grandchildren to bake with as soon as Dawn is old enough. She misses the days when she had four little kids to do things with, so she brought me a plate of brownies."

That got a real smile out of Sydney as she set two bowls on the counter. "I met Dawn at the hospital this morning, she's adorable."

"Yeah, she is." He smiled fondly as he pictured his tiny niece's tiny fingers and toes and soft, blonde fuzzy hair and big blue eyes. She would grow up to be the spitting image of her mother, and he hoped she had also inherited her mother's strength and ability to make the best of even the very worst of situations and still look for the good in life.

"How was the man from this morning, Spencer Wu?" Sydney asked as she dished the pasta salad into bowls.

"I'm sorry, Syd, it's not looking good."

"Oh." Her face fell, and he wished he could throw her a bone, but the facts were it was looking likely the man wasn't going to make it.

"Looks like he might have just fallen asleep at the wheel. We contacted his wife, and she told us he'd been held up at work and was in a hurry to get home because one of their kids was scheduled for surgery. He must have been driving all night to make it."

"That's so sad." The look on Sydney's face and the pain in her eyes said that she was upset about more than just witnessing an accident this morning and caring about the victim.

Once they were both sitting at the table and had started eating their meals he decided that now was as good a time as any to start talking. "You told me that your parents were both dead, but you never told me how they died."

Sydney faltered, her fork hovering in the air midway between her bowl and her mouth. He knew she wanted to talk, she was the one that had said she wanted to explain to him why him breaking their date had upset her, but he was sure that didn't make it easy. "My mom," she said softly.

"Your mom died in a car accident, didn't she?" he asked, putting two and two together.

"Mmhmm," she agreed with a nod. "I was eleven when she died, my sister was fourteen."

"That must have been rough to lose your mom at such a young age." He couldn't imagine what it would have been like growing up without his mother. After he came home from the military his father had been quiet, restrained, he'd take them camping and fishing, but he was reserved, and he didn't quite know how to connect with his kids. Mom had been the one to bring light and happiness and fun to their home, none of them had ever doubted how lucky they were to have her, and he couldn't imagine what would have happened to them if they'd lost her.

He had a feeling that whatever had happened to Sydney's family after her mother's death was worse than what he was imagining.

And he imagined some pretty dark stuff.

"It was hard," she acknowledged, suddenly very interested in the tomato on her fork.

The longer they put this off, the harder it would be. Sydney wanted to talk, and he was right here, ready to listen and do anything within his power to help her.

"Come here," he said, setting his own fork down and then reaching over to gently tug hers from her grip and pull her to her feet. He led her over to the sitting area and eased her onto the sofa, sitting beside her, her hand still in his. "Sydney, I know you said you want to give me an explanation, and you can one hundred percent trust me and feel safe to open up to me, but if you changed your mind, that's okay."

"I didn't change my mind," she said, chancing a quick look at him. "This is just hard."

"I know it is, sweetheart." He brushed his thumb across her knuckles as he tried to figure out how he could make this easier for her. "Tell me what you need me to do."

She gave him a sad smile, and he wondered what she was thinking, but before he could ask she started to talk. "I just need you to listen."

"That I can do," he assured her.

"My mom was cheating on my dad. The guy was someone she worked with, and she'd been having an affair for almost a year. I think she was planning on leaving my dad. I hope that she was going to take us with her."

The last was said with all the vulnerability of a child, and it sliced through him. He wanted to gather her into his arms and rock her and promise her that of course her mom wouldn't abandon her, but he wasn't sure it would do any good. He had never met her mom, for all he knew she *had* been going to abandon her kids. "I'm sure your mom loved you."

The shrug she gave said she wasn't altogether sure that was true. "My mom said she had to work late one night, it was a Friday, my sister and I were watching movies. It was late when they came to the door.

Two officers, they sat us down, told us that mom had been in a car accident and that she had been dead before help could arrive."

"I'm so sorry, baby." He squeezed her hands, trying to offer what comfort he could.

"She wasn't alone. She hadn't been working late she was at a motel with her lover. They were both in the car, he died too." She paused, and when she met his gaze her eyes were large and full of emotion. "It wasn't an accident, Levi. Someone messed with the brakes. I think it was my dad. I think he knew that she was cheating on him and he followed her to the motel. I think he killed her."

"Why do you think that?"

Sydney dragged in a long breath before answering. "Because he was a monster."

~

7:09 P.M.

Her father was a monster.

A *monster*.

It was as simple as that.

He was evil, and she was glad that he was dead.

Reaching over, Levi slipped an arm under her knees, his other behind her back, and lifted her over so she was snuggled on his lap. She wasn't sure if he realized but being able to have this conversation without having to look at his face made this so much easier for her.

"What did he do to you, baby?" Levi asked, one hand holding her securely against him while the other stroked her hair.

The endearment almost undid her and had her dissolving into a fit of tears. Sydney couldn't even remember the last time someone had used one with her, when someone had cared enough to. Even before her mother's death, neither of her parents had been the warm, cuddly, involved type. Her father had been remote, distant, spent most of his time at work. Her mom had a part-time job as a receptionist at a local law firm, neither had had a lot of time for their children.

"Sweetheart?" Levi prodded, his fingers brushing lightly across her temple.

"He did to me exactly what you think he did," she whispered into his chest.

Levi's arms tightened reflexively around her, holding her so tightly it was almost painful, not that she would ever ask him to loosen his hold. If she had to tell this story then this was where she wanted to be.

"I'm sorry, Sydney." Levi's lips pressed against the top of her head.

"I think he knew for a while that Mom was cheating on him, he was always so angry at her, blamed her for her death, said she got what she deserved."

"That's why you think he may have been involved?"

"Yes. After she died he became obsessed with me and Adelaide, my older sister. He took us out of school, homeschooled us himself, he never let us go anywhere, and when we did go out he always made sure we never left his sight." For a child who had mostly been left to her own devices the sudden stifling behavior from her father had been hard to take, and she had rebelled against it.

"You told me your father was dead. How did he die?"

That was a long story.

A long *unpleasant* story.

"After Mom's death, he started telling Addie and me that Mom died because she wasn't a good enough wife. He said he was our father and it was his job to teach us how to be wood wives, what we needed to do to please our husbands. He made us cook and clean and wait on him hand and foot, and he ... uh ... he taught us how to please a man in the bedroom."

A low growl rumbled through Levi's chest, and she stiffened.

She knew how that sounded. She hated that she'd been eleven years old and known how to give hand jobs and blow jobs. She hated that her father had stolen her virginity from her before she even really knew what it was.

But it was what it was, she couldn't change it, and she didn't want him to pity her.

Before he could say anything, she continued. "He remarried within a year of the car accident. He had been a teacher at the local high school, and he'd gotten involved with one of his students, she was only nineteen when he married her. He treated her more like a slave than a wife, he would punish her if she didn't do something the way he thought she should have, and he was always yelling at her that her job was to serve him. None of us were allowed to leave the house, he'd use us against one another, hurting one of us to punish another. He would make us go without food or without sleep as punishment for the smallest of infractions, and sometimes he'd hit us with his belt. He would always say he was doing it for our own good, so we would learn, so we wouldn't end up like Mom had. One day my stepmom managed to sneak us out a window, told us to go and get help, that she'd distract Dad so he wouldn't know we were gone. We went to a neighbor's, told them what was happening, by the time the cops got to our house he'd killed her."

"What was her name?"

"Priscilla, her name was Priscilla. She was like a big sister to Addie and me. She gave her life so we could live." Not a day had gone by that she hadn't spent at least a moment paying a silent tribute to the woman who had died so she could live.

"How did your father die?"

"The cops found him trying to clean up the blood, Priscilla's body was wrapped in a rug in his car, he committed suicide by cop."

"What happened to Addie?"

"I was fourteen by the time our father died, Addie was seventeen, we went into foster care, returned to school. I was quiet, shy, afraid of boys, part of me knew that what my father had taught me wasn't true, but too many years trapped in that house had made some of it sink in."

"You were just a kid," Levi reminded her, his hand resuming its gentle, rhythmic strokes along her hair.

"Addie didn't bounce back as well as I did. Just after she graduated she got involved with this man, he was controlling and abusive, but she'd been brainwashed into believing that was what men did to women. I tried to help her, I got her away from him a couple of times, but she always went back. As much as I want to help her, I had to accept that she had chosen the course of her life and that if I didn't put a little distance between us, her choices would end up consuming me. That was why I decided to move here, to start over with a fresh slate." Tears leaked out of her eyes as she thought of the mess she had left her sister in, knowing she couldn't force Addie to change didn't mean accepting it was easy.

"Aww, sweetheart." Levi's lips touched her forehead, then he tilted her face up, kissing her cheeks, catching her tears on the tip of his tongue, then his mouth hovered above hers as though unsure whether or not she wanted him to kiss her. "What do you need from me, baby?"

"I need you not to treat me any differently than you would any other woman. I don't want your pity, I went through a lot of therapy and worked hard to get where I am, I know I'm a victim, but I'm not a *victim*. I'm just me. Sometimes I'm going to be insecure because I haven't dated before, and sometimes my father's voice will get into my head, and he'll try to tell me that you're like him and that I have to do what he taught me to do." Dragging in a deep breath, she said what she needed to say, "If you can't deal with that I understand."

Levi growled again and then his mouth crushed down on hers, devouring her, kissing her hungrily like he could never get enough. Sydney lifted her hands, her fingers curling into his hair as she pulled him closer.

This was what she needed.

She wanted Levi to see her as the strong woman she had fought to become, not as some helpless damsel in distress who needed saving.

"You are different than any other woman," Levi told her as he tore his mouth away from hers. "You are the strongest woman I've ever met and I think you're amazing."

That was the nicest thing he could have said to her.

Moving around so she was straddling his legs, Sydney put her hands on Levi's shoulders and kissed him again. He settled one hand on her hip while his other dipped up under the hem of her t-shirt, his fingertips brushing softly across the bare skin on her stomach making her whole body vibrate with need.

Was she ready for this?

Her body wanted more, but her mind wasn't sure that the time was right, she had only known Levi for a few days, and even though what she felt for him was strong, and she believed he truly had feelings for her too, she thought maybe they should wait.

"We can stop here if you want," Levi said, obviously noticing the sudden tension in her body.

"I want you to stay tonight but ..."

"You're not ready for more, that's okay," he assured her. "We can just hang out, watch a movie, and sleep in each other's arms, or if you're not ready for sex, but you want to make out a little there are other things we can do."

Right.

Of course, she knew that.

Automatically her hands reached for the waistband of his shorts, intending to give him what he needed.

"Whoa." Levi grabbed her hands, pinning them against his stomach with one of his much larger hands. "That's not what I meant, sweetheart. I meant if you trust me I can do something for you."

"Trust you? I trust you," she said, nodding for emphasis. And it was mostly true. She *did* trust him, she was sure he would never do anything to hurt her, but she was so woefully inexperienced, and she knew he was not, which made her feel out of her depth.

"You can tell me to stop at any time, and I will," he told her as he stood with her in his arms and carried her upstairs to her bedroom.

"What are you going to do?" she asked breathily.

"Make you feel something I'm betting you never have before," he replied with a wink as he laid her down on her bed. "I mean it, Syd, you feel uncomfortable, or you change your mind, and I will stop immediately, okay?"

She nodded, not sure her voice would work at the moment.

Levi hooked his fingers in the waistband of her yoga pants, and when she lifted her bottom off the mattress he slowly pulled them, and her panties, down her legs, leaving her half-naked.

Her initial response was to cover herself quickly, but the appreciative look on Levi's face stopped her.

He met her gaze, and when she nodded he took hold of both of her knees and spread her legs wide open before settling between them.

Was he going to put his mouth on her?

Nervousness and anticipation warred within her.

Levi trailed a line of feather-light kisses up the inside of her left thigh, then paused and touched his lips to the part of her that was aching for him. At her gasp, he looked up at her again, "If you liked that you're going to love this." He repeated a trail of feather-light kisses up her right thigh, then the kiss he pressed to her center was firmer this time.

Like he couldn't wait a second longer, his mouth was on her, licking, suckling, teasing her until she thought she would burst. He slid a finger inside her, and then another, and then his mouth was back on her, and he was winding her so tight that she was sure when she finally came undone, she would shatter into a million pieces.

The pressure inside her grew, stealing her ability to think of anything but what Levi was doing to her, and then she was exploding into another world as wave after wave of pleasure buffeted over her.

By the time she was finally able to think again, her entire body felt limp and spent. Levi was watching her, a smug expression on his face.

"Feeling pretty pleased with yourself, huh?" she asked.

"A little." He grinned.

"You do know I have nothing to compare that to so even if you did a bad job I wouldn't know," she teased.

"Hey." He good-naturedly swatted her hip, drawing her attention to the tent in his shorts.

He'd made her come in a way she hadn't even quite believed was possible, now it was her turn to return the favor.

Sydney reached for him, taking him in her hands, only to have him quickly grab hold of her hands and remove them from his length.

Had she done something wrong?

She was experienced in pleasing a man. Didn't he want her to make him feel the way he'd just made her feel?

Did he change his mind and decide he wanted sex?

She hadn't thought he would force her, but what did she know about men?

"Relax, Syd." He smiled, and the look on his face and in his eyes said he wasn't going to force her to do anything she didn't want to so she relaxed a little.

"Don't you want me to return the favor?" she asked. "I know what

I'm doing, I might not be experienced at relationships, but I know how to pleasure a man."

Anger flashed across his face, and she shrunk away from him.

"I'm sorry," she murmured, eyes downcast.

"Syd, look at me." He waited until she somewhat fearfully lifted her gaze to find him looking at her tenderly. "That's not how things are between two people who care about each other. Just because I made you come doesn't mean you owe me anything. I'm showing you how it's supposed to be. I put my mouth on you because I wanted to, because I wanted to make you feel good, not because I expected anything in return."

"Oh," she said softly.

Levi removed his shirt then lay down, tugging her along with him. "Tonight was about you. I already know what that feels like, although I have a feeling that sex with you will be something different, something special. You're something special, you know that?" Taking her chin between his forefinger and thumb he angled her face so that he could kiss her. "You taste so sweet, like honey," Levi murmured against her lips.

"Thank you," she told him from the bottom of her heart, tears welling in her eyes. She had hoped that one day she might meet a man who could make her feel like she was as precious as a diamond, but there had always been that niggling doubt at the back of her mind that her father was right and the only way to get a man was to submit as his servant.

But Levi made her feel like she was worth all the money in the world.

He made her feel like she had been thrown into a fairytale and all her dreams could come true.

"You don't ever have to thank me for caring about you, Syd," Levi told her as he settled her against his chest. "Now, close your eyes and let me hold you."

Wanting this perfect moment to last forever, Sydney rested her head on Levi's chest, tucked her body close against his, and laid her hand on his stomach. She could get used to this.

Quickly.

~

10:38 P.M.

What was he doing?

This had to be the very definition of a bad idea.

Quite possibly the very worst idea that anyone had ever had, ever, in the entire history of the world.

So why was he here again?

As he sat in his car, watching the dark house across the street, he knew that he didn't have another choice.

He couldn't handle this on his own any longer.

That much was clear.

Evidenced by the dead body propped up in the seat beside him.

Scrubbing a shaking hand across his weary face, he sighed and had to fight back tears. He was at the end of his rope, and he didn't know what his next move should be. All he knew was that this had to stop.

It had to.

And it was time to make his move.

This was a dangerous game he had been playing, as evidenced by the marks on his face and arms. After the disaster that had been the last interrogation, he had been punished. He had tried to spare Wednesday Adams, he'd let only a little of the boiling water touch her skin, burning her but nothing compared to what the others had endured.

For that, his boss had him beaten.

That was when he knew.

If he didn't make his move now then they'd kill him.

Some of the things Wednesday had said to him had struck a chord. He knew that he'd hit her over the head and that she had been suffering the effects of a concussion when she had been spouting that there was no one else in the room with him, but when she'd said that only he could end this she'd been correct.

This was all on him.

His attempts to save Wednesday Adams hadn't worked. When he'd finished with his half-hearted attempt at questioning her, his boss' bodyguard had slit her throat because his hands had been shaking so badly he couldn't complete the job himself.

In fact his hands hadn't stopped shaking since.

This was killing him. Slowly but surely.

If he wanted to make it through this alive, he would need help, and he couldn't go to the cops. Not directly anyway.

The only way to accomplish what he needed was to try to do it as unobtrusively as possible, starting by leaving the cops a little gift.

Well, one specific cop a gift.

There was a new deputy in town. Sydney Clark. Twenty-six years old, brown hair, golden-brown eyes, sweet face, but tougher than she looked. After he'd tussled with her at Trina Liberty's house, he knew that she was the one. She'd managed to get away from him, and when she'd fought him, he had known there was something special about her.

When he'd known he needed to reach out for help it had been only natural that he would gravitate here.

If this didn't work, he would have to take more drastic measures, but he hoped this might be enough for now. If the cops caught his message, maybe they would be able to take over this investigation, leaving him off the hook.

Or dead.

No.

He wasn't going to think that way.

He would survive this, and then maybe he could finally go back to his life the way it used to be.

Maybe it was wishful thinking, but that was what he hoped would happen. If the cops caught him then he knew he would be spending the rest of his life behind bars, no matter that he had only been acting on someone else's orders and that he had been in fear for his life, but at least he would finally be free. If by some miracle the cops didn't connect him to the crimes, he would be able to reclaim his life and never take it for granted again.

Never.

To that end, he better get busy.

This would be tricky, it was late, but there could be people about at any time of the night, the last thing he wanted was to be caught right in the middle of leaving the body here.

As carefully as he could, feeling hyper-aware of every sight, every sound, every smell, he eased open his car door and got out. Although he knew it would look suspicious to anyone who might be watching him, he couldn't not stand and turn in a full three hundred and sixty degree circle surveying the neighborhood. The problem with small towns was that everyone knew everyone and anyone could be looking out of a window right now, and if they saw him standing here they'd tell the cops as soon as the morning light came, and the gift he had left for Deputy Sydney Clark became visible.

When he was satisfied that there wasn't anyone watching him for the time being at least, he circled the car to the passenger side and opened the door. Wednesday Adam's dead body drooped sideways as the window it had been propped against disappeared, and he quickly caught it before it hit the ground.

Unsnapping the seatbelt, he hoisted the dead weight into his arms. He was hoping that should anyone see him they would just assume he was carrying Sydney into her house. He hoped they thought he was just one of her colleagues, or a boyfriend if she had one, he didn't know and he didn't care, he just hoped they didn't get a good enough look at his face to identify him.

He felt a little better once he was across the street and in Sydney's front yard, no lights had come flashing on in any of the surrounding houses, and no one had called out anything, so he had to believe that this first step had gone smoothly. Now it was on to step two.

Quickly he scanned the yard, his eyes settling on what he had been looking for.

The pond.

He'd remembered the small pond because he'd been to this house many times before over the years he had been in River's End.

He carried the corpse over to the pond, which wasn't more than about seven or eight feet in diameter and roughly the shape of a circle. It might be small, but it was big enough to do the job, and he carefully set the body into the water. It was only about three feet deep, but he had to make sure that Sydney saw the body as soon as she left her house in the morning, so he grabbed some rope and tied it around Wednesday Adams' neck and secured it to a shrub that was nearby.

Then he stood and admired his handiwork.

Moving closer to the front porch, he pretended he was Sydney coming out in the morning, trying to make sure that there was no way she could miss the body. The pond was obscured from the street by the fence and trees and plants, but it was possible that a passerby might notice it.

That wasn't what he wanted.

It had to be Sydney.

She had to be the one to see it. She would get his message, he was sure of it.

Satisfied that he had done everything within his power to make sure that someone took over this investigation, he turned back toward the street. He should go back to his car, go home, try to get some sleep, hope that things looked brighter in the morning.

His feet didn't move.

Something was holding him back, and against his better judgment he lingered. The longer he stayed, the higher the chances that he would get caught. He couldn't afford that, and yet he didn't make a move to leave.

In fact, instead he turned and walked up the porch steps, stopping right in front of the door.

Sydney was in there, no doubt in bed asleep, there was only her car in the driveway so he assumed that she was alone in there. Maybe he could go in, talk to her, tell her everything and throw himself at her mercy.

His hand lifted and curled around the doorknob.

Should he do it?

It was risky, but he wanted this over more than anything else.

He waffled over his decision for more than a minute before he finally accepted that he couldn't go inside the house.

"Please, Sydney, please understand what I'm telling you," he whispered, pressing his forehead against the solid wood door.

If this failed, he didn't know what his next move would be. He didn't know that he would even have another move. This was it, he was playing big, and if it failed, he would have to face the consequences.

Slinking down the steps and along the garden path, he hurried across the street and into his car, anxious now to get away from here. He had done all he could, now things were in Sydney's hands, and he prayed that she had better success than he had.

June 14th
3:32 A.M.

"Mmm," Sydney groaned contentedly as she woke to find a warm body wrapped around hers.

Falling asleep in Levi's arms was everything she could have dreamed of and more. Somewhere along the way she must have rolled over in her sleep and was now facing away from him, but far from him letting her go, he had curled up behind her, spooning her against him, his arm wrapped firmly around her waist.

This was what she had longed for all her life, and it was hard to believe that it was real.

But it *was* real.

She was here, in her bed, with Levi holding her. They'd made out a little last night, and she hadn't freaked out like she had been afraid that she might. He knew about her past, he knew that she was both experienced and inexperienced when it came to men, he knew that there were going to be times where she blew things out of proportion—no matter how much she didn't want to, and got disappointed in herself for doing it—and he hadn't turned and walked out the door.

Sydney wouldn't have blamed him if he had.

It was a lot to ask someone to take on, she knew that, she was probably always going to have some residual issues as a result of what her father had done, and although she had promised herself it wouldn't happen there was always the possibility that she would be dragged back down the rabbit hole. None of that seemed to deter Levi, and that made her like him so much more.

She groaned again and snuggled deeper into his embrace.

"What are you moaning about?" Levi's voice asked out of the darkness.

"I thought you were asleep," she replied, turning to look over her shoulder where she could just make out his profile in the dark bedroom.

"Nah, all your wriggling made it impossible to sleep," he teased.

"You didn't sleep at all?" They'd gone back downstairs after a nap around ten to finish dinner before coming back to bed before midnight. Had he been awake all that time?

"Didn't want to miss out on a second of holding you in my arms," he explained.

Her heart stopped.

Why did he feel like he had to savor every second of their night together?

Was this just a one-time thing for him?

Did he think they would never do this again?

Trying not to let the fear she felt seep into her voice she asked, "Why? Was this a once-off as far as you're concerned?"

"No," he answered, nuzzling her neck. "As far as I'm concerned, this is no fling. We're a couple now, an *exclusive* couple, and we're dating with the understanding that unless it turns out, we're not as compatible as we think we are, that things will turn serious pretty quickly."

And just like that, she melted as though she was an ice cube and he was the sun.

In a lot of ways, that was kind of true. She had had to turn her heart to ice to survive what her father had done and the aftermath. It was why she had never acted on any of the crushes she'd had when she returned to school while in foster care or while she'd been in college. She'd known that opening herself up to the wrong person could crush her and so she'd kept her emotions tucked away.

Until Levi.

The spark she'd felt that very first time they'd met had jumpstarted something inside her, and the more time she spent with him, the more she felt the past melting away and herself becoming the woman she was always meant to be.

Love flushed through her, warming her from the inside out, constricting her throat, and making her stomach turn this weird little cartwheel. She'd never felt anything like this before. She'd loved her parents—even her father in a way—and she'd loved her sister and her stepmother, but this was different. This was so intense it had tears building in her eyes and her heart beating wildly in her chest.

"Baby?" Levi asked when a small shiver rocketed through her. "Is something wrong?"

"No, everything is perfect. Make love to me." It didn't matter that she'd only known Levi for a week or that it was too soon to know for sure that she loved him. What she felt for him was strong, all-consuming, and if she wasn't serious about him, she would never have told him about her childhood.

"Honey, we don't have to do that just because you can feel that I want to," he said, shifting his body slightly so his erection was no longer pressed against her back. "We're a couple, that means it's okay for you to say no or for me to say no."

"You're going to say no if I offer sex?" she asked on a laugh.

"Okay, so that's never going to happen." He laughed back. "But seriously, babe, if you don't want to we don't. Simple as that."

And she believed him.

She believed that in Levi's mind it was as simple as that, which was exactly what made her want to. He respected her, he was attracted to her, and she was ready.

"I want to, Levi. Make love to me, please," she ended on a whispered plea. Her confidence in herself was shaky and if he rebuffed her—even if he thought he was doing her a favor—it would hurt.

With a muted growl, he grabbed hold of her wrists and flipped her over onto her back. "You change your mind you speak up."

"'K," she replied breathily, her eyes wide, her entire body tingling in expectation.

"You're so beautiful," he said, staring at her with a wonder that touched her more deeply than any words he could say.

His mouth claimed hers, the kiss wild and passionate and everything that she needed. Levi balanced himself on one arm while his other hand dipped between her legs, and she curled her fingers into his hair and kissed him like he possessed the key to finally undoing the chains that had held her down for most of her life.

Sydney sucked in a breath as a finger slid inside her, his thumb attending to the bundle of nerves that would probably have her coming within minutes from his magic touch. When he added a second finger, angling it so he rubbed that place inside that had white dots appearing at the edges of her vision, she pushed him away.

"Levi, stop."

"You had enough?" he asked, and she couldn't help but smile. He really would stop right now if she asked him to no matter the fact that his body was clearly primed and ready to go.

"No, I just want you inside me when I come."

He shifted position but then stilled. "I don't have any condoms. I didn't come to your place last night for sex so I didn't bring any."

"I don't have any either, but I'm on the pill, and I'm clean, they did tests when my father died, and I haven't been with anyone."

"I was clean when they tested me when I was in the army, and I haven't been with anyone since Amy."

"Then I guess we're in luck." She smiled.

"Yeah, I'm pretty lucky." He smiled back in the semi-dark, his fingers caressing her face.

As his mouth trailed a line of kisses up her neck before settling on her lips again, he eased himself inside her slowly, inch by inch. "Levi," she groaned, lifting her hips restlessly as her fingers clawed into his back, trying to force him to hurry up.

"Patience, darlin'," he drawled with a chuckle.

"I'm not patient," she retorted, lifting her hips higher to take him deeper inside her.

"I can see that," he chortled, finally burying himself as deep inside her as he could.

"Ah," she sighed happily, this feeling of having the man she was falling for filling her up was something she couldn't even put into words. Every time she thought that what she was feeling was as perfect as things got, he made her feel even better.

He began to move, slowly at first, his fingers between them tracing lazy circles where their bodies joined. Sydney tangled her fingers in his hair as she drew his mouth back to hers, kissing him with an urgency that built as the feeling inside her began to build.

As Levi increased the pace, the pressure of his fingers increasing, the feeling inside her grew.

She was so close.

Teetering on the edge.

"Levi," she groaned against his lips, a plea for more, a plea for his body to make her tumble over the edge, a plea for him to never leave her.

His tongue plunged into her mouth as he thrust hard inside her, his thumb pressed firmly against her, and she came, flying wildly through another world that consisted of nothing but pleasure, as she screamed his name against his lips.

He came a second after her, continuing to move until he had wrung out every last drop of pleasure for both of them.

"That was out of this world," he murmured as he sunk down against her, pinning her to the bed with his much larger body.

She just hung onto him, not willing to let him go just yet, needing him to ground her now, convince her mind and body that this amazing feeling was even better because it actually meant something to both of them.

When he tried to move she tightened her hold, needing him still inside her. "I have to be crushing you by now, darlin'," he drawled.

"I don't care," she breathed, "I don't want you to let me go."

Levi rested his forehead against hers. "I won't, Syd."

A smile warmed her face, and she brushed her lips across his, once again he had pushed the bar of perfection even higher. When he told her he wouldn't let her go she believed him.

~

6:47 A.M.

"Ugh," Levi groaned, "I wish I didn't have to leave."

"Me too," Sydney agreed. She was standing in his arms, hers wrapped around his waist, her face pressed against his chest, and she nuzzled closer, her grip tightening, making it that much harder to drag himself away.

"I have to go to work, babe," he said, stroking his hand the length of her spine but making no move to let her go.

"I hate work," she muttered.

"Yeah, me too." He laughed. "If I don't leave now I'm going to be late." He'd already forgone his original plan to pop back home this morning to shower and put on clean clothes, instead spending a few extra minutes in bed with Sydney in his arms and taking a shower here, then putting on yesterday's clothes.

"Then you better go," Sydney said on a sigh.

Still, he didn't let her go. "One last kiss."

"Only one?" She pouted.

Levi laughed again. It was like once Sydney had unlocked the last chain holding her to her past, she felt free to just be herself. He wasn't so naïve as to think that things would be smooth sailing from here on out. Sydney had lived through something horrific, and she would always bear those scars, but now that he knew what had happened to her, he knew how to best support her.

"Come here you." Curling his hand around the back of her neck, he tilted her head up so he could mold his mouth to hers and kiss her like he never intended to stop.

And he didn't.

As far as he was concerned, Sydney was it for him. Unless they found out they weren't compatible as a couple, or there were some issues they couldn't overcome, then as soon as they got to know each other better he would propose. The amount of time they'd known each other didn't matter as far as he was concerned, it was about the connection they shared.

"If I don't leave now, I'm not going to." He groaned as he ended the kiss.

A smile graced Sydney's lips. "Then stay."

"You are a bad influence on me, missy," he said, swatting at her backside.

"I can't help it, you're irresistible."

"Sydney," he groaned, "you're killing me here."

"Sorry," she singsonged.

"You're not at all."

She giggled. "Okay, okay, I'll let you go to work. I have to go in soon anyway. Are we having dinner tonight?" A slight hint of uncertainty and vulnerability crept into her voice.

"Wild horses couldn't keep me away." He took her hand as he walked to the front door and opened it. It was a ten-minute drive to the hospital, he was cutting it close, but if he hurried he should be there by seven. It had been so long since he'd felt this kind of all-consuming emotion for someone, even the thought of not seeing her until tonight was almost enough to have him calling in sick to work.

Levi made it to the edge of the porch when he turned back around, unable to walk away without one more kiss, but something on Sydney's face sent adrenalin surging through him.

Running back to her side, he asked, "Syd? What's wrong?"

Her gaze was fixed on something off to the side, and he tracked it until his own gaze settled on the same thing.

A body.

Posed in the small pond in the corner of Sydney's front yard was a woman, her neck had been slit practically from ear to ear, and she was secured to a shrub with a piece of rope.

For the first time since he left the military, he missed having a weapon on him. "Syd, go back inside and call Abe," he ordered, his gaze scanning the yard, searching for any signs of the killer hiding watching them.

"Levi," she said with exasperation, accompanied by an eye roll and a wave of her hand, "*I'm* the cop, *you're* the doctor." With that she disappeared inside, returning a minute later with her gun in her hand, and the sight of her armed was the sexiest thing he had seen in a long time. She must have realized what he was thinking because she rolled her eyes again. "Really, Levi? That's what you're thinking about right now?"

"I can't help it that you look ridiculously hot holding that gun."

"You're incorrigible," she said but couldn't stop a small smile quirking her lips up. That smile faded as she approached the body, her watchful gaze keeping check on their surroundings. "It's Wednesday Adams," she said when she reached the pond.

"Who is Wednesday Adams?"

"The car accident yesterday morning, I was out there checking on an abandoned car, it belonged to Wednesday Adams. Search and rescue went out yesterday looking for her and were going to go out again today. We thought she might have wandered off and either gotten lost or gotten hurt. I guess we were wrong."

"She's the serial killer's next victim. Why did he leave her here? Why is he leaving you gifts?" There was not a single thing about this that he liked.

"How should I know?"

"Get inside, we'll call my brother and wait in there until he comes."

"Levi, that's ridiculous, he's long gone, probably dumped the body last night. I'm going to check out the scene while we wait for Abe and the others."

"No, you're going to go inside where you'll be safe." When he saw her mouth opening again, no doubt to argue, he warned, "You can walk in or I can carry you in."

"I get you're worried, but there's no need to go all protective alpha male on me, we're not in any danger—"

Reaching over, he snatched her up, slung her over his shoulder, and carried her back inside. Keeping her in place, despite her wriggling, he pulled out his phone and called his brother. "Abe, you have to get to Sydney's. The killer just left a body in her pond," he said without preamble.

"There in ten," Abe returned.

Comforted by the knowledge that his brother would be here soon, Levi set Sydney on her feet. She immediately shoved her hands onto her hips and glared at him.

"What do you think you're doing?"

"Keeping you alive."

"I can keep myself alive," she shot back. "I've been taking care of myself for a long time, Levi, and I worked really hard to get to the place where I can build a new life, away from my past. I have a job I love, a community that could become my family, and I'm ready for a relationship, I won't let anyone treat me like I'm some helpless damsel in distress, not even you."

If he'd thought she looked sexy outside with her gun in her hand, it was nothing compared to how she looked right now. Her eyes were sparkling brightly with a confidence that told him how she had survived everything she had lived through, her cheeks were tinted with pink, and those plump, kissable lips were pursed.

"You're looking at me like you want to kiss me. Didn't you hear a word I just said?"

"No, baby, I heard, come here." He reached out and snagged her arm, drawing her closer. "I couldn't be more proud of you, of how strong you are, of everything you've overcome. I don't doubt that strength, not for a second, and I don't see you as a damsel in distress." Sydney relaxed against him, and he kissed the top of her head. "But there's something you need to know about me, I'm *never* going to sit back when someone I care about is in danger. I protect what's mine. And, Syd, whether you want to admit it or not, right now you're being targeted by a serial killer so you can bet that I'm going to do whatever I need to, to keep you safe."

"So you've been hiding this protective alpha side under your charm, huh?" she asked but didn't sound particularly frustrated. Then she blew out a breath. "Look, I appreciate the sentiment, but don't ever treat me like I'm weak, I worked too hard to convince myself that I'm strong, and what you think of me matters to me."

"Babe, if you don't know your own strength by now you're crazy," he teased. Then gripping her shoulders, he pulled her back and bent his knees so they were eye to eye. "Sydney, you are one of the strongest people I have ever met. If you doubt that then I will tell you every single day until you get sick of hearing it."

She smiled up at him, and he knew he was forgiven. Capturing her mouth, he dragged her up against him and kissed her until a knock at the door disturbed them.

"Until tonight," he murmured, brushing his knuckles across her soft cheek.

"Yeah," Sydney murmured back. She shuddered in his arms, and he knew she wasn't as unaffected by what they'd found in her yard as her bravado implied.

Hooking an arm around her shoulders, they walked to the door together to find Abe standing there. "You're both okay?" his brother asked giving them both a once-over.

"Yeah, we're fine. He must have come sometime last night, probably once it got dark, he didn't try to come inside, just left Wednesday Adams' body and left," Sydney summarized.

"I don't like this, Abe," he said, his eyes boring into his brother's, begging him to make sure he did whatever it took to keep Sydney safe.

"I don't like it either," Abe said.

"I really don't think it means anything," Sydney protested.

"You've had contact with the killer twice now, once at Trina's house, and last night he sought you out," Abe said. "You, specifically. He could have left the body in any of our yards, but he singled out you. Until this situation is resolved I don't want you working alone, you stick with Fletcher."

Sydney stiffened at her boss' command, and Levi found himself torn. As Sydney's boyfriend, he wanted her kept safe whether she liked it or not, angry and dead weren't even in the same stratosphere, and yet he also wanted to defend her, tell his brother that Sydney was strong and tough and could take care of herself.

In the end, he kept his mouth shut.

He'd already lost two women he loved, and he wasn't going to lose a third.

~

7:19 A.M.

"You can go now if you want since the cavalry is here. You're going to be late, sorry about that," Sydney said to Levi. They were standing on her porch, and try as she might, she couldn't tear her gaze away from the pond and the body.

"You think I care about being late to work?" Levi growled, grabbing her and dragging her into his arms, kissing her fiercely before crushing her against his chest. "A serial killer left you a dead body as a gift, a killer who already almost killed you once. I'm not leaving your side until this guy is in custody."

"I really don't think that's necessary," she said, shooting a glance at Abe for support, but he just shot her a bemused smirk. Rolling her eyes and knowing that her boss wasn't going to offer her any help, she turned back to Levi. "You can't really be serious."

"Deadly, darlin'," he said, his hazel eyes hard, face set in an unyielding semi-glare.

"Levi," she said, exasperated. She understood this macho side of him, he'd been in the military, he had that innate need to save and protect, but she needed him to recognize that she was capable of taking care of herself.

"Sydney," he shot back, tone short.

"Fletcher is going to be with me today, and I'm guessing you're going to sleep here tonight since you're acting like a possessive jerk right now." There was only so much of this protective stuff she could handle. She knew what it was like to be stifled by someone who told you they loved you and were only doing what they had to do to help you, and while she knew Levi and her father were nothing alike, she couldn't help but be annoyed by Levi's decision that he knew what was best for her.

"A possessive jerk who cares about you," he corrected, pulling her closer when she tried to pull away.

Since she was pressed close to his chest and she could feel the tension flowing through his body, she let her irritation go. Truth be told, she was shaken up knowing that the killer had been in her yard and had left her a dead body. She didn't want to take out her fear on Levi, not when he was only acting all alpha because he was just as worried as she was.

Still as scared as she was, she had to prove to herself and to Levi that she was still in control. In her experience, the way to deal with fear was to acknowledge its presence and not give it the power to rule your thoughts and behaviors.

To that end, she gently eased away from Levi but took his hand so he'd know she wasn't angry with him. "You go to work, I'll be careful, I won't go anywhere on my own, I'll stick to Fletcher like glue. And if it will make you feel better I'll even ask him to drop me off at the hospital when we're done for the day and come home with you."

"We won't take any chances with her safety," Abe added, finally coming to her rescue.

"You don't go anywhere alone, not even the bathroom," Levi said, his voice fierce with a protectiveness she'd never experienced before. Her mom hadn't cared what the affair would do to her and Adelaide, and her father hadn't cared about anything but punishing them for their mother's actions, ever since her father's death she'd basically been on her own. It was weird having someone care so deeply about her, weird but nice, it gave her a warm, tingling feeling and she smiled despite herself.

"I *will* be going to the bathroom on my own, but I won't go anywhere else alone. I'm not stupid, Levi, and I don't have a death wish, I'm not some too stupid to live book or movie heroine, I'm a cop, and I won't take any silly chances," she promised.

"I guess I'll have to take it," he grumbled.

"Everything will be okay, go to work, I'll see you tonight." She stood on tiptoe and cupped his face between her hands, pulling him in for a kiss.

"Be safe," he whispered against her lips. "And you better not let anything happen to her," he growled at his brother.

Reluctantly, Levi released her and headed off to his car. Sydney watched him go, part of her wishing that he would stay by her side, just like he wanted to until the killer was caught, but the other part of her knew she needed to do this herself. For the last decade, her entire mission had been growing strong, overcoming, proving to herself and everyone around her that she wasn't going to be a victim for the rest of her life.

Fletcher's car pulled to a stop in the street outside her house as she and Abe both walked down the porch steps heading toward the pond. The medical examiner pulled in behind Fletcher, and seconds later, Will, Julian, and Beau were there as well as a crime scene unit. Her yard was buzzing with people, and it was nice to know she wasn't alone in this. For whatever reason the killer had decided to zero in on her, she knew her colleagues wouldn't let him get her.

"Did you hear anything last night?" Fletcher asked as he and Abe flanked her on either side.

"No," she replied. Maybe she might have if she'd been home alone, but she had been too preoccupied to notice anything. "Why this sudden change in MO? I know that he and I tussled the other day, but he tried to kill me." Her fingers fidgeted with the edge of the bandage on her arm. "If he tried to kill me, why is he now leaving me the bodies? What does he have to gain by doing this? This is more risky than leaving the bodies in the river. He wants to tell us something, he wants to tell *me* something, but I have no idea what."

"I don't like that he somehow feels connected to you," Fletcher said.

"I don't either, but I don't know that he's a danger to me, at least not yet. He could have broken in last night, come after me, instead he just left the body. I don't know what that means." She sighed in frustration. She needed a clue, but she didn't know where to find it. So far, the killer hadn't left any witnesses or any forensics, and she was starting to wonder if he ever would.

"He still left the body in the water though," Abe said thoughtfully. "I wonder why he didn't just leave it on your doorstep. What is it about the water that's so important? Is it just a forensic countermeasure or does it have a deeper meaning that we haven't realized yet?"

Before she could answer, the ME pulled the body out of the water, and Wednesday Adams' leg snagged her attention. "Look at this," she said to the others, walking over and crouching beside the body. "The burns are different than the others, not as bad, almost like he didn't really want to do it but felt compelled to see this through. I think the reason he changed his MO is because he wants us to stop him, he doesn't want to be doing this, but he can't stop, he needs us."

"Could be." Abe nodded slowly.

"But that still doesn't tell us if it's Dale Jacoway, Alan Dunkin, or someone else entirely," Fletcher said, sounding as frustrated as she felt.

"Remember that incident at the river that summer? I think you were about sixteen, Theo and I would have been twelve, that girl almost drowned. She was camping on the mountain with her family, hanging out with all the local kids. Word was that Dale was angry that he asked her out but she turned him down, and everyone thought that he tried to drown her but couldn't go through with it. We know he was around four of our victims before they died. We know he asked out three of them, maybe the water was a symbol of that and not anything to do with washing away evidence," Fletcher said, his blue eyes sparkling as he got excited about his theory.

"Go and pick up Dale, bring him in, see if we can get something from him," Abe said.

Full of hope that they were making progress and might even get this killer off the streets by the end of the day, Sydney followed Fletcher to his car.

"You really think it's him?" she asked as she slid into the passenger seat.

Fletcher turned the engine on and pulled out into the street. "Not sure, but this definitely makes sense. Now that we think that the water has some symbolic meaning and that this could be about being turned down like we originally thought, then I think all the pieces are finally starting to fall into place."

"I hope so."

"You know we have your back. You're one of us now, and in River's End that means something. Speaking of being one of us, I saw Levi drive off down the street when I pulled up. You guys together?"

A smile lit her lips at the memory of her wonderful night with Levi. She could hardly believe that everything in her life was falling into place. The new job, the new place to live, the new relationship, she had hit the trifecta when she decided to apply for this job in River's End.

"Yeah, we're together."

"I'm glad, it's nice to see Levi happy again. He's had it tough, losing two women that he loved, ever since Amy he hasn't let himself get close to a woman, that he's willing to risk his heart again should tell you how serious he is about you."

She knew that, but it was nice to hear someone else say it. "I'm pretty serious about him too."

"Good, I know it's none of my business, but Levi has been a friend since we were kids and I'd hate to see him hurt again. And although we haven't known each other for long I consider you a friend too, so if he hurts you, you let me know and I'll—"

Fletcher broke off abruptly as something shattered the back windscreen, and he slumped over the steering wheel.

Startled, Sydney spun around in her seat to see a car following them, a gun held outside the driver's side window.

Someone had shot at them.

Her partner was unconscious, she could see blood quickly staining his light blue shirt.

The car was swerving out of control. Thankfully they were now on the outskirts of town, heading for Dale's farm, so there were no houses or other cars out here for them to hit, but they were heading straight for a tree.

Flinging her arms up to protect her head as she prepared for impact, a moment later it came.

They crashed.

She was flung forward.

Pain exploded inside her skull.

A moment later, a tendril of blackness curled around and dragged her into the depths of unconsciousness, leaving both her and Fletcher vulnerable to the shooter.

~

8:01 A.M.

. . .

Walking away from Sydney was one of the hardest things Levi had ever done.

His gut had been screaming at him that it was a mistake, that she was in more danger than any of them realized. The last time he had ignored his gut Amy had paid the ultimate price.

Sydney had promised that she would play things safe, not go anywhere on her own, and he believed her because she wasn't the kind of woman who would willingly make a stupid decision. He also believed that his brother, cousins, and friends were capable of protecting Sydney, and they would do whatever it took to keep her alive.

Yet he couldn't shake this feeling of impending doom.

Levi pulled his phone from his pocket, toyed with the idea of sending Syd a message, just to check-in, but decided against it. He didn't want to do anything to distract her when one second of distraction could be the difference between life and death.

There was something about this woman who he had known only a week that touched him. She was beautiful and sexy, both of those things were true, but neither was what had attracted him to her. It was her strength. He'd sensed it the first time they'd met, and through each of those first few awkward meetings where she had been nervous and tongue-tied, which now that he knew about her past made sense. She was strong and determined, and had overcome so much that he couldn't not admire her.

She'd become very important to him in a very short amount of time, and now he couldn't imagine waking up tomorrow without her warm body tucked safely against his side.

If he lost her, could he really entertain the possibility of falling for anyone else?

After Missy, he'd been young, confident that despite the loss and the piece of his heart she had taken along with her when she'd died, that he would one day fall in love again, get married, have kids, die a happy old man who had lived a great life with the woman of his dreams by his side. After he'd lost Amy, he'd been older, and the loss coupled with his guilt had made him hesitant to get involved, preferring to flirt and have fun but not put himself in a position to hurt like that again.

Then he'd met Sydney.

From that moment on, he'd known he was hooked and that he was ready and willing to put his heart on the table again.

"Levi, we have a gunshot victim coming in."

He looked up from his desk where he was supposed to be catching up on some paperwork at the nurse who had just come rushing into the office. "Gunshot?" he echoed. That was practically unheard of in River's End, they had crime here, and sometimes it was a violent crime, but someone being shot right when the cops were working on finding a serial killer seemed so out of the norm.

His stomach dropped.

Could they be related?

Was Sydney the victim?

The killer had targeted her, and while he hadn't made any moves to hurt her last night that could change in a heartbeat.

Rushing into the ER, he headed straight for the doors that led to the ambulance bay and then stopped dead in his tracks when he saw who lay on the gurney.

Fletcher.

He'd known the other man most of his life, Fletcher was his younger brother Theo's best friend, and he wouldn't wish anything even vaguely unpleasant on him, but in this second, the only thing that ran through his mind was that if Fletcher had been shot and was here in the hospital then where was Sydney?

"I'm sorry, man." Fletcher turned his head and met his gaze, his eyes flaming with guilt and regret. "He shot me while I was driving, we didn't see it coming, I must have passed out, we hit a tree, and when I woke up she was gone. I'm so sorry."

Apologies.

How many times in his years as a doctor had he offered apologies to a patient's family and friends?

How many times had he tried to infuse his words with genuine empathy to try to offer at least a little comfort?

How many times had he heard the apologies of others after losing a loved one? The doctors after Missy had died, his colleagues after he'd finally been dragged away from Amy's lifeless body after performing

CPR for over an hour, they'd all told him how sorry they were for his loss.

Those words hadn't healed anything, and Fletcher's apology didn't either.

An apology didn't change anything.

It didn't change the fact that Sydney was gone.

The gurney was still being pushed toward him, and Fletcher's guilt-ridden eyes continued to bore into him, but he felt numb, empty, unable to move, barely able to breathe, and unable to think of anything but Sydney.

Where was she?

Why had the killer fixated on her?

How was he going to get her back?

He should have listened to his gut when it told him that Sydney wasn't safe. He should have insisted on staying with her. He should have told her that he was falling in love with her while he had the chance because he might not get another.

"We'll get her back," Abe said as he strode into the hospital.

Levi would love to believe his big brother's words, but the facts were that no one could promise him that because no one could predict the future.

"Levi, man, I'm really sorry," Fletcher implored as the gurney he was on was pulled to a stop in the middle of the trauma room.

He had to focus.

He had to pull it together.

Sydney was out there somewhere, no doubt injured, no doubt afraid, but he also had no doubt that she would fight as hard as she could, use every skill at her disposal, to find a way to survive just like she had found a way to survive everything else life had thrown at her.

"It's not your fault," he assured Fletcher as he moved into the trauma room. "How badly are you hurt?"

"Bullet was a through and through, left shoulder, he's lost a lot of blood, but it doesn't look like any major arteries were hit," a medic rattled off.

"Let's get him moved over, on three," he said to his team, and on three they moved him off the ambulance's gurney and onto one of the hospital's. Fletcher grunted in pain but didn't say anything else, his eyes still seeking his. "Let's get him hooked up," he said to the nurses, and leaving them to start monitoring his vitals, he pulled away the wad of bandages on Fletcher's shoulder. "Ouch," he murmured when he uncovered the torn flesh. "You were lucky," he said after probing the wound.

"Yeah, lucky," Fletcher muttered.

Abe stood behind Levi. "Run through again what happened."

"Sydney and I were driving out to Dale Jacoway's farm. We were talking through the case, then we were talking about you two." He waved a hand at him. "Next thing I know something slams into my shoulder. I don't remember anything after that until the car door was being wrenched open and EMTs were there."

"You were shot from behind," Abe said.

"From a car," Fletcher said.

"You think the shooter was the serial killer? Could he have been watching Sydney's house, followed you, and realized you were onto him? Is Dale the man you're looking for?" Levi asked, wishing he had fewer questions and more answers.

"Did you get a look at the car? Did you see a gun? Was there only the driver in the car, or one or more passengers as well?" Abe fired off a list of questions.

"I saw the car, and it wasn't Dale Jacoway's beat-up old truck," Fletcher told them.

"Who was it? Do you know who the car belonged to?" he asked, straightening and staring pleadingly at his friend. Fletcher was the only one who had been there when Sydney had been abducted. If they were going to find her then Fletcher needed to tell them something.

"I've seen the car around town before, it's Alan Dunkin's, he was the one who shot me."

"Are you sure?" Abe asked.

"Positive," Fletcher said firmly.

Abe shot a look at him, seeking confirmation that the bruise forming on Fletcher's forehead and the blood loss weren't impacting his ability to remember the events leading up to the crash. "His eyes are clear, vitals are all stable, words aren't slurring, he doesn't appear to be confused, if he says that the person who shot him was driving Alan Dunkin's car then I believe him."

"Seems too coincidental that the killer leaves a body in Sydney's yard, then just as we're leaving her place someone shoots at us and abducts her, for it not to be related to the serial killer case," Fletcher said.

"Agreed," Abe said. "The killer is Alan."

Now they knew who the serial killer was, they just had to find out where he had taken Sydney.

Before he killed her.

~

8:36 A.M.

She awoke groggy, drowsy, wanting nothing more than to curl back into her bed, bury her face in her soft feather pillow, pull the covers over her head, and go back to sleep.

Sydney tried to roll over, tried to reach for her soft Egyptian cotton sheet and the feather and down quilt that she alternated between pulling over her to stave off cold shivers and throwing away because it made her stiflingly hot. That was how she spent most nights, see-sawing between too hot and too cold didn't matter if it was summer or winter.

But for some reason, she couldn't seem to reach her covers.

Had she hurt herself?

Was she sick?

Maybe she had a fever, and her limbs were heavy and clumsy, not wanting to co-operate properly.

No.

That wasn't right.

She couldn't move her limbs at all.

And there was something scratchy around her wrists.

Panicked, Sydney snapped her eyes open only to wince and groan as pain stabbed through her skull.

Quickly, she shoved the pain away because to be honest, she just didn't have the time nor the luxury of dealing with it at the moment, she had to focus, and fast because she'd been kidnapped.

Everything came rushing back, her night with Levi, finding the body in her front yard, promising that she wouldn't go anywhere on her own, driving in the car with Fletcher, the gunshot, the broken back window, Fletcher slumped over the wheel, the car behind them, hitting the tree.

For some reason, the fact that she hadn't kept her promise to Levi to stay with someone hit her the hardest.

It was silly, she obviously wasn't here by choice, and she hadn't willingly broken the promise, but still, she knew how frantic he would be when he realized that she was gone and that hurt. Hurt worse than whatever injuries she'd sustained in the crash, which for now she couldn't even figure out. She kind of hurt all over, one giant throbbing mess, but adrenalin had to be coursing through her system, no doubt dulling things, making it impossible for her to pinpoint anything specific.

She would use that to her advantage.

An adrenalin crash could happen at any moment, and she didn't know if anyone knew who the killer was or where he had taken her, so she was on her own for the time being.

That offered her a measure of comfort.

She was used to being on her own, she'd had foster parents who had cared about her after she and her sister were rescued, and she'd had a therapist who had worked hard with her, but that wasn't the same as actually having someone in her corner who wouldn't walk away no matter what. If she'd wanted to overcome what her father had done she had recognized that she was the only one who could make it happen, so she'd thrown everything she had at it.

Just like she would do now.

Sydney had recognized the car that the shooter had been driving so she knew who the killer was, but did Fletcher? Was he even still alive? If he had been killed because the killer had fixated on her then that was a burden of guilt she would carry around for the rest of her life.

Shaking it off and ignoring the tears that burned the backs of her eyes, she surveyed the room. It was a large space, as she'd assumed she was tied to a chair in the middle of the room, her arms behind her back, rope securing her wrists, her legs were also secured to the chair's legs with rope and her feet, now bare, were sitting in a metal bucket.

Guess she now knew how the women had their feet and lower legs so badly burned.

Bile burned her throat, and she shoved it back down, worrying about what would happen to her was only counter-productive.

Clearing her throat, she called out, "Alan? Are you here? Do you want to talk?"

A moment later a man appeared in the doorway. Alan Dunkin looked wild, his hair was unkempt, his clothes were rumpled, his eyes were red, and dark circles marred the skin beneath them. In his arms he held a large book, it looked old, and she couldn't see a title, but she was sure that it had something to do with the murders.

"You want to talk?" he asked quizzically as he took a seat in one of two chairs that were over to the side, pushed up against one wall.

"That's why you brought me here, isn't it?" Now that she was face to face with the man she could see that his wife had been telling the truth when she'd mentioned that her ex-husband had been suffering from paranoia. Everything about Alan Dunking screamed unstable. Whatever his reasons for killing those women, she doubted it was anything that she and her colleagues had discussed.

"I wasn't sure you got my message," he said eagerly, hurrying toward her and squatting beside her chair. "We have to keep our voices down so *he* doesn't hear us."

He? Was there someone else here? Did Alan have a partner?

No, if he was paranoid then it was unlikely he could trust anyone enough to work with them. Delusional then, whoever he thought was here was likely nothing more than a figment of his imagination.

For now, it seemed best to play along, learn what she could, hope that she could buy herself enough time for Abe and the others to find her. She knew they had to be looking for her because whether Fletcher had survived the bullet and the accident or not, someone would have found the car. Since she would be nowhere to be found, surely they would assume that her disappearance was related to the serial killer.

"I need help," Alan whispered. "That's why I left her with you, I knew that you'd understand."

The beseeching way he stared at her and his imploring tone made it clear that he was desperate. That made him volatile and more dangerous because he was unpredictable and reacting to things that weren't real. She would have to tread carefully.

Going on a hunch, Sydney nodded. "You left her in the water."

"I had to," he said on a sigh of relief like he thought she understood what he was doing. "It's the only way to stop them."

"Right," she agreed, wondering what that meant. "The water stops them."

"It's the only thing that stops fire."

"Fire?" She couldn't stop the surprised word from sliding out and immediately regretted it when Alan's eyes narrowed suspiciously. Trying to recover, she added, "Yes, of course, that was brilliant thinking, keeping them in water so they couldn't catch on fire."

Alan relaxed. "It was the only way, if I didn't then they wouldn't have been stopped."

Stopped from what she had no idea, but she would have to wing it and hope that she continued to build this tenuous bond that was between them. "That was very brave of you to stop them."

"I had to," he hissed. "I didn't want to, but my boss said he'd kill me if I didn't get the information out of them."

His boss? Alan Dunkin owned a bookstore, he didn't have a boss, further proof that the man was living in an alternate reality. "And did you get the information?"

"They wouldn't give it up, but they knew, they knew when he was sending the attack that would end us all, and they wouldn't tell me. It's why I had to use the boiling water, cold water puts the avenging angels' fire out, but boiling water hurts them."

He said it so sincerely that her heart actually hurt for him. Alan truly believed that he was singlehandedly responsible for stopping an attack on the world. He didn't need prison, this man needed a psychiatric hospital. He had a brain tumor, or a disorder, or some sort of dementia, or something he needed treated, and she prayed there was a way to end this peacefully so he could get the help he needed.

"So you don't know when the angels are coming to attack?" she asked hesitantly.

"They wouldn't tell me." He threw his hands up in the air forlornly. "Which means my boss is going to kill me, please, I need your help."

"Your boss being ...?"

"Lucifer."

Of course.

The devil.

"And he's your boss because ...?"

"The book." He gestured to the one he'd been holding when he came in that he had set down on one of the chairs. "It was how I found out about the coming attack that God was sending. He came to me, told me that if I didn't help him find out when it was coming so he could stop it that he'd hurt my babies. I couldn't let him do that."

"Of course you couldn't," she clucked sympathetically.

"He told me I'd know one of God's angels when I saw them because they have a glow about them. When you were in the house the other day, you had a glow too, only it was different, that's why I knew you could help me. You *can* help me, can't you?"

"I can help you," she assured him.

How she had no idea.

She was tied up with her feet in the bucket so the idea of burning her was somewhere in his head. Her colleagues would be looking for her, but they had no idea where she was, and even if they did find her, when they came for her they would shoot Alan if he presented any threat, and given his delusions, he would no doubt react badly to a bunch of armed men storming this place.

Still, she wasn't about to give up.

Somehow she would find a way to get this man the help he needed.

~

11:27 A.M.

Raking his hands through his hair, Levi stared out the window of the conference room at the Sheriff's office.

Where was she?

This was hell.

Hadn't Sydney been through enough? Her father had taken out his anger on his wife for cheating on him on his two innocent daughters, sexually abusing them, and trying to warp their view of men and the world. Despite all of that, Sydney hadn't just managed to survive, she had managed to thrive. She was a smart and competent cop who loved her job. She had moved to a new town in the hopes of starting a new life, and even though he knew it had been hard and a little scary for her, she had opened herself up to him, not holding anything back.

Just this morning when he had awakened with her in his arms, he had felt like the luckiest guy in the world. After two losses, he was falling in love again, and he'd thought that he'd had the rest of his life to spend with Sydney.

Now she was gone.

And there were no guarantees he would get her back.

"Please tell me you have something." He spun around from the window where he had been staring out at the street, at the people going about their lives, wishing that he and Sydney were among them.

"We're doing everything we can to find her," Abe promised.

"I know that, but all we have is Fletcher's word that the car was Alan Dunkin's, that doesn't help us find him." He already knew that both Alan's house and the bookstore were empty, so where else could the man be?

As if reading his unasked question, his cousin Will said, "Julian and I spoke with his ex-wife to see if she had any idea where he might be holed up, she gave us a few ideas, and she gave us this." He held up a large old book.

"What does the book have to do with anything?" Levi asked.

"I think it has everything to do with this," Julian replied.

He and Abe both looked expectantly at their cousins. The brothers had driven straight out to Alan's ex-wife's house as soon as Fletcher identified him as the man who had shot him and kidnapped Sydney. Since Alan was already a suspect in the murders there was no reason to believe that the two weren't related. They needed every piece of information about the man they could get if they were going to find Sydney before it was too late.

Abe and Beau had filled him in on the case, some of it he had heard around town on the rumor mill, but what he'd been told was worse than what he had heard. He now knew what the killer had done to the victims, how he burned their feet and lower legs, the pain those women would have been in was excruciating.

Was Alan doing that to Sydney right now?

Had he already done it?

The man was fixated on Sydney. Had he hurt her worse or had he held off on burning her?

The idea that she had been hurt, that she was in pain, and he wasn't there to make things better was eating at him. This was his own personal hell. He hadn't saved Amy, and now he hadn't kept Sydney safe. He'd left her this morning even though he knew something didn't feel right. Now she was gone, and it was like his soul was gone along with her.

Fear was choking him, paralyzing him, stealing his life and he didn't know how to stop it.

"Hey, take a seat." Abe's hand closed over his shoulder and gently pushed him into a chair he'd pulled out. "We'll get her back."

He prayed that was true, but there was a chance they wouldn't. And there was a chance that even if they got her back she would never be the same person she'd been before. Burns were rough to deal with, and Sydney had no doubt been injured in the accident, leaving her vulnerable. Depending on how severely she'd been burned she could be looking at months in the hospital, years of skin grafts, her whole life changed.

Levi was full of so many emotions he didn't know how to deal with them.

It felt like they were strangling him. He wanted to scream, he wanted to cry, he wanted to throw up, he wanted to punch something, but more than anything else he wanted Sydney back safe and sound in his arms.

"Try to hold it together, man," Julian said, patting his arm. "I know it sucks, I know what it's like to be in your position, but you have to hold it together."

His cousin was right. Each of the four other men in the room knew what it was like to have someone you cared about in danger, but while they'd all got those people back alive it wasn't like things had worked out well long term for Julian or Will. That wasn't going to happen to him and Sydney though. When he got her back he would seal the deal, make things permanent between them. He wanted her to know that she wasn't just special to him, she was crawling inside his heart and making it her own.

Dragging in a breath, he tried to still the tornado inside him before it could toss him about and break him into a million pieces. "So what about this book?"

Will nodded and shot him an encouraging smile. "His ex-wife said that he found two copies of this book at a charity store about a year ago and became obsessed. He read them all the time, talked about them all the time, then a couple of weeks ago when he had driven down to visit the kids he brought one of the copies and asked her to hold onto it for him. She said he didn't say why, but that he was very insistent about it, told her the book was important and had to be kept safe. She said she took it because by that stage she was on the whole path of least resistance when it came to dealing with him."

"You think the book is what started this whole thing?" Beau asked.

"Yes," Will answered without hesitation.

"So is the book rare, valuable?" Abe asked.

"Not so far as we can tell, but what's in it might be the reason why he's been doing this," Julian replied.

"The book is about God sending his angels of fire to defeat the Devil. The victims were left in water. What if that's the reason he left the bodies in the water? If he thought that they were angels of fire then maybe he thought that was the only way to stop them," Will suggested.

"So that might explain why he killed the victims, and maybe even why he was torturing them, trying to find out about how or why they were going to formulate this attack, but what we need is something that will help us find where he is right now," Levi said, trying to reign in his frustration only because it wasn't productive.

"Maybe the book does tell us something that can help us find him," Abe said, a thoughtful look on his serious face.

"Care to share what you're thinking?" he snapped. It wasn't that he was angry with his brother, he was just angry with the situation and wanted to do something to resolve it.

His brother ignored his attitude. "Angels, God, the Devil, this is all circling around religious themes ..."

"The church?" he asked, then quickly answered his own question, "no, it can't be, the church is right in the middle of town, and people are in and out of it most days." Not only did the church in the center of town hold Sunday morning services, but there were meetings, both church and community ones held there almost every night of the week.

"The church is out," Abe agreed. "But there used to be another church in the area before water sports, hiking, and skiing had the town growing and the new church built. There was a small chapel, it's about ten miles to the north-east of the lake, about fifteen miles from town. The building was abandoned over half a century ago, it's secluded because it was originally meant to cater to the farms in the area, so there is plenty of privacy for Alan to have tortured the victims. If he sees this as some sort of epic battle between good and evil, then it could be the perfect setting."

As far as he was concerned, that was a good enough explanation of where the killer might be holed up. He was ready to get moving, the sooner they found Sydney the less chance that she would be hurt.

"I'm coming with you, no arguments. You're already down Fletcher, and I know how to handle a gun, I won't be a hindrance, and if this guy is unbalanced, you need all the people you can get. And if he's already hurt Sydney then having a doctor on scene would go a long way to dealing with the burns as quickly as we can."

"You assure me you can follow orders and keep your emotions in check, and you're in," Abe said.

"Deal." Following the others out, he murmured a plea to Sydney, "Hold on, Syd, we're coming for you, just hold on, baby."

11:50 A.M.

"She knows something."

Alan turned at the voice behind him, panic rushing through him, he'd gone to Sydney Clark because he believed she had the power to help him, but then this morning she had left her house heading in the wrong direction. He'd thought that she would know to head for the church, but she hadn't, and he'd been forced to take drastic action to bring her here.

He needed her.

Maybe it was unfair to drag her into this, but he had genuinely believed that she was the only person who could help him and he still did. She seemed to understand what was going on and he prayed that together they could bring this to an end.

"I don't want to hurt her, she's not one of the angels," he told Lucifer.

"She knows things, I need answers, get the water," Lucifer's hard voice replied.

"No, please." He was begging, and he didn't even care that it might result in a punishment of his own. "I don't want to hurt her."

"Alan?" Sydney called out. Her face was pale, making the bruises forming from the car accident seem so much more prominent, the bandage on her arm was soaked in blood, and her eyes were wide with fear. "What's going on?"

Her gaze was moving between him and the chair where Lucifer sat, and he was relieved that she could obviously see the man. Wednesday's adamant proclamations that there was no one else in the room had been beginning to get to him. For a moment he had almost started to doubt that all of this was real, but of course it was. It would almost be a relief to find out that it wasn't.

"Either you interrogate her or he will," Lucifer said with a nod of his head in his bodyguard's direction. The bodyguard gave him a sneer, and he knew that he couldn't let the man near Sydney. Maybe if he pretended that he was interrogating her but really tried to hurt her as little as possible, as he'd done with Wednesday, he could find a way to get her free.

"Okay," he nodded, pretending to look defeated. He walked into the kitchen to set the electric kettle to boil and tried to figure out how to make this happen. He didn't want to live under Lucifer's thumb anymore, he didn't want to live under the threat of losing his babies, he wanted to be free, and Sydney would help him do it.

The kettle bubbled and hiss as the water inside began to boil, absently he picked up the knife. It was the one he used when he had finished with the angels, and it was time to make sure they could never fulfill their plans. Maybe he could use it to get Sydney out of the chair, then together they could take out Lucifer and the bodyguard.

The switch clicked, indicating the water was boiled, and he pocketed the knife then carried the full kettle into the main room.

Sydney's eyes widened when she saw him, and she shook her head. "Please, Alan, you don't have to do this, we can find another way together. Together the two of us can figure out how to take down Lucifer, I promise you we can, you don't need to do this."

"Hurry up," Lucifer snapped, looking bored.

When he reached the chair Sydney was tied to, he leaned over, pretending to be checking that she was secured. He whispered in her ear, "I'm sorry, I'm going to have to pour a little water on your leg, I know it will hurt, and I wish I didn't have to do it, but it's the only way to keep him distracted. I have a knife, I'm going to slip it into your hand, try to get yourself free while I pretend to interrogate you. Once you're free we'll take them, I'll make sure there is still water in the kettle, and you keep hold of the knife. Together we can take out Lucifer and his bodyguard."

He carefully slid the knife from his pocket and passed it to Sydney, slipping it into her hand and praying that she would be able to use it to get herself free. Once she was then the two of them could take out the others, and he would be free, it would all be over, and while he didn't know what was coming next at least he knew it wouldn't be more of this.

"You need to tell me what you know," he said firmly as he straightened, holding the kettle above the metal bucket where Sydney's feet were.

"I don't know anything," she said, her face creased in concentration as she no doubt tried to maneuver the knife so she could cut through the ropes.

"I need to know when the attack is coming, how many of you there are," he said. He hoped when the attack did come that the angels would wipe out Lucifer and make him suffer. He also hoped they took mercy on him and knew he had only done this to keep his children alive.

"I already told you, I don't know," Sydney shouted back.

"If you won't talk willingly then I'll have to make you talk." With that, he began to pour water from the kettle, angling it carefully so that instead of going into the bucket where it would cover her feet, and she would be unable to get away from it, he let it trickle down the side of her leg and then onto the floor. It would still burn her, it would still hurt, but it wouldn't be as bad as it could have been.

Sydney's scream ripped through the old chapel as the boiling water made contact with her skin.

The sound hit him hard, and he winced at her pain, tears blurring his vision, and he quickly looked away, unable to look at the excruciating pain written all over her face.

"I told you that you will talk one way or another," he forced himself to say.

Panting and breathing hard, she looked him in the eye and gave a small nod, and he noticed that her arms, while still behind her back, were now at a different angle. She'd done it, she'd managed to cut her arms free, now all she had to do was get her legs free, and they could do this thing.

Alan moved a little so that he was between her and Lucifer, blocking their view of her so they wouldn't see when her arms came free, and she cut the ropes binding her legs.

Sydney's arms slowly moved forward, she winced at the movement and then paused to let the blood get flowing again.

"Are you ready to tell me what you know? We know an attack is coming, we know the angel is here, somewhere, waiting, watching, biding their time before they announce the coming of the war. Is it you? Are you the one who will herald it? Do you know when it's coming? Do you know how many angels will come? If you tell us what we need to know, then you'll be given a quick death, if you don't, then I will have to torture you until you are begging for death."

With a muffled groan, her face so devoid of color that he almost worried that she was too injured to be of any help to him, Sydney kept her body as still as possible and reached down with one hand to attack the ropes at her legs.

Hoping to buy a little more time, Alan held up the kettle. "Are you ready to answer some more questions or do you need a little more added motivation?"

"I don't have anything to tell you, I don't know anything, and even if I did there is no way I would share it with you," Sydney yelled at him. She met his gaze and held it, giving a small one-sided smile to let him know that she was still playing along.

They had this.

Adrenalin coursed through his system, energizing him. They were so close, Sydney just had one more rope to saw through and then she'd be free. As soon as she was they would make their move. Sydney had the knife, and he still had at least half of the water in the kettle that he could use.

"I'll take Lucifer, you take the bodyguard," he whispered. When she nodded, he held the kettle up again as though to pour more water into the bucket. "What's your choice? Are you sticking with being stubborn or are you ready to accept that you have lost and Lucifer has won, and tell him what he wants to know?"

"I gave you my answer, I'm not going to tell you a single thing."

The ropes dropped, Sydney was free, she clutched the knife in a white-knuckled grip, it was time.

Just as he was ready to turn and attack, he heard footsteps.

12:13 P.M.

She was free.

She was armed.

She was also dizzy with a pain that she had never felt before. It was so intense it was almost overwhelming and the only thing spurring her on and making her fight against it was Levi.

Sydney would do everything in her power to get back to him and while she didn't want it to end that way, if she had to kill Alan to do it she would. She hoped it wouldn't come to that, she was playing along with his plan to take out the imaginary Lucifer and a bodyguard. Her plan was as soon as they went to take down these characters she would use her knife to subdue Alan. He was much bigger than she was and she was hurt and shaky, so there was a chance that subduing him wouldn't work and she would have to go for the kill shot to make sure she got home to Levi.

With a prayer that wouldn't happen, she cut through the last of the ropes binding her, met Alan's eye, saw the hope there that she was about to help him end his nightmare, and just as they were about to make their move she heard footsteps.

A second later the door to the chapel where Alan had brought her was thrown open, and her guys came running through.

Without a conscious decision being made on her part, she flung herself at Alan, knocking him down before anyone could get off a shot. Alan had the kettle in his hand, and they all knew that he'd burned his victims, the others didn't know what was going on so they didn't know that the killer wasn't a threat to her right now, and she really didn't want to see the man hurt. He needed a lot of help, and yes he needed to pay for what he'd done, but he could do that in a psychiatric facility where he could also receive treatment. Killing him wasn't necessary, and it wasn't how this should end.

"Sydney," Levi screamed her name.

She wanted to answer, assure him that she was okay, but she wasn't okay, and the movement had stirred the pain on her leg from the burn and her injuries from the crash, and she couldn't focus enough to speak right now.

Alan panicked, dragging her to her feet along with him when he stood and held her between him and the others, the kettle still in his hand. "What is it? What's going on? Why are you here?"

"Alan, let Sydney go," Abe said, his voice calm, controlled like he didn't have a care in the world.

"No, I need her," Alan implored.

"Don't hurt him," she told the others. "It's okay, Alan, I'll still help you, you and me, we can do this."

"Sydney," Levi hissed, "what are you doing?"

She wanted to explain the whole thing to him, but right now, it was taking all of her energy to just focus on Alan and make sure he got out of here alive. "Alan, please, let's just tell them, they can help."

"We can't trust them," he muttered.

"We can," she promised. "Lucifer is still there, the others can't see him but we can. Abe, I need you to trust me," she said, meeting her boss' gaze and imploring him to do as she asked. "The seat over behind us, near the other door, there's a man sitting in it and a man standing beside him. I need you to shoot them both, okay?"

Abe gave her a funny look, his weapon still aimed at her and Alan, but with a curt nod, he shifted his stance and fired off two rounds, while Levi, Will, Julian, and Beau kept their weapons pointed at her, well at Alan, but since she was held pressed against his chest it felt like they were on her.

"See, Alan," she said, forcing a calm she certainly didn't feel. "It's done, Abe got both of them. It's okay now."

"It's over?" Alan sounded like he hardly dared to believe it was true.

"It's over," she echoed. "Lucifer is dead."

She felt the relief ripple through him, but then instead of loosening his grip as she had hoped now that his personal devil had been vanquished, he had tightened his grip so that it hurt. What was he thinking? What was his next move? He had to know that with five guns on him he wasn't walking out of here, and she wasn't sure he was rational enough to figure out a plan out of here. Given that he was delusional he could be seeing anything. In his mind, there could be more angels or devils in the room, more problems that only he could see.

That left her only one option.

The knife was still in her hand, thankfully she had managed to keep a hold of it when she knocked him down, and she was starting to think that using it was the only way out of this mess.

If she had to make a move to end this, she would, but she could at least make sure that she could take him down without him losing his life.

Before any of the guys could say anything, or anyone—including

Alan—could do something that couldn't be taken back, she shoved the knife into Alan's legs.

The man screamed and released her and without him holding her up her legs couldn't support her, and she crumpled to the floor.

Before anyone could get to her, pain speared through her lower back, and she cried out.

"Sydney?" Levi demanded as he dropped to his knees beside her. "Where are you hurt?"

"M-my back," she stammered, stunned. Alan must have pulled the knife out of his own leg and stabbed her.

"Hold on," he murmured as he lifted her into his arms and carried her outside. The feeling of relief that he was here was so strong that it sapped more of her strength. She closed her eyes and rested her head on Levi's shoulder as she felt herself slip into a weird sort of in-between zone. She wasn't really unconscious because she could hear what was going on around her, but she also wasn't really conscious, she was too numb and felt too disconnected to really be part of it.

Levi laid her down on the grass, and she gasped as the pain intensified in her back. His fingers pressed under her jaw to check her pulse before his hands ran methodically over her body from head to toe, checking her for injuries. While her whole body ached, there was nothing that was worse than anything else, except for the burn on her leg and the wound in her back.

Once he completed his examination, he grabbed the leg of her pants and ripped. Was it just this morning that she had put them on? In her house, with Levi, watching him get ready for work, still reveling in the night's lovemaking, excited to see how things progressed in their relationship, it felt like years had passed since then.

"I need water," Levi yelled.

She winced at the loud volume of his voice as it reverberated inside her head and he immediately placed a hand on her shoulder, squeezing firmly but not painfully.

Cold water began to flow onto the burn, and she cried out at the sudden onslaught of pain.

"Sorry," Levi muttered, then cursed. "I'm so sorry, baby, but we need to get some water on this while we wait for the ambulance. This is going to hurt, sorry."

Carefully he eased her onto her side and probed the sight of the knife wound. As soon as his fingers pressed close to the wound, she groaned in pain, her eyes falling closed as she struggled to breathe through the agony.

"I need something to put pressure on this," he called out, and a moment later something pressed tight against the wound, and she couldn't stop a scream from falling loose. "I'm sorry, honey, I really am, but you're bleeding badly."

Sydney wasn't so far gone that she couldn't catch what he wasn't saying.

She was bleeding badly enough that he was worried she would bleed out before an ambulance arrived.

"Can you open your eyes, sweetheart?"

His fingers caressed her cheeks, his touch melting away a little of the pain because she had been so scared that she would never see him again, never feel his hands on her, never kiss him, never get the chance to know if she was really falling in love with him.

"Come on, Syd, open your eyes for me, please, honey."

The imploring tone in his voice made her try. Summoning all her strength, she managed to force her eyes to cooperate, and as soon as they were open she saw Levi, on his knees at her side, one hand firmly gripping her shoulder keeping her on her side, his face close to hers, his pretty hazel eyes full of concern.

He forced a smile. "There's my girl."

"Kiss me," she said. Her voice was weak, insubstantial, even to her own ears, she could feel her life dripping away with each drop of blood, and all she wanted right now was to soak up Levi's comfort.

"Baby," he began.

"Please." She wasn't above begging. If she was going to die, she wanted one last kiss to carry her over to the other side.

Carefully, he leaned closer and feathered his lips across hers, the kiss was over quicker than she would have liked, but it was better than nothing.

"Is Alan all right?" She didn't think she'd got him in any major arteries, but she'd been woozy and in pain and knew there was a chance her aim had been bad.

"He's alive, and he'll make it," Levi replied.

"I'm glad, he's sick, he needs help."

"I can't believe you threw yourself on top of him," Levi growled.

"I had to. I was sitting down, he had the kettle, and you wouldn't have known that he wasn't a threat to me. At least not a threat to me at that moment," she amended because the man had been delusional and could have imagined anything at all happening.

"Don't you *ever* do anything like that again," he said forcefully, then leaned down and crushed his mouth to hers.

This kiss was what she needed. This was a real kiss, not the soft one he'd given her before, this kiss was full of fear and relief and all the possibilities that the future held. She lifted her hands and grabbed onto his shoulders, holding onto him, not letting him pull back because she needed him.

Most of her life she had made sure that she didn't need anyone, that she was completely self-sufficient, that she could handle anything and everything on her own, she'd thought that being independent was important. And it was. But she was coming to realize that there was a middle ground, maybe needing someone didn't mean not being able to carry the load alone it just meant having someone who could take it for a while to give you a break. That's how she saw things with Levi. She had proved that she could take care of herself, but having him here right now to hold her and reassure her felt so nice.

"You do know you have an audience, right?" Julian asked.

Reluctantly, Levi pulled away to shoot a glare at his cousin. "You couldn't just sit there quietly and pour water on her burn?"

Julian grinned. "Nope."

"Is the burn bad?" she asked hesitantly. If she survived tonight, she wanted to know if she had a long road ahead of her to heal.

"We'll see," he replied vaguely. "You have some bruises on your face, and I see the stitches in your arm split again, probably in the crash. I'm going to have to suture them for the third time," he teased with a tight smile.

So the burn was bad.

His non-answer was in and of itself an answer.

"Your wrists are a little torn up from the ropes," Levi continued, "and there's rope burn on your ankles as well."

"Fletcher?" She hardly dared to ask in case it was bad news.

"Is going to be fine," Levi assured her.

Sydney wanted to tell him that she was falling for him, she wanted to tell him how much he meant to her and the depth of the sense of loss when she'd woken up in the chapel and thought that she might never see him again. But she was scared, they'd only known each other a little over a week, they'd only been a couple for a few days, surely it was too soon to be saying things like that. She didn't want to scare him off, and given that he'd already lost two women he loved and very nearly lost her too she didn't want to put pressure on him to return her sentiment.

Her eyes sought his, and as though sensing that he looked down at her, smiled and brushed a hand tenderly over her hair. The look on his face said he was feeling the same way she was. Should she risk it and say something?

If she was going to die then she wanted him to know.

She tried to open her mouth but getting her body to obey was getting harder and harder.

A deep coldness seeped into her. Shaking followed, and she moaned low in her throat as pain arrowed from her back through her body.

"Hold on, Syd," Levi begged, his hand squeezing her shoulder tightly. "Does anyone know her blood type?"

"AB negative," Abe said, striding over.

"Trust you to have the rarest blood type," Levi teased, but the smile didn't reach his eyes. "I'm O negative, I'm going to donate now, get the first aid kit," he yelled to someone.

The cold was claiming her, taking her away with it. She couldn't feel Levi's hand on her shoulder, she couldn't feel the ground beneath her, she couldn't feel anything but pain.

Pain.

So much pain.

If it wasn't for the fact that she'd have to leave Levi behind she would almost welcome death if it meant being free of it.

"Honey, stay with me, okay? An ambulance is coming, and I'm

going to give you some blood now. When they get you to the hospital they'll probably rush you straight into surgery, until then, I'm going to keep you alive. You hear me?"

She gave a half-nod, the best she could manage.

"That's my girl. You just keep believing that, okay? I'm not losing you. I'm not losing another woman I love."

Love.

Had he just said he loved her?

A sharp prick on the inside of her elbow drew her attention, and she could feel Levi setting up an IV.

A wave of tiredness washed over her. "I'm sleepy," she mumbled.

"I know, baby. Try to hold on."

"Don't think I can."

"If you have to go to sleep, Sydney, then you keep breathing, okay? You keep that heart beating, and when you open your eyes again, I'm going to be the first thing you see," Levi promised.

He leaned in, touched his lips to hers in the lightest of kisses. Her lashes fluttered on her cheeks, she tried vainly to stay conscious so she didn't worry Levi further.

She lost the battle.

Darkness swamped her as she passed out.

June 15th
8:22 P.M.

A comfortable bed and a good night's sleep were what he needed right now, but that hadn't happened last night, and it wasn't happening tonight. Levi would be spending the night here in the hospital again, sleeping in an uncomfortable chair at Sydney's bedside.

It had been a long two days. Searching for Sydney after she went missing, finding her alive then watching her nearly bleed to death right in front of him. She probably would have bled out if he hadn't donated blood to her there on the grass in the woods outside the old church. She had been rushed to the hospital, taken straight to surgery, then kept sedated through the night as her body slowly recovered.

She would be kept here probably for another day at least. Thankfully the knife hadn't damaged her spine, and once the muscle and tissue healed, she'd be as good as new. The burn on her leg would take much longer to heal, she'd have skin grafts and multiple surgeries, but hopefully, her recovery would go smoothly.

While she slept, he'd snuck out to make a quick call to check in on how Alan Dunkin was doing and what the next step in his case would be. Sydney had saved his life by protecting him. By the time Abe and Beau had gotten him cuffed and under control he'd been ranting about the two of them plus him, Will, and Julian being the four horsemen of the apocalypse—it didn't seem to register to him that there were in fact five of them—and Sydney being the angel who was sent to start the war he believed was coming. The man was completely delusional which just made the whole situation that much sadder.

Striding through the quiet hospital corridors heading for Sydney's room, Levi felt that now-familiar ache in his chest that said he'd been away from her for too long. He never wanted to go through something like yesterday ever again in his life. That kind of fear and pain was too much, and it niggled at his brain telling him to cut his losses and run now before he got in any deeper.

He was tempted.

It would make life so much easier to just remain single, maybe when he was ready, date casually. Being ready to fall in love again and start a new relationship was different than having that woman snatched away from him and nearly killed.

For as long as he would live, he would never forget seeing Sydney throw herself over a suspect, especially one who had abducted her. And the feel of her blood slick on his hands as he watched her dying right in front of him was a nightmare he would never get over. His heart had been in his throat, and even now he couldn't quite get his hands to stop shaking and inhale a full breath.

But as much as fear told him to run he knew he couldn't.

He was already in too deep.

A life of fearing that he might lose Sydney was still better than a life without her in it.

Smiling at the thought of seeing her, kissing her, touching her, he'd pull his chair close to the bed and fall asleep holding her hand, and tomorrow night or the next night when he got her home and all to himself he would show her how much she meant to him.

Opening the door to Sydney's hospital room, he stopped dead in his tracks.

The bed was empty.

Sydney was nowhere to be seen.

Once again, his heart raced and panic clawed at his chest. Where was she? What had happened? He knew Alan was still here in the hospital and wouldn't be transferred to a secure facility until the morning, but he was cuffed to a bed, with an armed guard on his door, he couldn't have gotten free to get to Sydney. Could he?

If not Alan, then who?

And how could they have gotten her out of here?

The window was closed, the drapes drawn, and he was sure someone would have noticed someone walking through the hospital with a hostage.

Levi was about to spin around to go call Abe and rouse as many nurses as he could to see if anyone had seen anything, when the door to the hospital room's small bathroom swung open, and Sydney limped through it.

"Hey," she smiled at him.

In response, he stormed across the room, grabbed her and carefully dragged her into his arms, crushing her against his chest.

"What is it? What's wrong?" Sydney's panicked—and pained—voice asked as she curled her fingers into his t-shirt.

He didn't answer.

He couldn't.

He just held her tight and buried his face in her hair, breathing in her scent and trying to allow it and the feel of her in his arms to reassure him that she was here and she was okay.

"Did something happen?" she asked when he didn't say anything, and he could feel her anxiety levels rising.

"No, honey, I just panicked a little when I walked into your room and saw the bed was empty." It was silly, of course, nothing would have happened to her. She was safe here in the hospital, but he'd lost a lot, and it was hard not to let the worst case scenario be his first assumption.

"Sorry." She snuggled closer, tucking herself tightly against him and nestling her head against his shoulder. "If I'd known you were going to worry I would have left the bathroom door open so you'd know I was okay."

"Don't apologize," he told her, that wasn't what he wanted. "Sorry I freaked."

"Don't you apologize," she shot back. "I get baggage, I have mine and you have yours, and I think it's kind of sweet that you would worry that much about me," she finished shyly.

"Why are you so sexy when you're shy?" he groaned, wishing they weren't in a hospital right now.

Sydney laughed and eased back a little, her face sobering. "I know how hard it must have been for you when Alan took me, when you had to save my life, and I want you to know that there will be no hard feelings if you want to walk away. I get that maybe what happened made you re-evaluate whether or not you're ready for another relationship, and I promise I won't hate you or hold it against you if you want to end this ... thing between us."

Levi just stared at her.

How had she known exactly what had been going through his head when he was walking back to her room?

If anything, her words just made his feelings for her grow. There was pain in her eyes, and he knew it wasn't from her burns and the gash in her back, it was from the idea of losing him. And yet she was prepared to do it if it was what was best for him.

Sydney took a small step back, trying to extricate herself from his arms, her brave smile wavering, and he realized he hadn't said anything, and she had interpreted that as him wanting to pull back.

"No, Syd, no. No. I couldn't walk away from you even if I wanted to and I don't want to. This thing we have is real, and I meant it when I told you that we had something special going and as far as I was concerned it was permanent. And that's what I want, you and me, together. I know it's too soon to start talking about forever but ..."

"It's not too soon," Sydney blurted out. "I'm falling in love with you."

Those words were ones you never got tired of hearing.

They'd meant a lot when Missy said them to him, and they'd meant a lot when Amy had said them to him, and they meant no less when Sydney said them.

Picking her up, he spun her around—carefully because she was still attached to an IV giving her fluids and pain meds—making her giggle but then wince, and he realized he was no doubt hurting her. "Come on into bed with you. You weren't supposed to be up on your own anyway," he reminded her, carrying her to the bed and laying her down, putting the IV pole back in place beside the bed.

She kept hold of his hand. "Will you stay with me tonight? I mean not in the chair but in the bed with me?"

"You betcha." He grinned and climbed onto the bed, on the opposite side of her burned leg, and stretched out at her side. Sydney immediately curled into him, her face pressed against his neck, and he felt her sigh like a contented cat and snuggle even closer.

"I'm so lucky," she whispered into his neck. "I always wanted to meet a guy like you, but I wasn't sure I ever would."

"I'm the lucky one, honey," he corrected as he touched his lips to her temple. "I'm lucky that a beautiful, smart, caring woman like you wants to be with me. I'm lucky you looked past the charm and flirting to see what was underneath. I'm lucky that I got you back alive and mostly in one piece and I'm not ever letting you go."

Wetness on his skin told him that she was crying, and he of course got the immediate feeling of being out of his depth with a crying woman, but it passed quickly, and he kissed her temple again. He'd take tears if it meant that she was here, and he had a feeling that the tears were of happiness and maybe relief, that she could finally close the dark chapter of her past and look to the future.

A lighter future.

A happier future.

"Sleep now, baby, I got you."

CHAPTER *Ten*

June 17th
7:53 P.M.

"You are finally getting out of here," Levi said as he strode through the door to her hospital room.

"About time," Sydney said, slowly pushing herself to her feet. The knife wound on her back was healing as well as possible, and as long as she didn't put too much pressure on it, or bend or twist too fast causing the stitches to pull, it wasn't too painful anymore. Her leg hurt a lot, and she knew that the burns would take a long time to heal. She had a lot of doctor's visits coming over the next weeks, months, and possibly even years, as she'd be having skin grafts once the burn began to heal. Still, she could walk, she'd be back at work in a couple of days, and she had Levi by her side to support her every step of the way so she considered herself one very lucky lady.

"If you're up to it, I have something special planned before we go home." Levi reached for her hand and took it, entwining their fingers as he led her across the room.

"Ooh," she squealed excitedly. She'd been stuck in this room for the last three days and she was ready to be anywhere but here. Home had seemed nice because it would just be her and Levi without doctors, nurses, and friends popping in and out all the time. But as nice as home would be a surprise was an even better prospect. "What's the surprise?"

"Well, it wouldn't be a surprise if I told you now, would it?" Levi teased.

"I guess not," she grumbled, but she wasn't really annoyed. That Levi had planned something special for her as soon as she was sprung from this place just showed her what an amazing guy he was.

Hand in hand they left the hospital, walking through the parking lot to Levi's car where he opened her door, helped her in, taking most of her weight to relieve a bit of pressure on her leg, and buckled her in. As he started driving, he reached for her hand and again laced their fingers together. They sat in comfortable, companionable silence, she didn't feel the need to chatter away just to chatter, and truth be told she was still tired, so just relaxing here, holding Levi's hand, was perfect.

She dozed a little, but her eyes snapped open when she noticed that the car had stopped, and when she looked out the window she saw that they were in the forest, down by the lake. She hadn't been down here before, the lake was about ten miles north of River's End, and was how the town had gotten its name, being the end of the river.

It was beautiful here, quiet, peaceful, and exactly what she needed.

"From the look on your face, I'm guessing I made the right move by bringing you here instead of going straight home." Levi grinned.

"Yeah, yeah, you're a regular genius when it comes to women," she teased him.

Leaning over the center console, he pressed a hard kiss to her lips, then jumped out, walked around to her side, and opened her door for her. After he helped her down, he grabbed a picnic basket and a blanket, then took her hand and led her down to the dock.

"You have a boat?" she asked when she saw where they were heading.

"It's mine and my brothers' and dad's. We bought it together once me and my brothers moved back to River's End. I thought after everything that happened you might enjoy being out here, surrounded by nothing but nature."

"I would never have thought of this myself, but you're right, it's perfect and exactly what I need right now."

The boat was nice, big enough but not too big, and once Levi had helped her onto it and set the picnic basket down she sat in a soft leather seat and let Levi busy about getting the boat prepared and then turning it on and driving it out toward the middle of the lake.

He didn't drive too quickly, and she took the time to look around, soak in the scenery. It really was beautiful. Trees ringed the lake, except where the river ran into it, and the closer they got from land, the more she began to notice the sky. Puffy little white clouds chased each other across the expanse, and it felt like they were the only two people left in the entire world.

Arms wrapped around her, and she leaned carefully back against Levi's strong chest. "Enjoying it out here?"

"I've never been on a lake before, it's so pretty." She breathed, unable to wipe the smile off her face.

"Not as pretty as you." Levi tugged her to her feet and turned her around so he could kiss her.

As much as she loved having his lips on her, she wanted more. Needed more. "Levi, make love to me," she murmured.

"Syd," he started with that tone of voice that said he was going to slip into doctor mode any second now.

"Please, I need you, I want to feel you inside me, I want us to be joined together." Need was pulsing inside her, growing quickly, she knew there was only one way to quench it, and that was making love to Levi.

"I can't say no to you," Levi said, running his fingers through her hair as he touched his forehead to hers.

"I'll remember that."

"I bet you will."

Sitting down on the seat, he drew her down onto his lap, his mouth finding hers again as he pushed her skirt up around her hips. One large hand lifted to cup her face, while his other found its way inside her simple white cotton panties and began to tease her.

Not willing to be passive and just take what he was giving her, she reached out, unzipping his shorts and taking him in her hands. He was big and hard, and pulsing and she couldn't wait another second to have him inside her.

"Levi," she whimpered, he already had her teetering on the edge of ecstasy, and she didn't want to plunge off that cliff without him.

Hands circling her hips, he lifted her so he could shove his shorts and boxers out of the way, then set her down so she was straddling his legs. Last time she had let him lead, it had been her first real sexual encounter, and she'd been happy to let him be in the driver's seat, but this time she wanted to lead things. Levi seemed content to let her do things her way, his hands playing with her breasts as he continued to kiss her.

Moving slowly, she took him inch by inch inside her, letting her body adjust each time to the feel of him. He groaned when she sunk the rest of the way down, burying him deep inside her, and she smiled. Knowing that she had the ability to affect him, not because of what her father had drilled into her, but because the connection they shared filled her with a confidence she hadn't felt before.

That confidence spurred her on, and she began to move. Teasing him—and herself—as she moved up until just his tip remained inside then pushing back down until he was buried deep.

Up and down.

That magical feeling that she was just starting to understand grew inside her, and from the fervent way Levi kissed her, she knew that same feeling was growing inside him.

With a growl, Levi grabbed her hips. "You're killing me here, darlin'," he said against her mouth. He held her still as he pumped into her, harder and faster than her leisurely movements, and in mere seconds he had her screaming his name as she came in a flurry of passion and emotion that made it feel like this man had changed her whole being.

"I'm never going to get enough of that," she sighed delightedly as she rested against Levi, letting him hold her up.

"Lucky you don't have to then," he nuzzled the side of her neck. "You want to eat?"

"Not just yet. Can we just lie and look at the sky?"

"That's why I brought you out here," Levi told her as he gently lifted her up and helped her set her panties and skirt back in place.

"What?"

"The other night when we were walking to my place for dinner, you were all awestruck about the stars, and I thought after everything you've been through these last few days you deserved something special, and the stars out here, on the lake, surrounded by nothing but trees, the view is stunning."

Tears welled up. "You really paid that much attention to something I said that you brought me out here?"

"Of course, I'll always pay attention to the things you say." He kissed the tip of her nose, then grabbed a checked blanket and spread it out on the floor of the boat.

They lay down side by side. Sydney propped on her good side and tucked against Levi, her head on his shoulder, his arm around her, and watched as the sky turned from blue to black. The stars seemed to multiply every time she blinked her eyes until the entire dark expanse was filled with millions of twinkling diamonds.

The sight left her speechless, almost breathless, it was so beautiful and more than she had thought it would be. She didn't know how something so simple could touch her so deeply, but it did.

"I love you, Levi."

The arm around her tightened. "Love you back, Sydney."

Return to River's End as Will Black is in for the fight of his life to convince the woman he loved to give him a second chance after he abandoned her when she needed him the most in the sixth story in this gripping, emotionally charged romantic suspense series!

Some Truth Can Be Distorted (River's End Rescues #6)

Also by Jane Blythe

Detective Parker Bell Series

A SECRET TO THE GRAVE

WINTER WONDERLAND

DEAD OR ALIVE

LITTLE GIRL LOST

FORGOTTEN

Count to Ten Series

ONE

TWO

THREE

FOUR

FIVE

SIX

BURNING SECRETS

SEVEN

EIGHT

NINE

TEN

Broken Gems Series

CRACKED SAPPHIRE

CRUSHED RUBY

FRACTURED DIAMOND

SHATTERED AMETHYST

SPLINTERED EMERALD

SALVAGING MARIGOLD

River's End Rescues Series

COCKY SAVIOR

SOME REGRETS ARE FOREVER

SOME FEARS CAN CONTROL YOU

SOME LIES WILL HAUNT YOU

SOME QUESTIONS HAVE NO ANSWERS

SOME TRUTH CAN BE DISTORTED

SOME TRUST CAN BE REBUILT

SOME MISTAKES ARE UNFORGIVABLE

Candella Sisters' Heroes Series

LITTLE DOLLS

LITTLE HEARTS

LITTLE BALLERINA

Storybook Murders Series

NURSERY RHYME KILLER

FAIRYTALE KILLER

FABLE KILLER

Saving SEALs Series

SAVING RYDER

SAVING ERIC

SAVING OWEN

SAVING LOGAN

SAVING GRAYSON

SAVING CHARLIE

Prey Security Series

PROTECTING EAGLE

PROTECTING RAVEN

PROTECTING FALCON

PROTECTING SPARROW

PROTECTING HAWK

PROTECTING DOVE

Prey Security: Alpha Team Series

DEADLY RISK

LETHAL RISK

EXTREME RISK

FATAL RISK

COVERT RISK

SAVAGE RISK

Prey Security: Artemis Team Series

IVORY'S FIGHT

PEARL'S FIGHT

LACEY'S FIGHT

OPAL'S FIGHT

Prey Security: Bravo Team Series

VICIOUS SCARS

RUTHLESS SCARS

Christmas Romantic Suspense Series

CHRISTMAS HOSTAGE

CHRISTMAS CAPTIVE

CHRISTMAS VICTIM

YULETIDE PROTECTOR

YULETIDE GUARD

YULETIDE HERO

HOLIDAY GRIEF

Conquering Fear Series (Co-written with Amanda Siegrist)

DROWNING IN YOU

OUT OF THE DARKNESS

CLOSING IN

About the Author

USA Today bestselling author Jane Blythe writes action-packed romantic suspense and military romance featuring protective heroes and heroines who are survivors. One of Jane's most popular series includes Prey Security, part of Susan Stoker's OPERATION ALPHA world! Writing in that world alongside authors such as Janie Crouch and Riley Edwards has been a blast, and she looks forward to bringing more books to this genre, both within and outside of Stoker's world. When Jane isn't binge-reading she's counting down to Christmas and adding to her 200+ teddy bear collection!

To connect and keep up to date please visit any of the following

Printed in Great Britain
by Amazon